About the author

Oonagh Murphy-Jack lives in west London with her partner. She works for a national charity and is currently working on her second novel.

WAITING FOR ERIN

For my darling Eva, and to Emily, Louis, Mum and Dad, thank you for all your support and unconditional belief in me. To Kiera and Conlan, I am glad we have found one another again. And to my best friend Beth, for all the years of great friendship.

Oonagh Murphy-Jack

WAITING FOR ERIN

AUSTIN & MACAULEY

A CIP catalogue record for this title is
available from the British Library.

ISBN 978 1 905609 79 6

www.austinmacauley.com

First Published (2010)
Austin & Macauley Publishers Ltd.
25 Canada Square
Canary Wharf
London
E14 5LB

Printed & Bound in Great Britain

Chapter 1

'Mum!!' Orghlaith cried from the front room. 'Mum, I need you!!'
Dympna dropped the spuds she was peeling in the kitchen and
ran in to see her daughter.

'Oh, Jesus, Mary and Joseph! This is it!' Dympna shouted
out in her Southern Irish accent. A cross between a smile and
anticipation spread across her face. Dympna regained her senses
and took control of the situation. 'Right, we need to get you in
the car Orghlaith. Come on you need to move and quick,'
Dympna said firmly. Orghlaith took her Mum's hand and
managed to waddle herself into the hallway. They paused for a
second whilst Orghlaith caught her breath and Dympna picked
up the overnight bag.

'Aaaaaagh! Oh God Mum it bloody hurts!!' Orghlaith cried
out.

'I know me darling, I know, just hang in there for me.'

Orghlaith and the bump squeezed into the front seat.
Dympna started the car and said a quick silent prayer as she
reversed out 'Please God, please don't let anything go wrong...'
She had left her rosary beads on her bed which made her worry
even more. Dympna swore she put them in her handbag – she
always put them back in her handbag ready to go. 'Never mind'
she thought, 'if God isn't with us after all I've given him He can
feck off. Oh bejesus, I'm sorry God, I never meant to
blaspheme. Just look after Orghlaith, look after her and the babe.
Please.'

The sweat dripped down Orghlaith's forehead and Dympna felt quite helpless as she watched her 19 year old daughter writhe in pain and push with all she had as the nurses kept telling her it was nearly here. Dympna wiped Orghlaith's face and Orghlaith squeezed her hand tight. 'If you squeeze any tighter me bledy hand will fall off sure it will...' Dympna said smiling. Orghlaith looked at her Mum and managed to crack a smile amidst the pain of giving birth. Dympna wasn't pleased Orghlaith was having a baby so young but as a Catholic Dympna could never have let Orghlaith have an abortion. The babe was here now and they would just have to get on with it. Orghlaith had agreed to go back to University after a few weeks of being with the baby at home and Dympna was looking forward to having the little thing whilst Orghlaith was getting her education. It was going to be tough, but God didn't give us challenges without purpose Dympna reasoned.

Eighteen hours later a loud shrill scream bellowed out as Orghlaith's daughter made her entrance into the world. 'Congratulations. It's a girl,' the nurse said to Orghlaith, smiling. The cord was cut and the babe cleaned and made good for Mum to hold. Orghlaith was exhausted but managed to let the tiny bundle suckle on her breast for a while. Dympna kissed Orghlaith's forehead and said 'You're brave. You're really brave. And we're going to be fine. We are going to be just fine.'

Dympna knew only too well how physically drained Orghlaith must have felt. After all, Dympna had given birth to three boys all at 9lb and Orghlaith was just shy of 9lbs. Dympna smiled to herself as memories of giving birth to Orghlaith quickly ran through her thoughts. The babe had fallen asleep and the drained new Mum was ready to nod off too. Dympna took the tiny bundle all wrapped in crisp white blankets and placed her delicately in the hospital bed which Dympna thought looked more like a cheap plastic tub. 'Oh you're definitely an O'Meara...

Oh yes you are...' Dympna whispered to her grandchild, 'and you put up a good old fight didn't ye me little chicken – making Mammy work so hard.' Dympna stroked the mass of black hair on the babe's head. 'Oh if Grandad could see you he'd love ye so he would. He's back home in Ireland but Nanny D will call him and tell him to get his arse over.'

Dympna fell asleep muttering to herself and thinking of her ex husband Seamus. He had gone back to Ireland in the 70s when Orghlaith was a little girl and taken the boys with him. 'Come back with me D,' he'd said to her, ' London is no place to bring up young ones – especially a girl. Please D, come back home and we'll live in The Green, not in this grey shite of a city. London is no place for us.'

At the time Dympna knew Seamus was probably right but she couldn't go back after what had happened. 'I've no-one left Seamus. Don't you understand? I have no one there.' Dympna had explained through tears as she stood at the kitchen sink.

'Dympna you have everything there. The O' Meara's make the Green. Don't let what happened stop you from coming home.' Seamus had placed his hands on her shoulders for comfort but his words fell on deaf ears that night. Dympna made her mind up to stay in London.

Dympna woke in the hospital a little startled although everything around her was quiet and still. Dympna sighed, maybe if she had gone back to Ireland Orghlaith would have had a better upbringing and not got pregnant so young. Maybe she was just a bad Mother and hadn't guided Orghlaith enough. She knew the first thing Seamus would say to her would be that she should have gone back to Ireland all those years ago. Orghlaith would have been better off in The Green. But at the time she couldn't bring herself to do it – not after what had happened. As Dympna laid back in the uncomfortable hospital chair she recalled that night on the farm. The thing that had forced her out of Ireland and the home she loved so much....

The night that changed her life forever and eventually forced her out of Ireland and the home she loved so much.

The farm was beautiful. Acres of lush green land set apart from the rest of the town – away from the hustle and bustle and idle gossip her Mother Mary and Father Michael wanted no part of. Dympna and her brothers Donal and Kian worked with Michael maintaining the land and animals. 'Hard work is the making of a man – and woman.' Michael would tell his children in his soft Irish accent whilst they mucked out. 'But so is the craic!' he would say boldly with a glint in his eye, laughing as he dropped the cleaning bucket and would chase the three children across the farm until their legs grew tired and could carry them no further. Michael would carry Dympna back to the house for supper, the boys trying to keep up with his fast step.

Dympna's mother (being especially gifted at Mathematics) kept the accounts and bookkeeping up to date as well as the running of the house. 'Do you four do any work out there on that farm or is it all play and your poor Mam in here slaving over the stove ?' She would tease serving up their food, smiling across the table at Michael. They were all happy in that little world, their own cocoon on the farm in The Green. People in the town mocked and teased the O'Meara's reclusive lifestyle, often creating fairytales to entertain visitors and immigrants who had never met any of the O'Meara's; but those people were secretly jealous of the family whose lives together were seemingly perfect and who cared nothing for the judgement of others.

But this world was stolen from the O'Meara's that night. It was summer 1939, two weeks before Second World War would wreak havoc in Ireland's neighbouring country, separated only by a few miles of water. The horses outside were making a racket;

Dympna pulled her curtains back and looked out of her window wondering what the fuss was. She had a good view with her bedroom being at the very top of the farmhouse, the evenings stayed light for longer in the hot summer. It was near ten that night and the moonlight shimmered a strip of light across the field so she could just make out the figures of Donal and Kian running towards the horse stables thinking they were going to see to the unruly animals. Dympna jumped back nearly falling, startled by the gun shots. They were definitely gun shots. Her brother's bodies convulsed as if they were being electrocuted and they fell to floor helplessly. Dympna felt as if it were happening in slow motion. First Kian's stocky thick body followed instantly by Donal's long slender frame; Then they were gone, lost in between the long thick blades of grass and shrubbery and the summer night that was becoming darker by the minute.

She wanted to scream but couldn't find it in herself. No sound. She stood still and silent as if someone had pressed a mute button on her body. Seconds later Dympna snapped out of the trance and ran barefoot to the second floor to wake her Mother and Father. 'Da da!! Da!! Someone's shot the boys!! Someone's shot the boys!'

Mary and Michael had both heard the shots. Michael was out of bed already loading his rifle and ready to leave by the time Dympna got there. Mary was hysterical not knowing if her sons were dead or alive praying to God they were. 'Oh Jesus Michael! What's happened! What's happened!' Mary cried.

'I don't know.' Michael said loading the final bullet. 'Stay here and look after Mam he told Dympna.

'Yes Da.' He ran out in to the pitch black to find his boys.

Mary grabbed Dympna's tiny hand hurrying her to the basement at the back of the house, and guided her down the rickety stairs. 'Stay in here D do ye hear me?' Mary said cupping

Dympna's face with her palms. 'Stay in here and don't bledy move, I'm going with ye Da.'

'No Mammy, No!! Don't leave me here by me self Mam!' Dympna cried.

'I'll be back soon I promise.' Mary said hurriedly, once again holding Dympna's small face in her palms and kissed her daughters forehead.

Mary left Dympna in the basement, grabbed the rifle hanging on the wall, hands trembling and glanced back at Dympna once more telling her frightened little girl 'I'll be back soon I promise. I love you.' Mary closed the double doors of the basement praying her sons were still alive.

Dympna moved around the dimly lit basement room delicately, not sure what she should do, the picture of her brothers in the field re-played in her mind relentlessly.

She dragged some blankets from the shelf above, wiped the dust off and made a make shift bed in the corner. Huddled under the musty smelling blankets, Dympna held the Crucifix Mam had given her and prayed that He would look after her family. She tried to keep awake until they all came back but Dympna's eye lids grew heavier by the hour and eventually she fell asleep, curled in a ball clutching her Crucifix.

Dympna woke from her sleep disorientated but realising where she was she threw the blankets off and made for the door at the top of the old stairs. She crept around the silent house towards the dining room. Mary's naked body was draped over the dining room table saturated with bullet wounds. Dympna slowly walked around the room. She came closer to Mary and touched her face. It was still warm. Dympna realised her Mother's ears had been cut off and a note had been hammered into Mary's chest with a rusted nail 'Catholic fucking whore.' It read in faded black ink. Dympna ripped the note off and threw it on the floor tears blinding her eyes, the taste of the salty water dripping into her mouth. 'No! Mam! No No No!' Dympna cried out, her child voice echoing throughout the silent house. She walked just beyond the table to see her brother's bodies slumped one on the other on the floor. The same multiple bullet wounds had ripped through their clothes and their faces had been shot at so they were unrecognisable. A note was left on either body as it had been on Dympna's Mother. 'Dirty Catholic Bastards.' Each note read. Dympna couldn't reach her Father as he hung from the beam in the roof by his own belt. She had to get a stool and stand on it to get near him. There was a note attached to Michael's chest but Dympna couldn't see it properly. Dympna thought she would be able to get Michael down from the beam somehow but her Father's body was too heavy for her.

Dympna's recollection of that night was interrupted by the shrieking cry of her new granddaughter. The graceful woman gathered her thoughts and reminded herself that it was 1985, she was in London and she had just become a Grandmother for the fourth time. She pushed the memory of back home aside and picked up her Grandchild. Orghlaith came round and they discussed what the babe should be called. 'How about Erin? That's a lovely Irish name.' Dympna said to Orghlaith as the baby fed yet again.

'Yeah, I quite like that – I thought you may come out with a really awful name and we'd spend half the day arguing about it.' Orghlaith said laughing.

'I named you didn't I?' Dympna replied.

'Yeah exactly!' Orghlaith said in jest.

'Oh well it's a strong Irish name.' Dympna said. Orghlaith mimicked her Mother as she had heard Dympna say this a million times when Orghlaith had complained about her own name. The little babe was called Erin Siobhan O'Meara.

Chapter 2

Orghlaith bundled in to the lecture hall with the rest of the students for the first lesson of term. She was bright, motivated and wanted this degree so badly. English Literature had been her passion since school. Maybe one day she would be standing in front of 50 odd students giving a lecture on Studying the Novel. Orghlaith's thoughts on her future career were abruptly interrupted by a tall olive skinned guy 'Anyone sitting here?' He asked.

'No go ahead.' Orghlaith said looking up briefly from her notepad. Sit where you bloody well like, Jesus you don't need a written invitation, Orghlaith thought; but she didn't utter these words aloud lest she would cause offence to the arrogant shite sitting next to her. She could feel him staring at her and it was unnerving. He admired her dress sense – a cross between Madonna-esque and Fame: A grey off the shoulder sweatshirt slashed at the midriff to reveal a soft flat tummy. A chunky crucifix necklace hung around her neck with Jesus moulded in sterling silver and several other smaller crosses were entangled in the mass of necklaces making a knot at the top. Multiple silver bangles hung on one arm and black rubber ones on the other. He liked her eclectic style and the way her clothes showed off her pretty slim figure. Orghlaith looked to her left and caught his eyes giving her a good going over. Cheeky sod, she thought, but he was pretty damn hot and those big black eyes were cute. Anyway, no time for this she told herself, she had no time for men and flirting and all that jazz – she was a Mum now. No time for men. Most of them were full of shite anyway. And being a Mum at 19 was hardly attractive.

The lecture was coming to an end and the tall tanned guy slipped a note onto Orghlaith's folder, brushing her hand purposely. 'Come for a drink with me tonight. Max' he had written. Orghlaith half smiled – she was flattered for sure but she couldn't go, she didn't even know this guy. She wrote back: 'I can't. Have child to look after at home.' That should scare him off. 'What about tomorrow then? Get a babysitter.' Max wrote back. Orghlaith was surprised at his response. 'Not sure,' she wrote. Give me your number, I'll call tomorrow – see if you've changed your mind. Jesus he was persistent – maybe he just liked a challenge. He wasn't shy was he? She wrote her number down and passed the note back to him. The lecture came to an end. 'I'll call you.' He said, smiled and walked away. Ok so he was pretty hot.

Uni finished at four and Orghlaith headed home feeling shattered. 'I'm home!' Orghlaith called as she entered the hallway. The smell of homecooked Irish stew made her realise how hungry she was. She went into the large kitchen and gave Dympna a kiss on the cheek.

'How was Uni me darlin' Dympna asked kissing Orghlaith and keeping an eye on the stew.

'Oh yeah it was good, I'm glad I've gone this year. How's Erin been? Where is she?'

'She's just having a little nap...She went down an hour ago - I'll wake her soon so's she's not up all bledy night. She's been absolutely fine so she has – a dream. Oh bejesus she did a terrible whopper in her nappy today!' Dympna said laughing 'I thought one of the cats had done its business in the house it was so bad.'

'Oh God, is she ok Mum? Has she got a dodgy tummy?'

'Oh no me darling, everything is healthy and as it should be!'

The phone rang in the middle of dinner and Dympna answered the phone. 'Can I ask who's calling?...Right. Hold on a minute.' Dympna came back into the kitchen. 'A man called Max is on the phone for ye.' Oh God she didn't think he'd call this soon.

After a brief conversation and an agreement to go on a date the next evening which she didn't actually remember agreeing to, Orghlaith came back into the kitchen. 'Who was that?' Dympna asked curious to who the sultry voice belonged to on the other end of the line.

'His name is Max.'

'And does Max know you have a child?'

'Yes he does.'

'So what does Max want?'

'Max would like to take me out for a drink tomorrow night.'

Orghlaith you have a child to look after and Uni work to do – you don't have time for shennanigans with men – especially after what happened last time!'

Dympna raised her voice. 'Mum! I can't believe you said that!'

'Well he didn't stick around to see Erin did he? And she's not a few weeks born and you're off gallivanting with this Max! I need to pray I do!'

'Mum you're really blowing this out of proportion. It's just a drink.'

'Oh is that what Erin's father said to you as well.'

'I'm not putting up with this,' Orghlaith said. She went upstairs to see Erin not wanting to anger her Mother any further. She could see where Dympna was coming from – she was worried that was all, but it was just a date. One date!

Dympna agreed in the end to look after Erin so long as Orghlaith was home by 12 that night. Orghlaith felt like a young girl all over again with a strict curfew that she really didn't want to abide by. Ah well, she sighed. Orghlaith fed Erin her mushy dinner and placed her in the playpen whilst she painted her face and carefully chose her outfit. 'He's here,' Dympna said as she came into Orghlaith's bedroom and took Erin from the playpen 'Come here to Nanny whilst your Mammy goes out with her friend.'

'Thanks Mum.'

'Be good and get home safe.'

Max picked Orghlaith up in his black Jaguar and drove them up to the West End to a trendy bar with leopard covered seats and expensive cocktails. So I guess he likes to show off, Orghlaith thought. What the hell, he's gorgeous and it won't go anywhere so I'm gonna enjoy this Majito Cocktail or whatever it's called. The conversation was broad – he was an intelligent man and Orghlaith was enchanted – hooked. His wit and charm had bowled her over and before she knew it Orghlaith had agreed to another date with him the following night. He got her home on time as Orghlaith explained that her Mother was a devout Catholic Irish woman likely to chop his balls off and hang him from the street lamp post if he got her home late or tried anything but a kiss on the first date. Max laughed. He was half Irish and half Italian so he knew the women ruled the house regardless of whether there was a husband about or not. He didn't want to get on the bad side of her Mum so he got Orghlaith home at 11.55 sharp that night.

'So how was last night?' Dympna asked with a serious tone, hoping that Orghlaith would say he was not her type, she had Uni work and Erin, so would not be seeing him again.

'Oh it was lovely. I'm seeing him again tonight.' Orghlaith waited for Dympna to explode.

'Ok fine. I'll have Erin. I don't want her being passed to someone else to look after if you are going out with yer fancy man. At least come home and feed her tea before you go,' Dympna said.

'Mum you're behaving as if I don't spend time with Erin or look after her. Just because I am a Mother doesn't mean I can't have a life. I spent two months cooped up in this house looking after her and I don't think a couple of nights out makes me a terrible parent!' Orghlaith defended.

'Fine. Well, as long as you stay on top of Uni work and see Erin it's up to you what choices you make,' Dympna said.

'Oh of course it is – provided the choices are right by you.' Orghlaith fired back at her. She kissed Erin and said goodbye as she left for a day of lectures leaving things tense between her and Mam.

She got home and Dympna was feeding Erin. 'I thought you said you were going to wait so I could feed her when I got back from Uni?' Orghlaith said to Dympna putting her folders on the kitchen table.

'Well the child was hungry. She couldn't wait for you to decide when to come home,' Dympna said.

'The lecture ran over a bit – I'm not that late back. You could have waited.' Orghlaith sighed, feeling she hadn't seen Erin for a lifetime even though it had only been a couple of days. Orghlaith played with Erin for an hour before getting ready for the second big date with Max.

He arrived at half seven sharp with flowers for both Orghlaith and her Mum. 'Well if you think you're going to flatter me by buying me cheap flowers from the petrol station you have another think coming,' Dympna said to Max.

'Mum don't be so rude,' Orghlaith said taking the flowers.

'It's fine.' Max said. 'Come on, we'll be late for the theatre.'

'Thanks for tonight. It was perfect, it really was.' Orghlaith said to Max at the front door of her house .

There was another date the following weekend, and another after that. Dympna pleaded with Orghlaith to stay home with Erin and concentrate on Uni work but Dympna's pleas were met with the door slamming in her face and Orghlaith not to be seen or heard from for days. On Orghlaith's return the two strong willed women would argue ferociously, each protesting their case with harsh words and no empathy for the others circumstance or reasoning. Dympna attempted on yet another weekend to stop Orghlaith from leaving the house and to face up to her responsibilities but once again Dympna's words fell on deaf ears as Orghlaith said 'I'll be back tonight.'

Dympna looked at her with dismay burping Erin over her shoulder. 'Just go then Orghlaith, go.' Orghlaith shut the door behind her, the image of Dympna holding Erin as a Mother would play in her mind, but the pull towards Max was just too strong.

Orghlaith arrived at Max's Penthouse flat on the top floor in Chelsea, each time she came here it was as if she were transported into another world. The black leather sofas were so sleek and she loved the smell of leather; the huge glass coffee table with posh magazines arranged perfectly into a fan shape. She loved the feel of the carpet underneath her feet - made from Egyptian cotton it was light and soft and felt like heaven. She had the urge to roll around on it but resisted the temptation thinking Max might think her slightly deranged. The bedroom was equally stunning, everything black or white leather with smooth straight lines – nothing frilly or fancy and all items perfectly in place as if they were never used: aftershave lined up on the shelf in height order, followed by several bottles of hair gel and a box of tissues all in line with one another. Orghlaith lay on the King Size bed sinking into the crisp black duvet. Max entered wheeling a tray with champagne and two glasses sitting elegantly on board. Orghlaith laughed as he reminded her of an air stewardess. 'Is that all the thanks a man gets when he brings his lady champagne and sweets?'

Max smiled. 'Sweets?' Orghlaith frowned, wondering at the odd combination of sweets and champagne thinking strawberries would have been a better option. 'Sweets.' Max replied with a grin. He shook a small plastic bag of white powder in front of her.

'Oh my god... Is that?...' Orghlaith whispered. Max clambered on top of Orghlaith and ripped open her shirt pouring the white stuff on her bare chest. Orghlaith's shock at Max's rough tugging of her shirt soon turned to excitement as he rubbed the powder in her gums and let her wash it down with champagne. Before long, their clothes were strewn across the room, champagne glasses smashed in a sexual frenzy and the fairy dust that had so enchanted them both found its way into every nook and cranny.

Orghlaith woke feeling disorientated to say the least, and it seemed she had lost a day – it was Saturday. It was Saturday afternoon. It couldn't be – they had gone out early Friday evening. Surely they hadn't been in bed that long? She checked her watch again. Shit, Mum had expected her home last night! Oh God. Max was out to the world. She left him a note and said thank you for the mind blowing night of sex and drugs. She knew it was so wrong and so irresponsible given that she was a Mother but it all felt so good – like a whole life away from her shitty world as a single parent student.

Dympna's voice bellowed down the corridor from the kitchen as soon as Orghlaith walked through the door. 'What bloody time do you call this? Saturday afternoon you decide to stroll in? Are you taking the mickey out of me Orghlaith? Are ya?' Dympna said.

'Oh for God's sake Mum I stayed out over night – so what! I'm here now.'

'Jesus Orghlaith take some bloody responsibility. If I wasn't here to look after Erin then who would? I don't mind looking after her – I love it. But she's yours. Don't forget that.' Orghlaith and Dympna managed to make it up and Orghlaith spent the rest of the weekend doing Uni work and spending time with Erin. She loved Erin with all she had, she just wondered how different Uni would be if she were just a normal student with no responsibilities. Everyone else was at the student bar and going out after lectures but she had to come home and play Mum. It wasn't Erin's fault. She knew that. Bless her little self. But she couldn't get Max out of her head. She wanted to see him again and have that same explosive sex with him. He was like an addiction.

Orghlaith got to see Max in lectures that Monday and they had sex in the office of Dr Radipole who could have walked in at any moment. 'Where's the stuff? Have you got any of that stuff?' Orghlaith asked Max in the middle of it.

'I haven't got any on me. Come back to mine tonight – I've got something even better. It'll blow your head,' Max said finishing and doing up his trousers. Orghlaith didn't think about going home that night. She didn't call Dympna because she didn't want to hear the lecture. She didn't want to face that reality. Uni finished and Max drove them both back to Chelsea. Orghlaith felt alive with him in his fast car, driving through London living in this fantasy world. They were fucking before they even got past the front door.

Max got up after a while and poured them champagne which he brought in to the front room on a beautiful silver tray accompanied with a metal spoon and three plastic bags. Orghlaith sipped on the champagne 'What are these for?' She asked.

'These my darling are fresh needles – we are hitting the big time tonight .' Max said winking and stroking Orghlaith's face.

'Is that what I think it is?' Orghlaith said 'Is that… Heroine?'

Oh don't be scared beautiful… I do it all the time.' Max said reassuring Orghlaith that she wouldn't 'get hooked'. He tied a band tight around Orghlaiths left arm and looked for a fresh live vein. 'Relax,' he said to her as he pressed the fine needle into her skin and let the brown stuff razzle dazzle her. He sat back and watched her reaction. She was tense at first but after a while she looked like she was in heaven. He smiled feeling pleased with himself. He let himself have a little treat of the brown and slumped next to Orghlaith. There was no mind blowing sex that night. They were too high to do any of that.

Orghlaith woke in the early hours feeling like shit and after a few seconds looking around realised what she'd done. God it was better than the Charlie but it was so bad. Well it's not like I'm addicted is it, she said to herself. For God's sake you tried a bit if brown, everyone tries a bit of brown – I'm a bloody student – I'm allowed! Max drove her home early doors and said he'd see her in Uni later for the 1 o'clock lecture. She sneaked in around 6.00am and Dympna was asleep – Erin was in with her too. She might have had a bad night Orghlaith thought. She was so tired she flopped on her bed and fell asleep in her clothes and didn't wake up until two that afternoon – she'd missed her lecture. Damn. Dympna knew Orghlaith had missed the afternoon lecture but didn't wake her because she knew her daughter didn't get home until nearly seven that morning so she left her to sleep. She didn't want to ruin Orghlaith's life, and she knew she was still young but she needed to realise she had become a Mother which meant sacrificing some of the things any other normal 19 year old student might be doing.

Orghlaith spent some of the day being sick – it must have been some sort of reaction to the Heroine she thought. Orghlaith didn't tell Dympna she was feeling so rough in case she started to ask questions and she wasn't about to start filling Dympna in on what had happened. She knew her Mum would hit the roof, and she had every right to really. But Orghlaith couldn't stop thinking about the next time she would be at Max's place and what they might take or might do. It wasn't long before Orghlaith's question was answered... she got herself into Uni the next day and sure enough Max was there and straight after they headed back to Chelsea. Orghlaith couldn't wait – but she wasn't sure if she was more excited about the drugs or the sex with Max. It was everything. Max drove them through London and over Chelsea Bridge which was lit up and looked so pretty at night. Dympna and Erin flashed through Orghlaith's mind but she erased the thoughts because the bad feelings of guilt and shame would come streaming through her. She knew she should be home with Dympna doing Uni work and looking after Erin – trying to make a go of life. But this, this world with Max seduced her. With every ride in Max's Jag, every sip of posh champagne and wild nights of sex and drugs Orghlaith moved further away from the real world and it felt too damn good to let go.

They fooled around in the morbidly huge Jacuzzi like two kids without a care in the world, all responsibility delegated to those on the outside. As Orghlaith dried herself at the sink Max came behind her placing a diamond necklace around her neck. 'For you, because you're marvellous.' Max whispered in her ear. He pushed her wild black hair to the side so he could fasten the family heirloom. The necklace was far too big for Orghlaith's petite frame and delicate collar bone but she wasn't aware of this small indiscretion, overwhelmed by the dazzling jewels that sparkled so eloquently against her soft skin. Max stepped back admiring Orghlaith's reflection in the mirror; She stroked and touched the necklace as if it were a delicate creature, turning her body from side to side and her head this way and that attempting to become comfortable with something she felt stupidly in awe of. Max tilted Orghlaith's head back towards his chest as if she were a puppet easily manipulated and slid his forefinger across her gums feeding her the white candy. Max turned her around towards him, her chest against his. His movements hard and violent, her back hitting the sink again and again; Orghlaith's finger nails leaving trails of scratches drawn across Max's back in moments of unadulterated want. Minutes later Max playfully pulled Orghlaith into the bedroom. 'Come here, let's do up.' He said pushing Orghlaith on the bed; she fell easily into the soft bed covers. Orghlaith had no idea what Max was talking about. He held up needles in a plastic bag in one hand and his other palm faced upwards, a solid brown substance sitting innocently in the middle. 'We're going to have ourselves a bit of Harry Jones.' Max said, speech slurred. Aunt Hazel, Big Harry, Golden Girl, Black Pearl, Brown Sugar – whatever term was being used for Heroin it wouldn't matter because underneath these euphemisms and running through Orghlaith's veins would be a substance also known as Judas, masquerading as a friend, betrayal inevitable.

***

Orghlaith's eyes became sunken and she developed a glazed look that stared right through Dympna and Erin, unable to think of anything else but her next hit. Her lies knew no boundaries telling Dympna she was inundated with University work and exams and was simply tired and feeling ill when the truth was Orghlaith had quit Uni to spend her days with Max and Big Harry. Dympna was nobody's fool - something wasn't right, and if Orghlaith wasn't going to be honest than Dympna would have to find out for herself. Dympna came back home from her Wednesday morning cleaning job with a hungry Erin in tow. Once fed and watered Erin slept soundly in her cot, her Mother nowhere to be seen. Dympna took this opportunity to search

Orghlaith's bedroom – to search for anything – clues, hints at what Orghlaith was concealing from her. Dympna pulled out Orghlaith's drawers, grappled with the dust under the bed as she dragged out old magazines and several storage boxes rummaging through them furiously – letters, old teddy bears and dolls and odds and ends but nothing telling. Dympna attempted the two double wardrobes – searching pockets of clothes, the floor of the wardrobe and the shoe boxes stored at the bottom. Nothing. After several hours Dympna stood up holding her aching back caused by all the crouching and bending. The tired woman dusted herself down her hand brushed against the pretty jewellery box she had bought for Orghlaith's 18th birthday. It tumbled down from the bedside cabinet landing by Dympna's feet. The contents of the box came flying out across the withered carpet. Dympna was not prepared for what she found. Four needles, two in wrappers the other two stained with flecks of blood and a solid brown substance wrapped in foil. There were notes and love letters from Max all referring to 'doing up' and how he 'couldn't wait to party with the 'Big H', and of course lines and lines declaring his eternal love for her daughter. 'You are the best thing in my life. I'll be getting some more Golden Girl for you soon... Love M.' Dympna's heart was beating hard and fast, adrenalin firing through her body caused by a mixture of anger, worry and fear for Orghalith's life. She sat on the bed holding the needles and lump of Heroin contemplating how on earth she was going to broach this with Orghlaith. 'Max, Max, I'm going to feckin' kill ye.' She said aloud.

'Mum, Mum who are you talking to?' Dympha hadn't heard Orghlaith come into the house. Before Dympha could do anything Orghlaith walked into her bedroom. At the sight of Dympna with her stuff, Orghlaith began shouting hysterically, snatching the needles and Heroin from Dympha. 'What are you doing going through my stuff?! Why are you going through my things?! Is this what you do when I'm not here is it?!' Orghlaith was on edge, rage played in her eyes, a side of Orghlaith Dympna had never witnessed.

'I knew something was wrong Orghlaith, and you wouldn't tell me, you wouldn't tell me. What the Jesus are ye doing to yourself? Give me that shite!' Dympna wrestled her daughter to claim the needles and brown substance back, throwing them on the bed in disgust. 'Is this what you spend your time doing is it? This is why you look an absolute fright – Jesus look at ye – your skin, your hair – your – everything. You look as if life has been sucked from you Orghlaith,' Dympna cried. 'You're a bledy a Junkie – me only daughter is a junkie. Jesus. Jesus I can't believe it.' Dympna said shaking her head and wiping the tears from her face.

Orghlaith felt huge pangs of guilt as she saw how hurt Dympna was, she hugged her. 'I'm sorry Mum, I'm so sorry.'

'Oh Orghlaith.' Dympna sighed and hugged her daughter back. 'Let's throw this rubbish away – let us just throw it down the toilet never to be seen again.' Dympna said pointing at the bed. Dympna didn't know how to deal with this, she had been thrown many things in life but drug addiction was one she hadn't strayed upon. She naively thought Orghlaith could just stop taking the brown - that they would throw it away and the problem could be remedied. But it couldn't.

Orghlaith looked at her Mum in desperation, sweat beads penetrating through her skin, early stomach pains beginning. 'Mum you can't throw it away please... Please I need it, I need a hit now Mum. I'm starting to get stomach pains - you don't know what they're like, you really don't. Please Mum, just this once.' Orghlaith pleaded.

Dympna saw the desperation in Orghlaith's eyes and heard it echo in her voice. 'Oh Jesus Orghlaith come here.' Dympna hugged her daughter.

Orghlaith hugged Dympna back tight, crying, feeling ashamed and guilty but nonetheless needing, desperately needing to get that hit. The stomach pain was getting worse, she lay on the bed in agony crying out. Erin began to cry in the other room. 'Mum.. Mum please help me...' Orghlaith cried out.

Dympna held her daughters hand aware that Erin had now woken up too. The distressed Mother and Grandmother held her daughters hand. 'Now listen to me Orghlaith. Listen. I will help you this once, this once. You can have this,' Dypmna said holding the wrapped Heroin, her hand shaking, 'but afterwards no more, you have to promise me. We'll see the Doctor and get ye out of this mess.' Dympna could have been saying anything at that moment and Orghlaith would have said yes, ravenous for that brown sugar. Dympna couldn't believe she was actually going to allow Orghlaith to do this, but she didn't know what else to do, her poor little girl was in agony and there was only one thing at that moment that was going to stop the pain.

Dympna handed over the substance and needle to a desperate Orghlaith who grabbed at it as if she were a primitive being, uncivilised and starved. Her fingernails tore at the foil frantically, eyes darting to the needles, opening the wrapper with her teeth. 'Mum, Mum I need a lighter, this lighter doesn't fucking work.' Dympna ran to get Orghlaith a lighter from the kitchen downstairs; when she returned Orghlaith had tied an old dressing gown rope around her bicep and was now searching for a 'good' vein in her forearm, clenching and unclenching her fist.

Dympna put her hands to her face, she could still hear Erin crying in the background. 'I can't watch you do this.' Dympna left the room to get Erin crossing herself asking God to forgive her for what she was allowing to happen. Orghlaith crushed the brown, mixed it with water in the spoon and burnt the underneath until the solid substance became liquid. She filled the tube of the needle with the muddy brown liquid and tapped it several times to get rid of the air. Orghlaith's eyes rolled backwards, she slumped against the wall, sliding further down into her bed into an uninhibited state.

Chapter 3

The brown has a way of getting hold of you. It becomes the friend, the enemy, the sex – your life. It runs through your veins until there aren't any left and it's time to stop. But you can't stop feeling like you want to get to the next level of euphoria; the next level that's stronger than the last – and lasts just a little longer. For that moment in time, ah life is good – so damn good. But then it hits home; and before you know it your daughter's in hospital due to a drug overdose and the bastard who's supplied the drugs for the past few months is nowhere to be seen. Dympna got the call a few days before Christmas. 'Mrs O'Meara?' The throat cleared on the other end. 'Speaking' Dympna replied. 'Mrs O'Meara my name is Doctor Goodson, I'm calling from St Thomas' Hospital. I'm afraid your daughter has suffered a serious drug overdose. She is in intensive care.' The words didn't seem real to Dympna. She asked the doctor to repeat himself and asked whether they were sure it was her daughter. He confirmed that Orghlaith had come in with high levels of heroine and cocaine mixed with other substances. As soon as Dympna put the phone down she grabbed some of Erin's things as quick as she could and jumped straight in her car to the hospital. The Nissan Cherry was hard pressed to drive at thunder speed but Dympna put her foot on the accelator trying to get to Orghlaith as soon as she could. Dympna pressed harder on the gas and the Nissan tried to move faster along the busy

London roads. Everywhere was covered with Christmas lights, decorations and all things Santa, but Dympna was in no mood.

Orghlaith lay lifeless on the hospital bed with all sorts of tubes coming out from her nose and down her throat. As she held Orghlaith's hand the sleeve of her hospital gown slipped and revealed bruising and holes in the skin that looked as if a six inch nail had been drilled into Orghlaith's arm over and over in various places. It was the same on her other arm and on Orghlaith's legs. Dympna's mind raced over and over. 'I just want you back.' Dympna said aloud and cried into her hankerchief.

The plump blonde nurse in her blue uniform introduced herself as Angela and had been watching over Orghlaith the past few hours. She brought Dympna a cup of tea from the machine downstairs. 'Thank you.' Dympna said, taking the plastic cup and placing it on the cabinet next to Orghlaith's bed.

Angela touched Dympna's shoulder softly attempting to give whatever comfort she could to the poor Mother. 'If you need anything just call, I'm right here.' Angela said.

A tall grey haired man entered the cubicle. 'Hello, I'm Doctor Tomlinson.'

'Hello, I'm Dympna.. I'm Orghlaith's Mother.' Dympna replied bowing her head slightly. Oh God he thinks I'm a bad Mother.

The Doctor kindly explained that many parents go through this and it didn't mean she had done anything wrong. 'These things happen Mrs O'Meara, no matter how hard we try as parents believe me.'

'Oh maybe I didn't try hard enough...' It slipped out of Dympna's mouth before she even realised she had said it.

The silence was eventually broken by the Doctor clearing his throat. 'Your daughter has overdosed on a potent, very pure form of Heroin Mrs O'Meara - often referred to as black tar. We also found traces of cocaine and an additional substance called isobutyl nitrate.' The tall doctor towered over Dympna with his clipboard and pen and presented her with several leaflets for drug rehabilitation units. 'It is really worth considering for your daughter, maybe you could talk to her when she comes round? This place here,' he pointed to the picture of what looked like an old Victorian building, 'it's meant to be very good, please do think about it.'

Her daughter, Dympna thought, the little girl she had raised, that innocent creature was a drug addict? She turned to an unconscious Orghlaith and held the hand with the drip attached. 'What have you done to yourself?' She whispered, her eyes unable to hold back the well of tears that came tumbling down her cheeks.

'She's in good hands I promise and I'll be back every hour to monitor her progress.' The doctor said. He nodded at the nurse and pulled the cubicle curtain to. 'You should get some rest Mrs O'Meara.' The nurse said softly.

Over the next few days Dympna worked her cleaning jobs around visits to the hospital with Erin in tow at all times. Dympna had become accustomed to snatching sleep in the old chair in her living room or the awkward chair in the hospital with the ripped seat and exposed foam hanging freely; Rarely did she actually sleep in her own bed or retire at a decent hour.

Several weeks later Orghlaith was up and about and receiving daily methadone shots to substitute for the Heroin her body was crying out for. But Orghlaith wasn't coming home. Dympna had told her it wasn't an option – not after what had happened. 'You nearly died Orghlaith – you need to get yeself sorted out. This place the Doctor has recommended is meant to be very good so it is.' She explained. She was feeding Erin who sat blissfully unaware in her car seat perched at the end of Orghlaith's hospital bed.

'I'm not a fucking addict Mum... Not some scabby Junkie... I'm not going to rehab... I don't need to go... I don't need to go. It's a phase this has just been a phase Mum. I'll go back to Uni and I'll be fine, I'll get myself sorted out.'

'You are going into rehab Orghlaith. No questions.' Dympna looked her straight in the eye as she fed Erin the last spoonful. Orghlaith couldn't hold her gaze. 'This isn't fair on you, Erin or me.'

'Is that all you care about? Yourself?!' Orghlaith shouted.

'Ah Jesus Orghlaith did ye listen to a word I said? I don't want you in this mess, I want you to have a normal life – to enjoy life!'

'I'm a single Mum how can I enjoy life?' Orghlaith retorted.

The Doctor interrupted at that point, opening the cubicle curtain. 'Hi Orghlaith. How are you feeling?'

'Well how is a junkie supposed to feel?' Orghlaith asked defiantly.

'Orghlaith don't be so rude.' Dympna said sharply.

'It's ok Mrs O'Meara. It's ok' The Doctor said waving his hand and smiling, dismissing Orghlaith's retort. 'I understand that you are hesitant about this programme Orghlaith and I know all of this has been really tough, but I really do believe this place would be very good for you. You're twenty now yes? You want to be out there living life to the full, grabbing every opportunity that comes your way. And look at your daughter, isn't she lovely,' he pointed to Erin, 'she's lucky to have you as a Mum, and she needs you to around for a long time to come.'

'So do I.' Dympna said placing her hand on Orghlaith's. 'So do I Orghlaith.' She repeated.

'Here have my handkerchief Mrs O'Meara.'

'Oh thank you doctor.' Dympna wiped her eyes and blew her nose.

'Have a think about the rehabilitation. Please.' The Doctor seemed to have a way with words, his soft approach rubbed off on Orghlaith and she smiled at him.

'I'll think about it.'

Dympna took Erin home leaving Orghlaith to think about treatment. I'm not a drug addict, I'm not an addict Orghlaith repeated in her mind that night in her hospital bed. I have just had a few months of madness... But then all she could think about was a hit of Big Harry and how fucking good it will feel instead of this shit they were pumping her with – this methadone rubbish that didn't even touch the sides.

It had been such a whirlwind. One minute she had been at Uni and leading a normal life and the next she was headed off to the coast and labelled a 'drug addict'. Orghlaith couldn't get her head round it. She also couldn't get her head round the fact that Max had just disappeared – not one visit or call in the whole time she'd been in hospital. She was quite sure it was him who had dumped her on the steps of the hospital in the pissing rain. Bastard. Well I only have myself to blame for getting caught up with him. Then the memories of the past few months flooded back to her. The black Jag doing so many miles an hour in central London, the champagne in his flat, – oh the flat, with it's expensive smell and lush bed linen. The sex – the sex and... and the drugs. Which was the best bit? She didn't know. But the worst bit was missing out on time with Erin. And now the little girl wouldn't be fed or held by Orghlaith, wanting only the familiar hold and scent of Nanny Dympna. Orghlaith cried into the hospital pillow that night when they had gone. She never thought rejection from a child or the need for their love could be so painful. Angela came into the cubicle tentatively opening and closing the plastic curtain that mildly separated Orghlaith from the other patients. 'You awake Orghlaith? It's time for your medication sweetheart.' She said softly.

'Yes I'm awake.' The nurse could see the young girl had been crying.

'You o.k. lovey?' She rubbed Orghlaith's back and sat on the side of her bed. 'Going with the hardest decision is usually the best one.' Angela said as if she were reading Orghlaith's mind.

You sound like my Mum.'

'Well, judging from the way she has looked after you, that's not a bad thing. She seems like a good woman.'

'Yeah she is.' Orghlaith sighed taking a swig of water to wash down the methadone tablets.

'And your daughter is gorgeous.'

'Thank you, I know, I know... I should probably go to this rehab place... It just doesn't feel good admitting I'm a... You know, I have drug... Drug problems or whatever.' Orghlaith said picking at her nails.

'You are a strong cookie, I can tell, and once you get through this you'll come out the other side I promise.' Angela took the empty glass back.

'You think I should go to this place then?'

'Yes, yes I do, I think you have too much to lose if you don't. Far too much to lose.' Angela smiled and winked. 'Now you get some shut – eye madam.' She closed the curtains once more and Orghlaith could hear her flat rubber soled shoes squeaking as she walked off down the hospital corridor.

Dympna, Erin and Orghlaith drove in the Nissan to the remote countryside on a freezing day in January. The car journey was mostly silent as Orghlaith mentally prepared herself for the start of her six month drug rehabilitation and Dympna was bracing herself for a further six months of being a Mother to a young infant all over again. Dympna often felt like saying to Orghlaith to just get on with her life and Dympna would raise Erin as her own. She had wanted another girl but never had the chance. But she knew Orghlaith would not agree to it and now was not the time to ask. Many children back home in Ireland were raised by their Aunts and Uncles or Grandparents and it grew too complicated when the child got older. The child would suddenly find out at 17 or so that its Mum was its sister or its Aunt and the family often destroyed. Dympna didn't want that to happen to her family. She'd already lost a husband and two sons. She didn't want to lose anymore.

They drove through the winding tight country lanes following signs to Grogan House, Dympna and Orghlaith pointing out rabbits here and there along the way and other animals they didn't have the pleasure of seeing in London. A long steep hill and a narrow pathway finally led them to the restored Victorian mansion they had seen in the leaflet. 'Bejesus I can't believe this is actually for drug rehabilitation...It looks like a bledy hotel.' Dympna said pulling Orghlaith's suitcase out of the boot.

Orghlaith laughed, 'Well it's certainly not a hotel Mum that's for sure.' The building sat in the middle of acres of land closed off by tall well trimmed hedges, the neatly trimmed grass woven around the concrete walkways all leading to the front of Grogan House where grass and concrete were replaced by a wide pebbled drive. 'It's so quiet here.' Orghlaith said almost in a whisper lest she might disturb something or someone.

'I know. It's what you need though.' Dympna replied. The fresh air and tranquillity of the place reminded Dympna of back home; how things could have been had she returned... But not to think of that, we have to concentrate on the here and now she told herself.

Dympna and Orghlaith were welcomed by a friendly bald man with glasses called Mike, who was going to be Orghliath's key worker. 'Come in, come in.' Mike said waving his hands and taking Orghlaith's suitcase. He took them into a quiet room and offered them tea and coffee.

'Oh a cup of tea would be grand yes thank you.' Dympna said.

'And you Orghlaith?'

'Um... Yes, yes I'll have some tea please, thank you.'

Mike left the room to get some forms for Orghlaith to fill in and put the kettle on. 'Well he seems nice doesn't he?' Dympna said reassuringly to Orghlaith who had gone silent upon entry to the house. She had quickly looked through the small glass window into one of the rooms on the left which had a sign up that read 'Group Therapy In Session. Do Not Disturb.' Orghlaith saw a woman standing up talking and crying, looking down and wiping her face with a tissue offered by a man who was presumably another patient. Jesus Christ get me out of here she'd thought, but didn't utter these words aloud.

'Yes, Mike seems nice Mum.' Orghlaith replied thinking about what she had seen.

Erin slept soundly in the car seat. 'She'll be awake soon.' Dympna nodded at Erin.

'Mmm.' Orghlaith replied gazing out of the window.

Mike returned with a red plastic tray and three cups of tea. 'Here we are, something to warm you both up, it's so cold out there.'

The two of them thanked Mike simultaneously. 'So how does this work then?' Orghlaith asked.

She was thankful for the warm introduction but needed to cut the niceties and get to grips with what was going to happen to her for the next six months. 'Well, the aim of the rehabilitation is to get you living a normal daily life which does not revolve around your drug habit. You'll follow a daily schedule which will include activities, group and one to one therapy and of course a diet and nutrition plan to get your body back on track. Me and you will discuss more of this when you've settled in a bit better.' Mike explained. Orghlaith and Dympna sat silently for a minute.

Dympna put her arm around Orghlaith. 'Come here my chicken.' That was Orghlaith's pet name when she was younger; Orghlaith rested her head on Dympna's shoulder as if she were a little girl again.

'Do either of you have any questions?' Mike asked sipping his tea.

'Yes, will I be able to call Orghlaith and visit her?' Dympna asked.

'Um, now some patients find this hard but Orghlaith won't have access to our phone for the first two months and visits are also prohibited for that period.'

'What!?' Orghlaith sat up from Dympna's shoulder abruptly nearly spilling her tea everywhere. 'Two months?' They both said looking at each other then looking at Mike.

'I know it sounds rather harsh, I know, but we do it so that people who have friends and lovers who are addicts who are not in rehab can get better without the influence of those other people and that is why we do this.' Mike replied gently.

Orghlaith looked at her Mum, Dympna held her hand. 'This is tough I know, but it's about getting you better Orghlaith and giving you back your life.' Mike said.

'But I can't even speak to my Mum? She's not a bloody crack head is she?' Orghlaith said.

Mike smiled at Orghlaith. 'Um no, I'm sure your Mum isn't a substance abuser but this is our policy and we are very strict about it. If people break these rules then we take them off the programme and send them home.' Mike said in a more authoritative tone.

'Jesus.' Orghlaith said and sighed. She couldn't believe this was happening, get me the fuck out of here and get me some Big H. She wanted to run, get out of there. But she didn't. She gave Erin a long hard hug and said she'd see her soon. Dympna held on to Orghlaith hating that she had to leave her here but knowing it was the only way to get Orghlaith straight again. Dympna couldn't remember how many times they said goodbye or how many times she'd told Orghlaith she loved her in those last few minutes before she had to go back to London with Erin. They finally left Orghlaith at Grogan House and Dympna said a prayer for her.

Every morning before sunrise as Erin slept soundly in the small room next to Nanny D, Dympna would switch on her bedroom light – it still being dark at that hour hearing only the birds outside and the milkman driving his cart past her window, the bottles of milk clinking against one another. She would kneel at the bottom of her bed and look up at the Jesus and Mary moulds hanging from the wall adjacent. Clasping her rosary beads in between her hands and bringing them to her forehead she prayed for Orghlaith, Erin and for her two boys back home; And always a prayer for Seamus. 'It is God's will... This is all God's will.' Dympna would repeat to herself standing up and taking in a deep breath. 'What is meant to be is meant to be so it is.'

***

With Orghlaith being in rehab Dympna decided to go back to work. Dympna's savings were not enough on their own to support her and Erin as well as send Orghlaith money so she registered with Molly Maid cleaning agency and secured herself three cleaning jobs a week.

Seamus called that week. 'Finn tells me you've taken on the cleaning jobs again D? You know you don't have to.'

'Well I do actually, I do. Who else is going to keep me? Ah yes maybe me money tree in the back yard?'

'Oh D, don't be so stupid, you know I have more than enough for you, Orghlaith and the little one but ye so bledy stubborn you won't let me give it to you eh?'

'We have been separated for all these years Seamus Killoughery, you don't need to keep me.'

'You're my wife D.'

'Only on paper Seamus, only on paper.'

'How is Orghlaith?' Seamus changed the subject swiftly.

'Oh yes she's grand. Very grand. Everything is fine ye know the usual, she's out partying at all those University discos.' She lied.

'Ah yes that's my girl... And what about Erin, how's she, she must have grown so much, I'm sorry I haven't been over to see her yet D, the boys and me – we've been so busy here, ye know with the business and...'

'Ah yes, the business, the business.' Dympna said rolling her eyes to the ceiling and shaking her head. 'Well your granddaughter is fine, when you get the time you must come over and see her.' Dympna said, her sharp tongue stinging Seamus' conscience.

'Aye yes I will, I will, me and the boys will come over again soon to see all three of ye.'

'It's been months Seamus.' Dympna said in a softer tone.

'I know D, I'm sorry.' The silence indicated that it was time to go, they both said goodbye feeling as if there was so much they wanted to say, but didn't. Seamus put the phone down and looked out the window of his office across the farm, Con was speaking with a local client who needed more meat supplied and Finn was preparing the pig – feed in the outhouse. He thought about her. Every day he thought about her and what it would be like to have her there with him and the boys – Orghlaith and Erin too. It was just too late.

Dympna made herself a cup of tea and fed Erin. 'Ye granddad will come and see ye so he will, he will. He's just been a little busy my chicken, yes he has.' She said kissing Erin's forehead. 'But he loves you very much, just like Nanny D and your Mam.' Erin looked at the red plastic spoon Dympna was holding more interested in the food coming her way. Dympna thought about Seamus and the boys and wondered how she was going to tell them about Orghlaith being in rehab. She changed Erin, packed her food, clean clothes, nappies and the small Fisher – Price toy shaped like a ring that lit up and kept Erin occupied and out of trouble while Dympna went about her work. Sometimes she would have Erin on her hip as she polished and dusted, other times she would be lucky and Erin would sleep. But with Erin getting older and demanding to explore all the new places Nanny D was taking her to it got more difficult to keep her in one place and she was getting far too heavy to carry around for minutes at a time. 'I don't know what to do... She wants to climb into the cupboards and hide under the beds.' Dympna said to her neighbour Mrs Wallis over a brew that afternoon.

'Well I don't know why you just don't let Seamus help you out. But seeing as you're hell bent on doing this to yourself why don't you invest in the Porta- Pen.'

'And what the Jesus is that can I ask?' Dympna said as she sliced the soft white loaf of bread.

Mrs Wallis explained that the Porta – Pen was a playpen that folded down easily. 'Not as big as a normal one, you know, but big enough to keep young Madam in view and out of mischief leaving you to get on with your chores.' Mrs Wallis said in her cockney accent.

'And where do I get one of these Mary?'

'Oh I think Argos do them and that other shop , now what's it called?' Mary paused a minute to think and take a good bite from the ham sandwich Dympna had placed in front of her, she slurped her tea and let out a satisfied sigh. 'You make a good brew and ham sandwich Dympna... The other place is called MothersToBe on the corner just off the top of the high road. You might be looking at a few quid but I reckon it'll be worth it.'

On Mary's advice and kind offer to look after Erin for the afternoon Dympna went to hunt down a Porta-Pen and found herself amongst a sea of women with big round bellies wandering around MothersToBe, some cooing at the miniature clothes, others stocking up on breast pads and bonjela. Dympna wondered what Orghlaith was doing at that moment. She should be here now, in this shop with me choosing pretty things for Erin, pointing out the new pram she'd like and they would go and get a cup of tea and breakfast at Danny's Cafe afterwards. Dympna sighed, her fantasy interrupted by the sales assistant asking if she was paying by cash or card. 'Oh, um cash, cash.' She replied. Dympna thanked the assistant for helping her take the Porta-Pen to the car. He said once it was out of the packaging she would be able to carry it around no problem and open and fold it with ease. 'Let's hope I haven't just bought a load of shite eh.' Dympna said to herself as she drove home.

The Porta-Pen was God sent, although it took a while for Erin to get used to the confines of the hexagon shaped play pen Dympna knew where the little one was and could keep an eye on her while she worked. And so they developed a routine together, cleaning jobs in the morning where Erin would be content in the Porta-Pen (she had finally succumbed, no longer crying for Nanny D to take her out); Wednesday afternoons was reserved for the park, sometimes Mrs Wallis would come with her youngest. Playgroup was on Thursdays, it had been a while since Dympna had had to sing Humpty Dumpty and Heads Shoulders Knees and Toes but here she was twenty years later singing as she did all those years ago with Orghlaith and the boys.

One day Dympna sat watching Erin become familiar with the new entertainment blanket she had bought her. Erin amused herself for an hour or so and Dympna laughed out loud at the look of surprise that took over Erin's face each time she pressed the red button and the green frog popped up excitedly from underneath the shiny material. 'Oh if Mammy could see you, she'd be so proud eh, so proud. Ah God Orghlaith, why can't ye be here.' Dympna would say holding Erin in the air. 'She'll be home soon don't you worry me little chicken.'

Orghlaith had sent several short letters but didn't say anything about how she was finding the treatment other than it was a nice place and the staff were really friendly, the letters didn't sound like her Orghlaith. Dympna knew she'd be having a hard time of it but it was the only way, it was the only way she could get off that shite.

Erin was now a year old – sitting up and walking (when she felt like it) otherwise shuffling along on her bum. Dympna looked at her in the high chair and wondered at the little thing who had grown so quickly and changed so much in a year. Erin couldn't get her porridge and banana breakfast down quick enough and Dympna was talking to her about Orghlaith as she had always done explaining that Mummy was away but that she would be home soon. No sooner had Dympna said this than Erin pointed at her and said 'Mum' in that still baby-like gurgle. Dympna nearly scolded herself dropping her tea.

'No, I'm Grandma. Say Grandma.' Dympna said and pointed to herself repeating the word Grandma – hoping Erin would repeat it back; but she just sat looking rather confused. Dympna stroked Erin's head and said 'Grandma' one more time in a softer tone. She wondered what it would be like when Orghlaith got back from rehab for good... She'd have to let go of Erin – oh God she didn't want to think about it. The thought of giving her up made Dympna's insides churn.

The phone rang: 'Hello... Hello Mum...?" Asked Orghlaith.

'Orghlaith! Oh Orghlaith sweetheart how are you? Ah we've missed you terrible' Dympna replied. It had been three months since Dympna had heard her daughter's voice. Dympna held back tears so as not to cause any upset with Orghlaith.

'It's been really tough Mum but I'm doing ok... I just want to make sure Erin is alright – is she alright Mum?' Orghlaith asked in a desperate tone.

'Sweetheart don't worry Erin is doing really well. Really well.'

Orghlaith couldn't get her words out quick enough – overwhelmed to have some contact with her Mum and somebody who was in the outside world which already seemed so alien to Orghlaith. 'Oh Mum you can come visit me now... I'm allowed visitors and I can see Erin at last...' Mother and Daughter arranged a visiting time for the next week and Orghlaith got to speak to Erin briefly before her time on the phone ran out. Dympna and Orghlaith said goodbye and put the phone down simoultaneously. One sat in their age old chair and cried. The other sat on a chair in a room away from the other patients and the nurses and cried too. Both women wondered why it had come to this.

Dympna got herself together, applied her rouge blusher and lipstick and adjusted the cross on her neck. She looked smart even when she was cleaning. She left the house that morning with Erin in tow ready for her cleaning job over in Maida Vale and with Orghlaith at the forefront of her thoughts. She was startled by a man in his 50s sitting on the wall of the house next door. 'Good Morning... I'm ye new neighbour. Dooley McGuinness.' He put out his hand to shake but Dympna was not in the mood for pleasantries either so he got a curt response

'Nice to meet you.' And she smiled – at least he thought it was a half smile anyway.

'Where you off to so early?' He asked with a big grin.

'Some of us have work to go to. Have a good day.' Dympna pushed the pram forward and set off to work. She wasn't sure why she had been so short with him when he'd been so friendly and polite. Perhaps he had reminded her too much of back home or too much of Seamus. Yes, she thought to herself, never trust a good looking Irish man – they think too much of themselves and the accent alone will get you into bed and into all sorts of trouble. But still, he had been polite and Dympna resolved with herself that she ought to apologise to him later for being so abrupt.

Dooley McGuinness could not get his next door neighbour out of his mind. What a feisty woman. I like that, good looking too – fabulous combination. She could be no more than 45 he thought. Shiny hair so black and wide brown eyes to match. Dooley McGuinness pleasantly surprised to say the least at his fair neighbour, although he wasn't surprised that she was Irish given the big Irish community in Kilburn but he didn't expect that. Didn't expect that at all. Dooley concluded that Dympna was rude to him purely because she had found him charming and probably hadn't had any male attention for a while. Dooley McGuinness loved women, and, most of the time, women loved him and didn't he know it.

That evening Dooley put on his best suit and checked his reflection in the mirror. He combed his thick grey hair back and smoothed down the slightly unruly eyebrows. He wondered why his eyebrows had stayed brown whilst his hair had gone so grey – why couldn't he have kept his hair colour instead he thought. But he decided that the grey hair made him look demure and more handsome anyway. 'Oh you've still got it... you've still got it old boy!' Dooley said doing a little two and fro dance in front of the mirror. He polished off his look with a few (too many) dabs of aftershave that burnt the living daylights out of his freshly-shaved face but he laughed it off 'No pain no gain.' Gritting his teeth and slapping his face where the aftershave was still stinging him like mad.

Dympna put Erin to bed and sat in her favourite chair ready to watch that murder mystery programme at eight. 'Oh bejesus it feels so good to sit down.' She said softly to herself. She sipped on her tea and sat back pushing each shoe off with the other foot. 'Mmm.' She closed her eyes for a moment. The doorbell rang. 'Ah Jesus.' Dympna sat for a moment contemplating not opening the door, but it might have been someone in need or something and she'd never forgive herself so she opened the front door. It was the man who had startled her this morning.

'Good Evening,' he said taking his hat off.

'Can I help you?' Dympna said in a tone that didn't exactly scream friendly.

'Well I thought seeing as we are now neighbours I should come and introduce myself properly and we can get acquainted Mrs O'Meara,' Dooley said edging himself towards the step. Dympna thought back to how rude she had been and decided that she should let him in. Dooley sat down in the kitchen and Dympna made a brew. It was supposed to be a quick cup of tea but it was gone half eleven by the time Dooley had left. He told Dympna about his move to England many years ago and funny stories about being an altar boy and stealing the bread from Church because his family were so poor. Dympna laughed until her stomach hurt because his stories were told in such a way that you couldn't help but laugh. She told him about the first time her Father made her milk a cow and she fell over into a bucket of shite and her brothers chased her all over the farm with cow shite for days after. When he left she sat down and sighed and realised that she hadn't laughed like that for what felt like a lifetime.

Dympna began to prepare herself for the trip up to the country to visit Orghlaith at Grogan House emotionally and practically. Of course it was easy to pack Erin's nappies, a change of clothes and her liquidated babyfood for the next day. But the hard part was to think of what state Orghlaith may be in and the fact that in three months she would have finished treatment and be coming home to claim back what was rightfully hers – Erin. Dympna loved the little girl so much, and she loved Orghlaith too. She'd have died for them both. She wanted Orghlaith to be young and free and live her life and not be tied down to being a Mother so young. But Dympma knew she had also grown so attached to Erin that she couldn't help but want her as her own.

Dympna pushed that thought as far back into her mind as she could and felt an overwhelming amount of guilt for thinking such a terrible thing. 'Oh God please forgive me in these times of madness. I pray that Orghlaith is well and Erin will be blessed. I love them both with every bone in me body.' She crossed herself and thought it would be a good idea for all of them to go to the Chapel together at Grogan House. Dympna wished her daughter had more faith but Orghlaith was not convinced that God existed and rubbished the Catholic religion. Even at her Holy Communion Orghlaith ran riot and tried to set fire to her own dress that Dympna had paid a fortune for. Dympna laughed at this memory although remembered feeling absolutely mortified at the time, but it was Orghlaith's free spirit and rebellious nature that Dympna secretly admired. She loved her for that, although she would never let on to Orghlaith.

Dympna fell asleep in her armchair for an hour or so until was abruptly woken by the doorbell. She bolted upright and immediately started cursing 'Ah bejesus Dooley McGuinness... You have woken me out of me sleep...' But as she looked through the glass in the front door it was a figure that was too slight to be Dooley's – far too slight to be Dooley.

Dympna opened the door and there stood Orghlaith. Dympna's mind ran through a million possibilities of what could have happened but her question was answered. 'I ran away Mum,' Orghlaith said sullenly. 'I am clean and everything, I just couldn't stay in that place anymore. I just couldn't do it anymore.' Dympna held on tight to Orghlaith in the hallway with a mix of feelings washing through her but so glad that she was able to hold her and that she was back home.

They sat in the kitchen, Dympna made them tea. 'I am clean Mum. I have been for most of the treatment there. I just wanted to come home and get on with my life normally. I needed to be with you and Erin and start living normal life. I need to be here Mum.'

Orghlaith looked so well – better then she had in months. Dympna had her daughter back again and now she was here she didn't want to let her go again, but she was worried that she hadn't completed the treatment. 'Orghlaith sweetheart, it's so good to see ye but you haven't finished your treatment have you? Are ye really ready to come home? Are ye off that shite Orghlaith?'

'Mum I haven't taken anything in months.'

'Yes, but is that because they have stopped you? Can you control this yourself Orghlaith?'

'Yeah, yes I think I can.' Orghlaith replied with not as much conviction as Dympna would have liked. 'Don't you want me here Mum?'

'Oh Orghlaith don't be stupid, of course I do, I've missed ye so much I can't tell you. I just need to know you're not going to go backwards.' Dympna stood up and kissed Orghlaith's forehead, cupping her face with her hands. 'You'll always be my baby, my little chicken. I suppose I better call Grogan House and tell them you're here safe and sound. Did you tell them you were leaving?' Dympna said with her hand cupped over Orghlaith's.

'Yeah, I told Sue my keyworker.'

'What did she say to you?'

'She said she couldn't force me to stay but that I would be better off finishing the treatment.' 'She was probably right,' Dympna said. 'Look I'll call them now and see if I can have a chat with Sue.'

'Yeah thats fine Mum, but I really don't want to go back.'

'Did anything happen there?'

'Like what?' Orghlaith said sharply.

'I don't know,' Dympna said wondering if there was another reason why Orghlaith was so adamant not to return to Grogan House. She spoke to Sue who confirmed that Orghlaith had made good progress but stressed that she should complete the programme to prevent relapsing in the future. Dympna resolved that Orghlaith would stay with her and that if there were any problems she would be in touch.

'I understand you must be pleased to have Orghlaith back at home Mrs O'Meara but she is much more likely to stay clean if she finishes the whole of her treatment here,' Sue repeated again. 'At least think about it.'

Dympna had decided that Orghlaith was clean and she should stay at home with her and Erin and so the decision was made. Grogan House was no longer a part of the lives of either Dympna or Orghlaith. 'Thanks Mum. Thank you.'

'I'm just glad to have you back my love, but you have to stay clean do ye hear?'

'Yes, I know.'

Orghlaith looked in on Erin before going to bed and couldn't wait to get reacquainted with her daughter again. She was astounded at how big she had gotten in little under four months. She went into her Mum's room to say goodnight. 'Mum I called Dad when I was in Grogan House. He's coming over to London with the boys.'

Dympna was unplaitting her long black hair in front of the mirror. She turned to Orghlaith. 'You invited Seamus over?'

'Yes Mum, he wants to see us – so do Finn and Conrad.'

Ok my love. That's fine. When are they due over?'

'Well he said about two weeks time although he still thinks I'm in rehab so I'll have to call him and let him know I'm back home. He said it would be good to see you too Mum.'

'Well, yes it will be good to see them all. You get yourself to bed my love, I'll call you in the morning.' Dympna was glad that Seamus and the boys were coming over. She had never wanted them to be such a divided family. The boys wrote frequently still and phoned every other week but it wasn't the same, it had never been the same since Seamus took them to Ireland. She missed them terribly, oh God how she missed them. The visits to London had got less and less the older they became and the more responsibilities they got with life as men. Dympna couldn't find it in herself to tell them what had happened – she didn't want the boys and especially Seamus to think she had been a bad Mother and had let Orghlaith down. But now they knew, they knew that not only was Orghlaith a single parent but had just spent the past four months in rehab.

Chapter 4

Seamus, Finn and Conrad had booked themselves in to the Hotel Beaumont near the Kilburn High Street. They were successful businessmen and had done well from the farm back home in Ireland. They had the money to stay in such an expensive hotel so they indulged themselves and each had their own room complete with en suite bathroom and a generous mini-bar. Dympna and Orghlaith walked through the posh doors greeted by the hotel men in their red and gold uniforms. Orghlaith was pushing Erin in the pram. Dympna was pleased Orghlaith had bonded so well with Erin in the past couple of weeks and that she was still managing to spend time with Erin herself. But Dympna was missing not pushing her in that pram and not making up the baby food as often or going to see Erin in the night when she woke up crying – the little things that she missed already and it had only been a couple of weeks.

The boys met Orghlaith and Dympna in the foyer of the hotel. 'Oh Orghlaith it's so good to see you – and who's this little mite..Hello me little darling,' Seamus said as he bent down to Erins height and took her out of the pram. 'Come and see Grandad, and how are you Dympna – looking very well, so ye are.' Seamus said with a cheeky smile.

Dympna had just finished hugging the life out of Finn and Conrad. 'I'm very well Seamus thank you. It's grand to see you all. Just grand.' Dympna couldn't believe she had all her family in the one place – well, apart from the grandchildren and wives of the boys but nevertheless she felt that warm feeling inside. Seamus treated them all to lunch in a posh restaurant in Knightsbridge and everyone got on well. Dympna looked around the table at Orghlaith laughing with her brothers, and Seamus holding Erin. This is how it could have been if we had stayed as a family Dympna thought to herself – it could have been like this...

Orghlaith and the boys stayed in Knightsbridge for a few drinks whilst Seamus, Dympna and Erin went back to Dympna's house. 'It will give them a chance to really spend some time with one another. They're getting on so well,' Dympna said in the cab on the way home. 'And we could have just jumped on the tube you know... This cab is going to cost a bloody fortune Seamus.' Dympna smiled shaking her head.

'Only the best for my girls.' He said back.

Erin went for a little sleep when they got home and Dympna put the kettle on for a brew. The doorbell went and Seamus opened it. He was surprised to see a man standing there behind a massive bunch of flowers. Dooley McGuinness came into the hallway and presented them to Dympna. 'Well thank you Dooley, thats very kind of you.' She placed them down on the kitchen table. 'This is my ex husband Seamus, Seamus this is Dooley McGuinness my next door neighbour.' The two men nodded at one another and grunted a slight hello. 'Seamus is over from Ireland for a week with my two sons visiting.' Dympna explained.

'Well I'm sure you have a lot to catch up on so I won't stay for a brew. Nice to meet you Seamus. Dympna I shall pop in during the week.' Dooley gave her a sly wink and then placed his hand out to Seamus. They shook hands and Dooley made his way out.

'So you've got yeself a little fancy man so you have. Dympna O'Meara I never thought you'd have it in you ye dark horse!' Seamus winked at her and laughed.

'He is my friend Seamus, nothing more.' Dympna said clearing her throat.

'Ah friend my arse! You fancy him!' Seamus was laughing.

'So are ye jealous Seamus, eh?' Dympna said placing her hands on the table.

'Me jealous? Never. Why would I be jealous – what's he got that I haven't?'

'Ah Seamus be quiet and drink your tea and stop being a macho man. Bejesus you're going to drive me mad in this next week you're here,' Dympna said laughing.

'Well I could always stay in your bed Dympna and drive you mad there.'

'Seamus stop talking that filth. I'll wash your mouth out with soap and water so I will,' Dympna said.

They sat down at the table in silence for a minute or two until Seamus broached the subject of Orghlaith. 'Why didn't you tell me what had happened with her? You didn't even tell me she was pregnant. And then I find out not only have I another grandchild but my daughter is in rehab. Why do you think you can do everything all on your own D?' Seamus said touching her hand.

She pulled it away instantly. 'Listen to me Seamus Killoughery... you have lived in Ireland with the boys and I have raised Orghlaith and I was not about to ask for your help or anyone elses help for that matter – I am not a bad Mother,' Dympna replied with a sharp tongue.

'No one said you were a bad Mother D. I'm not saying that. You just should have told me so I could have been involved. Maybe I should have stayed in London all those years ago but I couldn't – this isn't home D. It's not your home either. But I know why you didn't come back to the farm. I know why and I have always understood that.'

'You could have stayed in London, Seamus. You could have stayed. But that's neither here nor there anymore. The main thing is that the boys and Orghliath have a good relationship with one another and we keep this family alive,' Dympna said.

Erin started crying so Dympna went up to take her out of the cot. She came back down to the kitchen with a sleepy-looking Erin. 'So you looked after her while Orghlaith was in rehab?' Seamus asked.

'Yes I did. And you came with me to me cleaning jobs didn't you Erin? And then we would go to the park afterwards or paint with our hands and feet eh.' Dympna said holding Erin in the air.

'That was a lot to take on D – you should have called and told me. I would have got straight on that plane and come over to help – financially and otherwise,' Seamus said.

'You wouldn't have left the farm for too long Seamus or the businesses. I know what you're like.'

'D that's really unfair, if I had have known things were that bad I would have come in a flash,' Seamus said.

'Well things are fine now and Orghlaith is clean and has been really good with Erin since she has been back so hopefully things are back on track.'

'Yes Orghlaith seems really well so she does and that's just grand. You seem to have come out the other side. You can see that little one adores you so she does. Is Nanny D the best nanny in the world?' Seamus said gently shaking Erin's little hand. 'She's a good Mammy and a great Nanny eh?' He said smiling.

Seamus left Dympna and Erin a little later after they'd had supper to head back to the hotel. He had missed her all of the years they had been apart. That's why he had never remarried. Sure, he'd had his flings and one fairly long term relationship but no one ever matched up to Dympna. No other woman had made him feel alive and she still made him feel like that. He remembered seeing her for the first time on the farm back home running away from her brothers who were chasing her with cow shite. He helped her hide from them. He was infatuated with her then and had loved nobody else in his life the way he did her.

Two weeks with the boys and Seamus gave Dympna a taste of what it could have been like had they stayed together. Finn and Conrad were protective over Orghlaith and the little babe and it was as though they hadn't grown up apart. They went sightseeing and ate out as any normal family would. Seamus regretted what he had left behind and when he left Dympna to return home with the boys back to the business he didn't want to leave her. But he didn't tell Dympna that. He smiled and gave her a tight hug. 'I'll be back to see ya D.' And then in seconds the boys and Seamus were gone and Dympna and Orghlaith both felt the emptiness left in the house.

***

Dympna came back through the door ready to cook dinner but found Orghlaith slumped on the sofa in the front room and Erin in the playpen. 'Orghlaith!' Dympna cried out. 'Orghlaith,' she shook her and shook her again but she didn't wake up. She checked her arms and the needle marks were fresh but she couldn't see any instruments or drugs as she quickly scanned the room. 'Oh Jesus!' Dympna called 999 and asked for an ambulance to be sent to the house. 'Yes my daughter has overdosed on heroine.'

Three hours later Orghlaith came round. 'You're going back into rehab.' Dympna said firmly 'You can't keep doing this to yourself or to Erin and I can't take it. I love you and I won't watch you kill yourself anymore.'

'Mum it's only been a few times... Please Mum I can't go back into rehab I won't be able to hack it. Please.'

'A few times is enough. Jesus, Orghlaith don't do this. Apart from yourself you have to think about Erin - you're her Mother! Look at her. You left her in a pissy nappy and hungry while you were off your face – do you think that's fair on her? It's not fair on you either. What did I do? What did I do to make you go down this route? Did I raise you badly...? What did I do? What did I do that was so wrong?' Dympna held back her tears. Orghlaith had to stay over in hospital while the drip cleaned out her system and an appointment was made to get her back into rehab. Dympna kissed her daughter's forehead. 'I love you. I'll be back in the morning,' Dympna said and got a cab back home.

Orghlaith's keyworker Sue and another keyworker from Grogan House, Michael, came to collect Orghlaith a couple of days after she had been sent home from hospital. Sue spoke to Dympna and said how important it was for Orghlaith to complete the full treatment no matter how much better she felt after a couple of months of being there.

Dympna agreed and said 'All I want is for her to get better again.' Sue and Dympna went into the front room where Orghlaith was sat on the sofa with her things packed chatting to Michael. Orghlaith stood up and hugged her Mum. Dympna didn't want to let her go but she knew she had to. Orghlaith then picked up Erin and held on tight 'Mummy will be back soon I promise. Don't forget me.' Orghlaith couldn't hold back and the tears kept coming. She placed Erin gently in the playpen and turned to Dympna 'I'm sorry Mum, I really am sorry. I'll do it this time I promise. For you and Erin.' Orghlaith left and this time it was going to be for a minimum of nine months.

Dympna was surprised at how quickly she adapted to looking after Erin again as well as her cleaning jobs. She had kept two cleaning jobs when Orghlaith came home but had dropped the other three because she wanted to be with Orghlaith in the first few months of her being out of rehab. It was the same again as it had been only a few months before and Dympna got herself and Erin into a routine.

It had been a week since Orghlaith went into rehab and Dympna knew she had to call Seamus and the boys and tell them what had happened. She thought she had been a bad Mother and this was God's way of punishing her. If she had just gone back to Ireland all those years ago and raised Orghlaith in The Green with her family none of this would have happened. Dympna was ashamed to tell Seamus but knew that she couldn't keep it from him as she had done before. The voice on the other end was definitely his smooth southern Irish accent that made his words sound like he was singing. Dympna blurted it out that Orghlaith was back in rehab and before she knew it tears had welled up in those pretty eyes. 'I'm glad you told me this time D. I'll take some time out and get myself over to London, the boys can look after the farm and the business here and I can help with Erin. I'll book a flight for the weekend, what do you say D?' Seamus was surprised that Dympna didn't protest his coming over.

'Yes it would be good to have ye over Seamus, sure it would.' Seamus felt like saying pack your bags and come back home but he knew that would be unwise right now. What was he thinking? They had been apart for nearly 20 years – they were so much older now and she wouldn't want him back would she? She had good old Dooley McGuinness to keep her company anyway. Dooley McGuinness my arse, thought Seamus. She's my woman, and too bledy good for you that's for sure.

Dympna put the phone down and actually felt relief that Seamus was coming over and would be around for a little while. Just to have another adult in the house who she knew so well and who knew her well was what she needed. She wasn't sure why she had felt so compelled to call Seamus this time around and felt uncomfortable that she was excited about him coming to stay. 'Don't be a silly old fool,' Dympna said aloud to herself. His voice and the feelings that came back to her sparked off memories of back home on the Green when they were dating. All the girls fancied Seamus Killoughery and were terrible jealous when Dympna and Seamus became an item. He still had a good head of hair on him as he did all those years ago – red hair with flecks of blonde and emerald green eyes. He was Celtic through and through. Dympna liked the freckles on his hands and the fair hair on his thick strong arms. Seamus was always broad and muscular from working on the fields and playing too many sports. She fell in love with him instantly and thought they would stay on the Green forever. She snapped herself out of this daydream and went to answer the door.

'Dympna! How are ye!' It was Dooley McGuinness in a suit where the trousers were far too high up the waist and jacket sleeves too short.

'Bejesus Dooley that pink shirt would blind anybody – where did ye pick that blighter up from?' Dympna said laughing. Dooley looked surprisingly hurt by Dympna's reaction to the outfit he had spent hours deciding over. She detected his embarrassment 'I'm only kiddin' ye. It looks grand so it does.'

'Ah you had me going there D so you did, I thought you really didn't like me new suit... Now can I come in for a brew... I'm dying of the thirst,' Dooley said, with a bright large smile now Dympna had approved of his attire.

'Well I can hardly say no can I?' Dympna said laughing. Dympna and Dooley drank their tea while Erin had her nap. She told him about Orghlaith and explained that Seamus was coming over at the end of the week.

'Ah sure things will be fine Dympna. You're a strong woman and you'll get through it, although I'm not sure about this Seamus fella taking me place you know!' Dooley laughed.

Dympna laughed too 'Do all Irish men have such a wicked tongue on them?!'

***

Seamus arrived at Gatwick Airport on the Friday night. He couldn't understand how Dympna had managed to stay in London all these years – how had she put up with it – especially Kilburn, it wasn't pretty or beautiful – not like The Green. Seamus had never wanted to live anywhere else – his heart and soul were in The Green and he would no doubt spend the rest of his life there. The thought that Dympna would come back home quickly ran through his head as Seamus waited for his luggage. The cab to Kilburn took Seamus through London as it was at night. Ok so at night it looked quite beautiful all lit up and Central London was bursting with people everywhere... young girls in their micro – minis and stilettos with big hair and heavy make-up. One girl had a t-shirt on with the boys from Wham plastered all across it in bold colours. Jesus, Seamus thought to himself – what was happening to music these days – Wham my arse. He laughed at his take on young people and their taste in the current music trend and shook his head 'You're getting old Seamus aren't ye...' But he still resolved that music today was not as good as it was in his day and London was no match for The Green.

Dympna had prepared a good Irish stew and Erin was still awake when Seamus arrived at the house in Kilburn. 'Oh that's just what I need – I'm ravished, and that plane food is terrible D honestly!' Seamus left his suitcase in the spare room. On his way downstairs he passed photographs that Dympna had kept of them together when they were younger. She had photos of the boys and Orghlaith too, and of course the new edition to the family – Erin. He picked up the photo of Dympna – the photo was at least 30 years old and she was wearing the dress she wore to the first disco Seamus had taken her to. She looked beautiful.

'Come on Seamus ye stew is getting cold!' Dympna shouted up the stairs to him.

He put the photograph down and joined Dympna and Erin in the kitchen. 'Ah D this stew is lovely...' Seamus said touching her hand.

'Would you like some of the bread I made?' Dympna asked pulling her hand away swiftly. He shouldn't have done that Seamus thought to himself, he didn't want to make her feel uncomfortable and he knew they weren't together but he couldn't help it, he just wanted to touch her and it had felt like an eternity since he had held her or felt her skin. It seemed easier to get on with things living in Ireland away from her but now he had started to see and speak to her more often Seamus realised how much he had missed Dympna. They cleaned the dishes away together and bathed Erin. Dympna put her nappy on and fresh babygrow while Seamus entertained Erin so as to distract her from trying to pull her nappy off. 'Is that better me little love? Are ye nice and clean now?' Dympna said giving Erin a big cuddle.

'Ye're great with her D, you really are, and it's been a while since you had to change any nappies and look after a young one eh?' Seamus said. 'Here pass her over and I'll get her to sleep – you go and have a cup of tea and watch your show.' Seamus said. Dympna wasn't sure, she didn't trust anyone else with Erin and felt so protective with her – but she handed her over to Seamus – he was her Grandfather after all. Dympna went to boil the kettle. Ten minutes later Dympna went up to check on Seamus and Erin. She popped her head around the door and Seamus was tucking Erin in. He kissed her forehead. 'Goodnight me little chicken,' he said. Dympna and Seamus retired to the front room and watched D's favourite murder mystery show accompanied by a good few cups of tea and chunky biscuits.

Dympna had never left Erin with anyone else before and was petrified of the thought of anyone else changing her or holding her. But that Saturday night Seamus had persuaded Dympna to come to the theatre with him so she had put her trust in her neighbour Mrs Wallis who was a part-time childminder and very well qualified. Nevertheless, Dympna still checked her credentials and made sure Mrs Wallis produced all her documents to prove she was up to the job of looking after children. 'Honestly Dympna, she's in safe hands, you know I've raised five of me own God bless 'em and they've all turned out alright. Been lookin' after kids since before Jesus was born.' Mrs Wallis said in her cockney accent. Dympna thought she was a lovely lady and had the odd cup of tea and a chat now and then with her, but could she trust her with Erin? Seamus and D left Mrs Wallis' shouse with Dympna resolving to call her later if she needed a babysitter in the end. The fact is, she did need a babysitter, but she didn't want to leave Erin. 'D don't be so ridiculous, she's your neighbour who ye have known for bledy years now! And a qualified childminder! Erin will be fine – it's only for a few hours D and we can collect her after the theatre. Come on, let your hair down woman.' After several cups of tea and a couple of chunky biscuits Seamus managed to persuade Dympna to let Mrs Wallis babysit for Erin while they went to the theatre. Dympna felt a huge amount of guilt though – how could she be going out to the theatre when her daughter was in rehab and leaving her Granddaughter with a stranger. She told Seamus. 'So what are ye to do Dympna? Stay home until Orghlaith comes back? Stop punishing yourself D, you're a good woman and deserve to have some of the good life.'

Dympna left Erin with Mrs Wallis and gave her the phone number to the theatre they were to be in so Mrs Wallis could call if there was an emergency. D left Erin a selection of dinners and desserts in case she 'didn't fancy the chicken stew one'. Mrs

Wallis had to practically push Dympna out of the door, but eventually she left Erin with the kind neighbour and walked back to her house. 'Go and get yourself ready D, we haven't long until the show starts you know.' Seamus said as she walked in. 'I know, I know.'

'She'll be fine, D. I promise. Now go and get dressed up...'

Half and hour later Dympna returned in a little black number with a short black jacket and matching black heels. Her hair had been taken out of the braided bun she wore it in so often and fell gracefully like black cloth down her back. At 50, Dympna looked as if she were still 35. Seamus felt like it was their first date all over again with his heart in his mouth and his stomach flipping over and over. He was actually taking her out again after all those years. There is the frequent argument that love dies or fades as we age, but If it's the real stuff – really the real stuff then it should last. And that's what Seamus felt. She didn't look the same as she did when she was 18 – and neither did he. But it didn't matter, the physical chemistry was shooting off the walls that night.

Chapter 5

The phone rang whilst Dympna was in the bath so Seamus picked it up. 'Hello.' The voice on the other end belonged to Orghlaith's keyworker Sue. She had some bad news for them. Seamus didn't want to reiterate it to Dympna but knew he had to, it would mean a visit to Orghlaith and talking some sense into her.

'Who was that?' Dympna asked as she came in to the kitchen towel drying her hair.

'It was Grogan House – Orghlaith's key worker wants you – or us to come and visit Orghlaith.'

'Oh Jesus whats happened?' Dympna gasped. Seamus explained what Sue had told him. 'Right. That's it. We're leaving soon. I'll get Erin's things together. Can you call them back and tell them we're on our way. It's about a two hour drive so tell them we'll be there by twelve to see Orghlaith.' Dympna placed Erin gently in her playpen in the front room and rushed upstairs to get the essentials – change of clothes, nappies... Next trip for Dympna was to the kitchen to get bottles she'd made the night before and the Bolognese she had made and squished into a less solid substance.

No sooner had Seamus made the call to Grogan House than Dympna was packed and dressed and ready to go with Erin on her hip on one side and baby bag and car keys in the other hand – Dympna seemed to have it all under control. Seamus gently took the baby bag and the keys and placed his hand on her shoulder. 'Let me take that. And I'll drive,' he said. 'Although I think my street cred might be lost after driving that old banger,' he said smiling.

'Now don't knock that car Seamus. It's got me from A to B plenty o' times and I've never had a complaint from it,' Dympna said laughing. But she felt pangs of guilt for laughing. How could she smile? How could she even laugh when this was going on with Orghlaith. 'Anyway, we need to be getting on.' She said in a more serious tone.

'You can laugh D' Seamus said. 'You can still laugh. It's not a crime.'

They arrived at Grogan House at mid-day as Dympna estimated. Seamus was surprised that the old Nissan actually had a bit of bite to it but he did laugh at how ugly the thing was. Dympna should be driving a classy car, he thought. She should be driving a beautiful car down the country lanes in Ireland living a grand life. But she wasn't and he cursed himself for leaving her and Orghlaith in London and taking the boys. All of this was his doing he thought.

He placed his thick stocky arm around Dympna's shoulder as she pushed Erin in the pram and kissed the side of her forehead pulling her into him tightly. She glanced up at him and he gave her the look that said 'I'm here.' 'Come on lets' be going in D.' Seamus grabbed the bottom of the pram whilst Dympna held the other end and they made their way up the stairs to the grand door of Grogan House.

Dympna and Seamus were greeted by Sue and taken into one of the rooms for visitors. Grogan House was indeed a beautiful building in stunning surroundings but the inside was painted with sad faces illuminated by the cream and beige walls that were in desperate need of a repaint. Several patients walked past Dympna and Seamus as they waited in the hallway, staring at them, wary of their presence. Dympna wondered how old the man with the pony tail was who offered them tea and the woman with the bleach blonde hair and gravelly voice who asked them why they were there. A history of addiction that started at 14, an abusive Mother and years of prostitution had clearly aged the blonde woman well beyond her 30 years, though she didn't reveal this to the polite Irish strangers visiting their grand-daughter. Dympna wheeled the pram two and fro looking around the place nervously, anxious to see Orghlaith. Seamus shifted uncomfortably, rubbing his chin with his hands then putting his hands in his trouser pockets. One of the patients had had an accident further down the corridor, a nurse came to the rescue 'It's ok, Sam, it's ok' she said softly assisting the skinny young man to his room and came back to clean up where he had defecated. 'Sorry about this.' She said to Dympna and Seamus with a weak smile as she got the bucket and cleaning stuff out from under the stairs. The atmosphere was unnerving and a sense of the unpredictable lingered throughout.

Orghlaith was in the middle of a group therapy session when Sue interrupted. 'Sorry Simon, can I borrow Orghlaith for a moment please?' she asked the therapist.

'Of course, of course.' Simon replied looking at Orghlaith. Sue smiled at her and led Orghlaith to the room where Dympna and Seamus were anxiously waiting.

She was quiet and withdrawn when she came into the room. Dympna just about recognised her: Orghlaith's black hair was scraped away from her face in a tight pony tail and looked like it needed a good wash. Her face was pale and lifeless and dark circles dominated around her eyes. Erin sat on Dympna's lap as they all congregated around the table. Dympna broke the awkward silence. 'What the Jesus is going on here? I mean what are ye doing to yourself Orghlaith?' she asked, as she entertained Erin with a small toy simultaneously. Orghlaith didn't answer.

Sue proceeded to explain exactly what had called for the emergency visit... 'One thing I want to stress is that we don't want Orghlaith to leave the unit. That's the last thing we want – really. We want her to get better, she's a great girl with so much going for her – and we keep telling her that.' Sue touched Orghlaith's knee reassuringly and smiled. 'But,' she continued, 'but she has broken serious rules here and potentially put other patients at risk too.' Sue explained to Seamus and Dympna that Orghlaith had smuggled drugs into the unit two nights ago – and a man was found in her room.

'What!?' Dympna shouted. 'Who was the man Orghlaith? Oh what have I got to do? You're here to get better and you're bringing men and drugs in? These people are trying to help you and you put two fingers up to them? I am trying to help you too Orghlaith. I am trying...' Dympna didn't finish her sentence as she choked and the tears streamed down her face. Seamus hadn't seen this coming and was somewhat surprised that the strong woman next to him looked so broken and at a loss.

'The man was Max if you must know,' Orghlaith said defiantly. 'It was Max and he fucked me all night and brought me my stuff. So what?' Orghlaith finished.

Dympna just stared at her. Was this really her daughter saying this? Is this who she had raised? What a terrible Mother she had been, she thought. A terrible, terrible Mother. Seamus placed his arm around Dympna. 'It's ok, D, it's ok,' he whispered.

Orghlaith threw her mug of tea against the wall in a rage and started shouting. 'It's ok? It's not fucking ok is it?!! Don't you dare turn up here like you're the supportive Father and Husband – you haven't been here for most of my life – piss off back to Ireland "Dad".' Orghlaith quoted "Dad" using her fingers as speech marks. 'And you Mum? All you care about is Erin. You couldn't give a shit about what happens to me – you never have.

All you did was work and drink. Work and drink, work and drink. What sort of a Mother is that? And now Dad comes back and you two think this is happy fucking families? I get this lot whilst my brothers grow up on the farm and work in the family business with you in Ireland. You wonder why I'm so fucked up? Take a good look at yourselves,' Orghlaith said.

'Now just a minute,' Dympna said placing Erin on Seamus' lap; She leaned across the table so she was closer to Orghlaith. 'Just you wait a minute young lady.' The room went quiet as her firm tone of voice took over. 'I raised you the best I could and I worked my arse off to put food on the bledy table and send you to a good school. I taught you right from wrong and that good old thing called morality. Now listen here: my family were murdered when I was a girl and I'd give anything to get them back – even for just a second. So do you think that I'd have a child of me own only to not love it and not want the best for it? Do you? I have loved and raised ye with all good intentions I swear by God so don't ye dare sit there as if you know what hard done – by is. Have you spoken to the other patients? Have you? Have you asked them what they've been through? I'll bet you've had a walk in the park compared to them yet still you insist on putting that shite into your body.' Dympna returned to her seat exhausted by what she had just said.

'Oh you're such a bloody martyr aren't you Mum? You were a cold cow to me all the time and you know why? Because I wasn't like you. I wasn't a cold emotionally detached bitch and I didn't believe in your religious bullshit you tried to brainwash me with!' Orghlaith shouted at Dympna.

Dympna got up and slapped Orghlaith hard across the face. 'How dare you!?' Dympna shouted.

'Woah woah!' Sue jumped up. 'Ok, ok guys I think we need a breather. Let's take a break shall we.' Years of experience with the families of addicts had taught Sue alot, she knew Dympna was in pain, they all were. Mother and daughter looked at each other and looked away eyes filling, Orghlaith holding her face where Dympna's handprint remained. Dympna immediately regretted the hasty action.

Sue led Seamus and Dympna to another room and brought them some tea and biscuits. 'Just take some time out, calm down and come back and meet Orghlaith and I in the other room when you're ready,' Sue said softly.

'I'm so sorry,' Dympna said to Sue.

'Don't worry Mrs O'Meara, these are difficult times for everyone. It's hard for the families involved as well as the patient and a lot of underlying stuff tends to come out whilst the patients are in therapy. Don't worry,' Sue said reassuring Dympna.

'I wouldn't be here if I didn't care,' Dympna said shaking her head and wiping her eyes. Dympna turned to Seamus 'I did the best I could with Orghlaith. I love her Seamus... Maybe I was too cold... Maybe I didn't show her enough love and pushed too much with the Church... Maybe'

'Stop it D. Orghlaith's saying all that because she's angry. She's angry and frustrated and probably angry at herself for being here too. Whatever you did or didn't do is not the reason Orghlaith got on the drugs D. You can't blame yourself. If anyone's to blame for this whole mess it's me, I should have taken you all with me to Ireland – she would have loved it there,' Seamus said it before he could stop himself.

'I know it would have been different... I know if I had come with you and the boys then we wouldn't be sitting here now and Orghlaith wouldn't be in such a state,' Dympna said.

'I didn't mean it like that D,' Seamus said. 'Come on we better go back in and see her. See if we can help her to stay here.'

Dympna said touching Seamus' knee. He wanted to hold Dympna and kiss her and tell her it was all going to be alright and Orghlaith would recover and they'd all go back to Ireland

and live happily ever after. He really wanted that to be true. They went back into the room. Orghlaith had been crying, her eyes red and slightly swollen. Dympna went straight over and gave her a hug. 'I never meant for this to happen to you. But look – look at her,' Dympna pointed at Erin. 'Isn't that enough to make you want to get better?'

Erin was sitting on the floor amusing herself with an odd looking toy oblivious to what was going on around her. Orghlaith looked at Erin and went to pick her up. Erin began to cry and Orghlaith immediately put her back down on the floor to play. 'She doesn't even know me. It's you she goes to now Mum,' Orghlaith said sitting down. 'It's because she's got used to me. Get better Orghlaith and then you can come home and bond with her and bring her up. She's your daughter Orghlaith and I'm only looking after her until you get better. Would you prefer it to be a stranger? Of course not,' Dympna said.

'I spoke to the rest of the team about Orghlaith's situation when you wre having some time out and it has been agreed that Orghlaith be on her final warning but has another chance to stay and complete the programme if she wants to,' Sue said.

'Well that's great news,' Seamus said. 'The sooner you get better the sooner you can come home and start living your life,' he finished.

'What life?' Orghlaith retorted. 'I'm a single Mum with no qualifications and no job. What life is that to return to?' Orghlaith said.

'What incentive is that?' 'You chose to get pregnant,' Dympna said.

'Did I?' said Orghlaith. 'I didn't have much choice about having it though did I Mum? But I'll stay and do the programme. I'll do it for Erin.' Orghlaith picked Erin up and held her tight covering her in kisses. 'I'll see you soon sweetheart.' Orghlaith said. 'Meeting over,' Orghlaith concluded, and she left the room without saying a word to Seamus or Dympna.

Seamus and Dympna sat in the car outside Grogan House taking in what had just happened with their only daughter. Seamus had not seen Dympna so emotionally drained in a long time – it was a rare thing for D to fall apart and he was surprised she was letting him see how upset she was because it just wasn't like her. 'I haven't seen you so down in a long time D,' Seamus said stroking her hair.

She let him stroke her hair – it felt good. 'Maybe I was a cold Mother to her... And I was forceful with the Religion. All the things she said were true Seamus. But I didn't have anyone to tell me how to raise a daughter on me own. So much had happened in my life and I wanted her to be strong and deal with life and all the shite I knew it might throw at her but I sent her the other way. I loved her in the wrong way – I was cold and too harsh when she needed softness and a Mother's touch, and now she's full of anger and bitterness. I put her in that rehab unit all by myself.' Dympna cried hard into Seamus' shoulder. He leaned across his driver seat and manouvered himself so he could give her a good hug. She felt comforted and safe in his big arms and his familiar smell made her cry even more.

'You are a great woman and you were a great Mother to Orghlaith and still are. It's not just you she blames – it's me too and for that she's right. I should never have left and taken the boys and not her. I just thought a girl needed her Mother and the boys needed a Father figure. I ended up ruining you and her. I don't blame Orghlaith for feeling like that towards me. You brought her up the best way you know how D. Parents make mistakes – it's allowed. I don't know many Mothers would look after their daughter's child so she could get an education,' Seamus said. 'And from the sounds of things this Max fella or whatever his name is has had a pretty big influence over her.'

'Oh Seamus he's an absolute gobshite – a smarmy git, he says he's got Irish blood in him but I can't believe that – for the Love of God he's the worst man I've ever met – other than you,' Dympna cracked a smile through the tears.

'Well I'll give you that one D, I'll give you that one. I've had me moments that's for sure, but I'm not all that bad I promise,' Seamus said laughing. 'Now let us get you home. We could sit here talking forever about whose fault it is but the main thing is that Orghlaith gets better and we make sure she does it,' Seamus said.

'Why are you doing this Seamus? Why are you back after all these years?' Dympna asked.

He knew she was going to ask that question at one point. He hadn't visited for this long or spent so much time with Orghlaith or D since Orghlaith was a little girl. 'Because my little girl is in rehab and you need my support. I should have been there more over the years and now is my chance to make it right.' Seamus said. 'Raising Finn and Conrad was no easy game either D. They were little bastards at times I tell ye!' Seamus said laughing through tears.

Orghlaith had missed her brothers all these years, she envied their life over there too, it hadn't been enough seeing Finn and Con and her Dad only occasionally. And what had been wrong with her anyway? Why did Dad take the boys and not her? She remembered all the times Seamus had visited with Finn and Con, crying hysterically when they left for the airport, tugging at Dympna's clothes begging for them to go back to Ireland with the boys and Dad Dympna crying never explaining why they couldn't all be together. Seamus remembered those times too as they drove back from Grogan House that day. Before long the boys had grown and joined Seamus to help run the farm business and of course the three year gaps when they were at University and a year for travelling so Seamus and the boys saw even less of

Orghlaith and Dympna. It killed Seamus to see Dympna or hear her voice on the phone. Not seeing her made it almost more bearable to be without her. But now things had changed and Seamus knew this was his chance to bring his family back together and more than anything, he wanted Dympna back. He had to have her back.

Chapter 6

Dympna put Erin to bed and retreated to her chair in the living room, it was old and worn and she had sat in it so many times over the years it had moulded to fit her shape. She collapsed into the chair letting it take the weight of her exhausted body and heavy head. Seamus brought in the tea. The only sound in the room was the clinking of the teaspoon as Seamus stirred the sugar in his cup. Dympna switched on the television and leaned forward to take a sip of her tea. *'And the main news today is of course the bombing in County Fermenagh.'* The newsreader said solemnly. *'Authorities have confirmed 11 people have been killed and over 60 injured. Among those killed were a married couple, a retired policeman and a nurse.'*

'It's the IRA Seamus I'm telling you, it's them,' Dympna said sighing. 'They do us no justice by behaving in such a manner. I'm ashamed to be a Celt at times – do you know how many looks and comments I get when people hear me accent over here? Everyone thinks I'm hiding a bomb in me knickers I swear. Organisations like that do nothing for the reputation of good Irish people, and where has it gotten them Seamus really? Where has it gotten them? Ireland is no better off politically then they were twenty years ago – if anything they've made it worse. God forgive them.' Dympna said shaking her head.

'I think they've done what they've been forced to do D. I don't agree with killing innocent civilians but Ireland doesn't belong to England D. For the love of God can they not see it needs independence and it needs people to fight for that,' Seamus said.

'Yes well, fighting for it is one thing, but murdering people for it is another.'

'Do you feel no loyalty to your country anymore D?' Seamus asked.

'It's not about loyalty.' Dympna pointed at the television screen footage of bodies being pulled from the rubble of the building the bomb had gone off in. 'You call that loyalty? That is no more and no less than barbaric Seamus, and I love my country with all my bones but that is no way to deal with political matters. I wonder if they even know what they're fighting for anymore,' Dympna said.

Seamus lay in bed in the spare room unable to sleep with all the thoughts whirring in his mind. He could hear Dympna's movements as she washed in the bathroom and moved into her bedroom where she switched on her radio. Ella Fitzgerald's voice came floating out and Dympna was soothed at the sweet sound. Seamus thought Fitzgerald's songs were too sad and her voice so beautiful it made you feel too much without even knowing why. It's called emotions Seamus Killoughery, he could hear Dympna saying to him. That's what happens when you hear a beautiful song or read a great novel. He smiled as he imagined Dympna saying her piece to him so intense with feeling about the things she believed in. Her music continued to play and Seamus could hear the sounds of her drawers open and close and then just the sound of Ella's voice. She must be undressing, Seamus thought. He wondered what Dympna's body would look like naked now – it had been years since they had seen each other naked. He could tell through her clothes she had kept herself lithe and trim – her well fitted blouses and skirts skimmed a beautiful hourglass figure which he tried to admire with as much discretion as he possibly could. Seamus closed his eyes and tried to shut out the overwhelming need to go into the room next door and devour every inch of her. He fought the mental pictures and the aching between his legs – he tried to think of more practical things like the business back home or buying Dympna a new car but he couldn't push her out of his mind or how much he wanted her. He went to the bathroom and on his return passed Dympna's bedroom where the door was slightly ajar. He peered through the crack in the door and could just see D in front of her mirror brushing her hair. Seamus was surprised that a woman of 50 could still have such a figure. Age and life are not always merciful on the human form, every smile, every frown, days spent in the sun, late nights, early starts with too much coffee to see us through. Such things sketch themselves across our form and if you look close enough reveal tell tale signs of a life lived this way or that. But Dympna's love of whiskey or two and thick slices of white bread ham sandwiches had not done her any harm. Her body was trim and lithe and skin still glowed. She moisturised her body and face unaware of Seamus' presence outside her door. Seamus held on to the crotch of his trousers – he felt silly. He looked down to the floor and shook his head at himself feeling that he had behaved like a foolish schoolboy, what was he doing behaving this way he thought. But an impulsive change in thought led him into Dympna's bedroom and before he could stop himself he'd walked in and blurted out. 'I love you D.'

Seamus what are you doing?' Dympna shouted alarmed. She put down her hairbrush and grabbed her dressing gown tying the belt so tight it strangled her stomach. Her cheeks blushed.

'Ah don't worry D I've seen it all before, we've had three kids together!' He hadn't meant to make her feel uncomfortable, but he needed to talk to her, he needed to.'D come on, ye know what's going on between us. Are ye saying you don't regret all these years being apart?' He sat on the end of her bed and looked around the room. 'Bejesus are you sure you have enough pictures and moulds of Jesus and his Mam? Maybe I should buy you a few more – just in case you run out,' Seamus smiled.

Dympna laughed. Her room was covered with religious paintings, statues and ornaments of all shape and size. 'Now don't be taking the Michael out of me Seamus Killoughery, sarcasm is the lowest form of wit did ye know that?' She smiled at him. They looked at each other in silence for a moment, the banter easing the awkward atmosphere.

'Sit down here, sit down a minute D please,' Seamus patted the space on the bed next to him. She succumbed and sat down. 'I don't bite,' Seamus smiled.

'Ah but I think you do Seamus, I think you do - all that bledy charm and your sparkly eyes, I'll not be falling for it so I won't do ye hear? Do ye hear?' Dympna said arms folded across her chest. 'I fell for it once and look where it got us.'

'Why are you fighting us? You won't let it happen will you? You just won't let it happen and I can't understand why,' Seamus said in a slightly softer tone.

'Because you left and I can't forget that, you broke my heart – I'll not go through that again,' Dympna said firmly.

'I left D but you didn't come with me did you? What's the difference? I couldn't stay in London and you couldn't stay in Ireland. We left each other,' Seamus replied.

'No Seamus, I couldn't go back there after what happened to my family and you know that. You could have stayed here it's just that you wouldn't and there is a difference between couldn't and wouldn't. You chose to go.'

'We can argue this until the cows come home but the fact is we've a chance now, a chance to make it right,' Seamus said touching Dympna's hand.

'Seamus I have so much going on with Orghlaith – she needs my support; and I have Erin to look after as well as me cleaning jobs. I'm not about to up sticks and move to Ireland and you're not about to move to London so we can be together are you? It's bad timing – it always has been with us.' Dympna said these words with her rational mind. Dympna sat on the bed with her dressing gown still pinned to her for dear life. Seamus next to her.

'If you don't want me D that's fine, I'll deal with it but don't use Orghlaith and Erin as an excuse. I will be here to support you through it all – the boys are well able to keep managing the business for me back home,' Seamus said. He knew now he needed to be there more than ever, he just hoped she would let him in.

'I'm not giving you excuses Seamus. Starting something now would be foolish on both parts. But I'm glad you're here, your support has meant so much. Thank you,' Dympna squeezed Seamus' hand tight and smiled at Seamus letting him know she still loved him – it was just the wrong time.

He gave a long hug and kissed her forehead lightly. 'I'll let you get some sleep.' He went back to bed glad that he had acted on impulse and gone into her room because if he hadn't he would never have realised just how much she still loved him. She was right though, he thought to himself, she was right – as with most things. The timing was all off – there was too much going on. But when would it be good timing? When would they be together again? At least now though, at least now he knew she still cared and that was enough for the present time.

Neither Dympna nor Seamus slept well that night both churning thoughts over in their minds of what had happened that evening – the what ifs, the possibilities, the whys and why nots... The following morning was slightly awkward and in an attempt to remedy this Seamus offered to cook that evening. 'That would be lovely, thanks. I'll be home from me last job about half six. Now I can leave Erin with Mrs Wallis or you can take her for the day Seamus? I know you have phone calls to make to the boys about work but if you'd like to spend a bit of time with her on your own?...' Dympna asked.

'Oh I'll have her of course I will D, it will be my pleasure. I can make the phone calls to Finn and Con as well – us men can multi task at times too you know,' Seamus smiled.

'Well I wouldn't be putting any of me betting money on that one Seamus but I'm sure you'll be fine with Erin.' They both laughed and the atmosphere at once lightened. Seamus had been left strict instructions about what Erin should eat and should not eat. 'I've left it all in the fridge and labelled it so she has the lasagne for her lunch and a bit of that cake for pudding ok. When you speak to the boys send them my love and tell them I'll call when I get in tonight.' Dympna left for work. Seamus checked in with the boys at home and they were doing just fine. Finn's wife was pregnant again and he was over the moon. 'Wait 'til I tell your Mother... She'll be so happy! That's great news – congratulations son! Just make sure you don't go and get too pissed celebrating tonight and leave the business to ruin! I know the pair of you will be going straight down to the Rose and Crown for a few pints after that news!' Seamus said.

Seamus looked at Erin and imagined all of the family in one house together – like it should be. He sighed. 'Right me little chicken, we need to go and get some meat if Grandad is to cook a good meal for Nanny D tonight.' Erin looked up with big brown eyes and laughed innocently. She was two now and had a mass of black hair that D had made into a French plait that day. Seamus took her on a little trip along the Kilburn High Street to the butchers D had pointed out to him before. Don't get the meat from anywhere else, D had said to him. But the butchers had run out of beef and he wanted to make a Bolognese. He managed to find another butchers further on the high street.

'Hi how are ye, I'll have a pound of that mince beef... that ham looks good as well – I'll take a few slices of that too.

Thanks.' Seamus said to the man in the white coat behind the counter. Erin's face was squished up against the glass that shielded the customers from the field of meats on display.

'No problem.' The butcher wrapped his hand in a fresh white bag and grabbed the slabs of meat from the display. 'Must be difficult having that accent after what your lot have done.' The butcher said as he wrapped the meat in cellophane.

Seamus looked at the man shocked that someone could make such a blatant insult. 'What do ye mean us lot?' Seamus said holding himself back from smacking this fella in the face.

'Well incase you ain't heard the news there was that bombing that killed a load of innocent people on our Remembrance Day, and they reckon it was, you know, the IRA,' the butcher whispered.

'Ah yes the bombing,' Seamus said with an intended condescending tone at the man's ignorance. 'Yes it was a terrible thing. Terrible.' Seamus handed over the money in exchange for the meat.

'Oh, so you don't agree with it then?' Butcher man said.

Why would I agree with it?' Seamus asked becoming more agitated at this man. 'Well, I don't know, I just thought you would... You know...' The butcher man said.

'Well no I don't. I don't agree that innocent people were killed – I'm sure most people don't. Ask her there what she thinks why don't ye?'. Seamus said pointing at a random customer. He left the shop pissed off with the conversation he had just had. He wondered if the butcher actually knew he had insulted him or if it seemed natural to ask an Irish person what they thought about the recent bombing – ok natural to ask maybe, but to assume he agreed with it annoyed Seamus. We are all tarred with the same brush by certain people he thought. D was right.

It had started to rain heavily. Bustles of people on Kilburn High Street were knocking into one another and umbrellas were colliding as the little ants ran for cover under the bus stop shelters or tried to make their way home a little quicker than usual. Grey clouds covered London town and the thunder and lightning came every few minutes. Seamus pulled Erin's raincover over her buggy and double checked she was strapped in before pushing her at extra speed to get home quicker. It made no difference – Seamus was absolutely drenched by the time he got back home.

Dympna came to the door. 'Oh come in – you're wet through aren't ye. Go up and get changed Seamus – I'll take Erin.' D said.

'You're home from work early.'

'Yes I finished early so I just missed the rain. Did you get the meat?' she asked. Seamus pointed to the undercarriage of the buggy and hurried upstairs to change from the soaking clothes. He had a quick shower – the hot water on his skin felt so good – especially after being in the freezing cold.

They prepared the meal and Seamus told D what the butcher had said. 'See, I told you didn't I? Didn't I tell you? That's how some people think of the Irish Seamus,' D said knowingly.

'I know D, I just didn't expect that. I suppose it is ignorance – lack of knowledge as to what's really going on and the complexity of the situation.'

'Well yes, that's part of it. It's implying that we all advocate terrorist behaviour. I don't and neither do a lot of the Irish community here that I know of either.'

'But then that's the ignorance of people like that – it's not our fault.'

'No it's not our fault Seamus. But it doesn't help when our own people are killing each other let alone the English. It makes me so angry. Murdering each other is not solving anything. I don't know why there can't be some sort of resolution,' D said as she cut peppers on the chopping board. 'Pass us the onions over would ye.' They chopped the veg and made dinner together discussing the political state of Ireland right through to Dympna's love of murder mystery shows. Erin sat in the playpen in the kitchen amusing herself for a while before demanding attention from one of the adults.

The night ended with D and Seamus drinking tea and eating biscuits. 'I must call Grogan House tomorrow to see how Orghlaith is ye know... I hope she is trying to get herself on the mend,' Dympna said sighing.

'She'll be fine D. She'll come through it and things will work themselves out – they always do,' Seamus said reassuringly.

Chapter 7

'Seamus! Oh Jesus, Seamus! Wake up!' Dympna cried. 'Oh God! Please No! No!' Seamus jolted upright and sprung out of the bed. Dympna explained to Seamus through tears and a near panic attack that Erin was gone. He managed to take the note that Dympna gripped so tightly in her hand and make sense of the situation:

Dear Mum,

Firstly, I am clean – no more drugs. I didn't need to finish the programme because I got myself together really quickly and didn't want to stay longer with the rest of those losers in there – I couldn't take it. But I'm taking Erin – she's all I have. She is my daughter and I couldn't let you take her from me and play happy families with you and that shite of a Father of mine. Decided to come back after all these years did he? A bit too fucking late weren't you Seamus?

Anyway Mum, don't worry about where we're staying or anything – Max has sorted us out a lovely place to live and things will be just fine. I know you don't approve of him but he's not a bad man – got a good heart. I just want some space and to live my life as I want. I'll be in touch.

I love you, Orghlaith.

Seamus finished reading the letter. 'How did she get into the house D? I can't believe we didn't hear her or hear Erin cry... I can't believe it,' Seamus said to Dympna.

'The letter doesn't sound like her Seamus – it sounds like it's been written by another hand – not by my Orghlaith. Maybe I just don't know her anymore – maybe I never did,' Dympna said. She raised her hand to her forehead and rubbed it in disbelief – she felt helpless. D wondered why Grogan House hadn't called her when they discovered Orghlaith had gone... She had the right to leave the unit but surely Sue or Mike could have called to say Orghlaith had quit yet again. Maybe they had given up on trying to make her stay. 'I'm phoning the police Seamus. I'm phoning the police and I have to tell them Orghlaith has kidnapped Erin. What else can I do?' D said.

She ached for an answer – for someone to tell her what was the right thing to do. 'What about the social services D? They might be more helpful than the police?' Seamus said.

'Yes. Yes, social services. Right.' Dympna went straight downstairs to get the phone book out from the cupboard under the stairs... There were so many social service listings so she called the main line and they connected her to the services local to Kilburn.

By the time she actually got to speak to the woman she needed she had been connected and reconnected six times. Dympna tried to control the unsteady hand that held the 1970s phone and took a deep breath to control the overwhelming emotion building up inside her. 'Hello... Yes. Well the situation is that my Granddaughter ... Yes my daughter has taken her – kidnapped her from the care of myself and her Grandfather... No I am not the legal guardian of Erin... Right. Ok. But my daughter has just left a rehab unit. She didn't complete the programme. She is a drug addict and so is her boyfriend and they have my granddaughter!' At this point Dympna started crying.

Seamus took the phone from her. 'Hello, yes, I am the Grandfather... So exactly what rights do myself and my wife have over our grandchild?... Well that's really bloody helpful isn't it.' Seamus said anger mounting at the unhelpful monotonous voice on the other end of the line. 'Well if I knew where my daughter was then I would be going to get her and my Granddaughter wouldn't I? This is why we're on the phone to you people thinking you might bledy been able to help. But obviously not,' Seamus said. He slammed the phone down in frustration.

'I thought it was easier to say we were both looking after Erin – less complicated,' D said staring out the window.

'Oh yeah I know. But it doesn't seem to matter anyway D. We – or you have no legal rights over Erin anyway,' Seamus said.

'Can you believe that? I can't believe that after all this time of looking after her I have no rights and they are just not willing to do anything. I told her Erin was at risk because Orghlaith is an addict and you know what she said Seamus? She said she would take down that I had reported possible neglect of a child but there was not a lot she could do especially because we didn't know where Orghlaith was living,' Dympna said, shaking her head. 'I have to call the police now Seamus – that's the only way we'll have any chance of finding them both. I'm worried for them both. Jesus.' Dympna cupped her face in her hands and Seamus hugged her and kissed her head. She was comforted by his strong hold and the familiar scent of him. At least she wasn't facing this alone. She looked up at Seamus. 'Do you remember when we lost him?' she said. 'If I lose these two it means God would have taken three of my children. Three he has taken on me. He took me family and now he takes me children. Am I such a bad person Seamus? Am I? Maybe I am blind and stupid to believe still.'

'Don't lose your Faith just yet D.' Seamus said still holding her. Memories of the baby boy who had died of meningitis flooded the heads of Seamus and Dympna... How close they had both gotten to him only for him to leave them so suddenly at just under a year old. He was their first. Neither had ever forgotten.

Seamus broke the silence. 'Come on D, we need to sort this out.'

Dympna wiped her face and pulled her shirt straight as if to get control of the situation. 'You're right, you're right. I'm going to call the police,' she said in a firm authoritative tone.

Two police officers arrived that evening – a detective and a sergeant. They took details of Orghlaith, Erin and Max as well. Orghlaith and Erin were placed as Missing Persons with Erin being described as a child at risk. An investigation into their whereabouts would begin straight away and the detective – Paul Knight seemed a good guy with genuine concern over the safety of both the girls. He was one of the few people Dympna had told about Orghlaith's drug addiction that didn't pass judgement on either Orghliath or Dympna which surprised D. People were quick to judge and seek someone or something to blame but Detective Knight had a compassionate side which left Dympna and Seamus with a little hope that they would find the O'Meara girls and bring them home. Once Paul Knight and his sergeant had gone Dympna headed off to Church. Seamus stayed home thinking she probably needed a moment to herself and with Him upstairs. Religion had phased out of Seamus' life but he knew it meant a lot to Dympna; He had a great admiration and respect for the commitment and strength of her belief, even at times like this when she must have felt that He was letting her down – again. Indeed, Seamus could not have read Dympna's feeling any better. She walked down the aisle in the Church between the two sets of Pews separated by a few feet of each other, her heels making a clink clinking sound on the worn out wooden floor. The ceiling was held by monstrous pillars of concrete and decorated with biblical scenes; archangel Gabriel appeared more than once surrounded by beautiful Cherobs with cute chunky bodies and golden ringlets. She then came face to face with the statue so familiar. Easily recognisable to those who believed, who didn't believe, historians, archaeologists, writers and people alike. The crown of thorns on the head, the bolts through the hands holding up the arms' and the ankles bound together attached to a cross. She looked with questioning eyes, crossed herself once more and knelt praying for her girls. But she also questioned Him, she whispered and sought to find the answers to a world she could no longer make sense of. She didn't find her answer that evening, but found the silence and beauty of the Church as a cushion for the blows she had taken that day and many a time before.

Chapter 8

Orghlaith opened the door to the flat after taking Erin to the park that day. She knew that only a few miles away in Kilburn Dympna had realised by now that Erin was gone and she was probably heartbroken. Not heartbroken that I have left your life too though, eh Mum, Orghlaith thought. How wrong Orghlaith was, if only she knew. She put these thoughts aside and focused on the fact that she had Erin back. She was hers after all. 'Welcome home sweetheart.' Orghlaith whispered in Erin's ear as they entered the beautiful apartment Max had bought. Orghlaith loved it, especially after living in the rehab unit for what felt like eternity. Orghlaith's crucial weakness was her lust for the hedonistic lifestyle of all things wonderful and feel-good without any rules or discipline – it was her Achilles heel and she knew it. Max knew it as well, too well. He had showed her the flat after she had broken out of Grogan House – the best feeling she had had since her first hit. The flat, with its super-modern style blew Orghlaith away. The French doors in the living room that led on to the balcony spying over London town, the seduction of the blood red sofas arranged in a square surrounding the big fluffy white rug, the remote controls for everything from the windows to the cabinet filled with fine wine (recommended to Max by the local Italian restaurateur), and their bedroom, ah the bedroom with a four-poster oak bed draped in velvet red curtains complemented by the oak floorboards that ran throughout the apartment – Orghlaith thought it was fabulous. Max had laid a beautiful corset and knickers on the bed with intricate patterns and matching stockings for her to wear on their first night alone in the new flat. The sex, as usual, was so damn good it came close to a hit of Big Harry. But nothing was better than that. So she was like a kid with the key to every sweet shop in London oblivious to the fact that the owner of this store, Max, was no Willy Wonka – there would be no Golden Ticket in anything she unwrapped from him.

Orghlaith's favourite room was the bathroom which had a huge Jacuzzi and an incredible mirror with light-bulbs surrounding it – just like the movie stars had in their dressing rooms in the old films. She remembered Marilyn Monroe and Doris Day combing their blonde locks in such a mirror and admiring their beautiful reflection. D loved those films too. They watched them together on Sundays. Orghlaith would apply make up in the glamorous bathroom whilst wrapped in soft white towels purchased from Jacque Blanc & Co. She was worth a million dollars in that bathroom, just like the Hollywood starlets.

There was the extra room that had been made into Erin's room – it was very girly – all pretty in pink and just what Orghlaith thought a little girl's room should look like. Max had kitted it all out as he said he would as they had planned over the phone whilst she was at Grogan House: she would get out of that dive, go to Kilburn and take Erin using the keys she still had to Dympna's house. They would be a happy family – start again in this wonderful new place without her interfering Mother and her good for nothing Father as Max had described Seamus and D. Orghlaith felt a twinge of guilt as these words left Max's lips but she nodded in agreement and came to believe that they were wretched parents who cared nothing for her – only Erin – who wasn't even theirs anyway. She was clean now, and that was it. She had to make this work this time so she could have the family she wanted. All that mattered to her right now was Max and Erin

– they were going to have it all. She would look after Erin until she was old enough for nursery and school and then she would go back to University and eventually to full-time work. In the meantime, Max would be the main source of income. Erin would want for nothing, Orghlaith reasoned, Max was loaded. Inheritance money from his Uncle had assured him four properties in the UK and what appeared to be an infinite amount of cash in the bank. And ok, he still dealt the drugs here and there with some Arab guys she'd met a couple of times on the Kings Road but it was nothing major – he did that just to get some more cash in – he did it for them. Sure, he'd been out of order in the past but he had wooed her back – come all the way to Grogan House to see her with huge flowers... Found the room she was in and crawled through the window – how romantic Orghlaith thought as she briefly reminisced back to the night he persuaded her to leave the unit and come back with him to London.

Orghlaith placed Erin on her brand new play mat with all sorts of shiny objects and furry animals Erin hadn't seen before – this was different to the one she was used to at nanny D's which explained the bewildered expression on Erin's face, her little hands hesitating at the giant green frog with boggly eyes. Erin did not befriend the rather ugly frog and instead opted at looking in the mirror at herself touching her reflection and laughing. Orghlaith gazed around the room and realised how much effort Max had put in to the room for Erin – he must really care, really want us both she thought. 'Look at your new room sweetheart,' Orghlaith said kneeling down to Erin's level. 'Look how lovely it is – Max did all this for us – all for you my darling.' She picked Erin up and hugged her close but Erin began to try to wriggle free so she took the playmat and Erin into the living room to keep an eye on her whilst she made a late lunch. Orghlaith continued that day to try and reacquaint herself with a daughter she hardly knew. Erin spat out the cheese sandwich Orghlaith had made her and cried. 'I don't know what you like sweetheart... I don't know – how am I suppose to know?..' Orghlaith said aloud frustrated and upset. Of course I don't know, Orghlaith thought to herself – how could I know when good old nanny D sent me off to rehab so she could have you to herself and get back with good old Daddy Seamus. Yes, Orghlaith thought, that was one thing Max was definitely right about – she had tried to take Erin from me – my own daughter and raise her as her own like they all did back in Ireland when they were too ashamed to admit their daughter was a single parent with a bastard child. She didn't care about me – just herself and her religion – what sanctimonious bullshit Orghlaith thought.

Orghlaith managed to satisfy Erin's appetite with a lasagne ready-meal mashed up into a mushy substance easier on Erin's few teeth and the others yet to cut through that had left the little mite in bouts of pain adults soon forgot about until their wisdom teeth appeared in later years. The little one was satisfied with this meal and took her late afternoon nap with a warm, full belly. Whilst Erin slept soundly Orghlaith sat watching television but it might as well have been a blank screen as her mind wandered off to thoughts about Max's whereabouts – he said he only used now and again and he was selling for the money but how long did it take to make a couple of deals – he'd been gone since early that morning... She thought about Dympna and resolved that D didn't give a shit about her and when things got tough took the easy option and carted Orghlaith off to rehab so she didn't have to deal with it. Good parenting Mum, Orghlaith thought, shaking her head. She contemplated how different things could have been had she not got pregnant – if she could have gone to Uni and been a student without the pressure of being Mum too. Would she have had Erin if Dympna hadn't laid on the guilt about abortion so much? Who knows, it didn't feel like it was her

94

decision to make at the time anyway – Dympna had made it for her. But Erin was here now and for Erin's sake Orghlaith had to make sure she stayed clean. But with Max dealing and using himself (he wasn't an addict he said, only used recreationally) Orghlaith was going to have a daily battle against the brown – and the Charlie and the pills, but the brown was the hardest to leave alone. The biggest war for Orghlaith, however, was not tangible or edible or available as liquid, solid or powder or pills. It wasn't wrapped in anything or disguised as something else and no one else could see or understand it. The greatest war she faced reader, was against the demon wedged deep inside her, it kicked and thrashed around stamping it's clawed foot as a three year old child would hoping if it went on for long enough you'd snap and give in if only for a few seconds you could relieve the torture and have some peace. But every time you give in to the child it simply repeats the tantrum knowing eventually you will cave. Each tantrum gets worse and each demands a bigger and better reward. Orghlaith's demon seems to know when she is at her most vulnerable and pokes at her during these times, encouraging her to fuck it all, be reckless, be impulsive, tighten the belt around the arm and inject the magic of mind blowing euphoria – just this once. Just this once. But like the child, the demon wants bigger and better each time and just once will never happen – because it will happen again and again and again. Orghlaith knows this, which is why she tries to keep the beast inside under lock and key. Every day a war wages between him and her with Orghlaith so far the undefeated.

Chapter 9

'*A young Mother and her daughter are still missing after 3 months. Detective Paul Knight is leading the investigation into their disappearance.*'

Max switched the television off. 'She knows you're not bloody missing for God's sake, you left her a note. It's not like they don't know you're with me is it. They can't force you to be in contact with your Mother if you don't want to be. Anyway, look what I got this morning,' Max said, waving a wad of cash in front of Orghlaith's face. She was still thinking about the news bulletin – there had been several since she had taken Erin – especially in the beginning. Max was so worried the police would find them and he would lose the girls (well that's what he told Orghlaith anyway) that he made Orghlaith hack off her beautiful black mane of hair and bleach it. She now sported a blonde bob and the weight had dropped off again from her once curvy, slender frame. 'Well at least no one will recognise you now – hopefully. And I think the blonde bob looks incredibly sexy,' Max had said that day. She no longer wore her bangles and rubber bracelets or the ripped t-shirts she had loved so much. Max had said they looked 'common' and bought her clothes and jewellery to create what he called 'a more refined wardrobe.' Her bracelets were replaced with a single gold bracelet – small and delicate with a diamond in the middle and the ripped t-shirts replaced with shirts or camisoles and cardigans. The sexy mini dresses she wore out partying were gone for good. The metamorphosis had happened so gradually Orghlaith had not realised the changes she had gone through with Max always encouraging how 'fabulous' she looked and how much more mature she had become since they had been living together. 'You are even beginning to pronounce your Ts properly – it sounds soo much better.' Max would say.

The chocolate maker is a clever, manipulative man moulding his creation with precision and delicacy. He gets it at the right temperature and at just the right time to have it look and taste as he should want. And here she was – the final product, originally named Orghlaith with her manufacturer yet to find her a more fitting name. He was the bearer of all things wonderful and Orghlaith embraced the wealth and the lifestyle – made easier perhaps, because it came wrapped in a middle class bow with an Oxford educated accent. He continued to wave the wad of cash in Orghlaith's face and dismiss the news story that had clearly pricked at her conscience. 'Just forget them Orghlaith, forget Dympna and fucking Seamus, look at us – look at all that we have – our own family, a beautiful place, and so much fucking money it's ridiculous. You don't need them. Tariq and Karim say hi by the way.' Max had just made yet another deal with the two brothers. The set up had been very lucrative with Max using a contact in the States to get pure heroin smuggled in from Columbia. It made its way to London via America by anyone willing to risk a hefty prison sentence for a few thousand pounds or dollars. The third brother Hamza, was a thrill seeker and had smuggled a kilo or two in the past three years just for the buzz.

Tariq and Karim on the other hand, were not prepared to swallow packets of heroin or insert them up their behinds for love nor money – and neither was the delightful Max. The wedge of notes he was flashing in front of Orghlaith came from a recent deal split between Karim, Tariq and himself, and Max was clearly pleased with the result. 'Get out that bottle of bubbly – this is what it's all about beautiful...' He kissed Orghlaith hard pulling her aggressively towards him. She thought he had probably had a bit of coke that day – the white stuff always seemed to make him aggressive after a while. 'Jesus Max, what are you doing? You've got ridiculous amounts of money in the bank and all the properties...' Orghlaith said, following him into the kitchen. He opened the champagne grinning. She took two glasses from the cupboard, becoming agitated but not quite sure at what she was agitated with.

'To us,' Max said and raised his glass expecting her to chink his glass – which she did. She half smiled at him and shook her head.

'You don't need to deal Max, especially with those guys – they're the big time boys – you don't know what you could get yourself into. What's the short one called – Hamza is it? Not sure about him, seriously, something not right there.'

'They're the only people I deal with Orghlaith, I'm not some scummy dealer off the street – I buy and sell high quality stuff and they know the right people to get it over to London for me and more importantly – who to sell to. They're harmless guys, don't worry so much and enjoy it. Here – this is yours,' Max handed her two thousand pounds. The crisp notes in her hand felt so good, she couldn't deny it – she felt empowered by the money and thought where she might take Erin that day or what they might purchase as they strolled along the famous Kings Road... but she also thought about the families and the girlfriends and boyfriends who used to visit Grogan House – they would curse the drug dealers: Orghlaith remembered one of the Mums in a group therapy session saying 'That fucking dealer – he wouldn't leave her alone – he knew she would get back on the gear and be straight back to him. Bastard. I'll never forgive him.' On the other hand, Orghlaith knew that she, like many others were addicts and there was little anyone else could do if they wanted a fix – how could they blame the dealers? She didn't blame anyone else for her addiction, she had an addictive personality and that was it. Black and white wasn't it? There would be no supply if the demand wasn't there – and this is how Orghlaith justified Max's drug dealing, he was just delivering the goods and that was it. It's a shit world and we've all got to survive Orghlaith reasoned as she put her MaxMara coat on and headed out with Erin for lunch. Max said he'd meet her later because he was picking more gear up from Hamza in a bit, Orghlaith nodded and left.

While Orghlaith drank over-priced coffee from Maison Vert and treated herself and Erin to even more over-priced clothes, Max made his way to Hamza's flat in Knightsbridge. He was impressed by Hamza's taste – simple and elegant, but even more impressed with Hamza's sister. She was staying with Hamza for the Easter holidays until she returned to study in Manchester. Max had not seen anything so beautiful and enchanting since he had first laid eyes on Orghlaith two years before. 'Hi, I'm Max, I have a business meeting with Hamza.'

'Hi, I'm Saffanah, Hamza's sister – he said he's stuck in traffic but he shouldn't be too long – come in, come in.' Saffannah offered Max a drink.

'Jack Daniels on the rocks would be fabulous.' Max said feeling awkward with her. Her presence was powerful – feminine and strong.

'So what do you do Max?' Saffanah asked, light green eyes staring straight at him.

'I am a property developer,' He lied. He didn't know how much she knew through her brother but he wasn't about to tell her that he dealt drugs – even if she knew her brother did.

'Funny, that's what my brother says he does for a living to strangers, when we all know he deals,' Saffanah said letting Max know she knew the score.

'Well, property is a lucrative business these days Saffanah, very lucrative. Won't you have a drink with me?' Max asked taking his.

'I drink too much at University – Hamza would kill me if he knew, but one drink won't kill me will it Max?' She said smiling. She was beautiful, without a doubt, her skin very light olive and crystal clear – not a mark or blemish on it and her large green eyes cat-like in shape decorated with long thick black lashes. Her nose pointed downwards slightly and was a little flatter than the Western noses he was used to – but beautiful still and fitted perfectly on her face. Her off the shoulder red jumper allowed Max a glimpse of her collar bone and his mind wondered as to what it might be like to take that jumper off. Three Jack Daniels later and some more of Max's charm and that red jumper was off as was every other piece of clothing owned by them both – scattered across Hamza's apartment in urgency.

'You can't tell Hamza about this,' Max said afterwards, pulling up his trousers and searching for his other sock.

'You think I'm fucking stupid? My brother is paying my University fees. There is no way he'd be doing that if he found out about this.' Saffanah said, pulling her jumper over her head.

'Well, at least that's sorted then. Where is your bloody brother anyway?' Max said looking at his watch.

Ten minutes later Hamza finally turned up and gave Max the brown that Karim and Tariq had got for him. 'Get rid of this as soon as,' Hamza said. 'We don't need any trails, Karim and Tariq had a tough time getting this through,' Hamza said. 'So you met my sister then?' Hamza said briefly, as he unwrapped and re-wrapped the brown, showing it to Max. 'Hey little sis, you better have been polite to my friend – she can be a bit of a moody one at times,' Hamza said, smiling at Saffanah. 'But she's a good girl, studying at University to become a lawyer – so she can get me out of trouble – ain't that right sis.' Saffanah smiled a knowing smile and looked at Max. Max looked at her. Hamza didn't have a clue about his sister did he, Max thought, and that's how she wanted it. Max wasn't too bothered about their family set up anyway, he had had some fun whilst waiting and now he wanted to get out of there and get rid of the stuff. Pound signs were ringing in his eyes already.

Max headed towards the Jewel Bar tucked away behind the Kings Road – an exclusive, members only place with famous faces popping up here and there. It was early afternoon so the bar wasn't that busy and Max could see the three buyers on the table in the corner drinking and laughing with two women. He made his way over and they immediately stood up to shake his hand – he liked this. Money and drugs – ah, what power they could give one person. 'Gentlemen,' Max said taking the chair and centre of the table. 'Here is the sweetest brown sugar you're ever going to get your dirty hands on.' Placing a thick plastic bag on the table. The women were ushered away while the men did business.

'I'll be seeing to that one later,' Frank said in his husky voice. They all laughed on cue. Frank was the oldest of the three, an old school cockney brought up in the east end with good contacts who liked a bit of the brown and a pretty woman by his side. 'If I've got those two things I'm like a pig in shit,' he'd often say aloud. The woman Frank had been talking to was a sexy blonde thing Max thought, before pushing that distraction aside and getting on with the deal. He was one of the few people Max knew who managed to control his addiction but Max knew that never lasted. What were they – fucking stupid? That's why Max tried to stay away from the brown now he was clean – he tried to. If you were taking the stuff eventually it would take over you. End of story. It was only a matter of time before Frank's need increased and Max would, of course, provide him with the brown sugar to ease the pain – for a price. Frank was into the shoulder pad jackets (he had a silver-grey one on today sleeves rolled up to his elbow) which Max thought looked ridiculous but who was he to argue with one of his best buyers about his dress sense. Frank thought he looked the business and Max didn't want to spoil his fun. The other two men at the table – James and Ben were wealthy boys originally from Chelsea, back in London for the weekend partying and needed their usual fix for themselves and whichever girls they were planning on putting their charm on. The boys had never been too keen on the brown and steered clear but Max told them they should try some as well as giving them the usual white stuff these yuppy boys loved so much. Cocaine was the big thing right now – snorting it, licking it, rubbing it in your gums or even smoking it, whichever way it was going in it was a good fucking drug. No hangover to deal with the next day, no dirty needle marks and the best sex enhancer ever made. But it couldn't beat the brown Max concluded in his head, it couldn't beat the brown. No way. This was going to blow these boys away and get them back for more. Line my pocket thank you very much, Max said to himself, holding back a smug grin.

Frank and the boys hooked up every other weekend for several days of absolute carnage with Max being their first port of call for the best stuff in London. Why do you deal when you're absolutely loaded already Orghlaith often asked him. Why the fuck not? Max wanted to retort. He had told Orghlaith it was good to have some extra cash for all of them – and that was true. He did want extra cash for himself and her. But he didn't need it. Truth is, Max knew no better. He never finished any of the University courses he was forced to start by his parents and he'd never held down a 'normal' job. He remembers his Father getting him an internship at a law firm in the city hoping Max would have a flying career – that Max would 'make something of his life.' Max rebelled. He sabotaged the office he was working in so badly it looked like the firm had been burgled, and walked out of Demonte and Tyler Associates vowing he would never want a normal job with these people who thought they were something just because they worked for a pathetic firm in the City.

Max wanted thrills, danger, excitement and money – without the nine to five regimes of every day jobs or the pressure to 'make something of his life.' But he couldn't tell his Mother and Father what he was doing – he knew their disapproval might cut off his allowance and take him out of the will. They were pleased when he said he was settled down with Orghlaith and Erin and running a small restaurant business. They relocated to L.A. so were none the wiser. Max could have said he was running half the Kings Road and they wouldn't know – or care. As long as Max wasn't damaging their reputation in London the folks were content – which is why he had to keep the drug stuff away from circles which might report back to his Father. The last thing he needed was Max senior turning up and screwing everything for him.

Max wrapped up the deal with the boys. 'Thank you very much,' Max said placing all the cash in a plastic bag – the buzz was incredible. Not so much from the money but from knowing that what he was doing was wrong.

'Max, Max, stay for a drink mate,' Frank said, lifting his glass up. 'I think my friend over there likes you. Alex come here babes. Come here,' he motioned to the blonde woman with his hand. 'And you Francis, don't be shy.' The two women giggled and walked over to the table. 'I want you to say hello to my friend Max. He's a very very nice boy, ain't you Max,' Frank said laughing.

'Oh yes I am. The nicest boy you'll ever meet,' Max said, smiling at Alex. Alex had big blonde wavy hair. She reminded Max of Michelle Pfeiffer in the film he couldn't remember the name of – bright blue eyes and cheekbones you could chisel diamonds with.

'Let Max buy you a drink,' Frank said. Max and Alex went to the bar and before Max left the table Frank let him know that there was a room across the way if he wanted to entertain her. Max didn't know what to think. He'd just come from having sex with one of his best contacts' sister, and now here he was being offered it again. I wouldn't be doing this if I was in a bloody law firm all day Max thought to himself. He couldn't resist a beautiful face and before he knew it he'd taken the blonde to the room at the back of the bar.

Jesus, Max thought, as he left Jewel Bar and headed back to the flat, 'Jesus Christ,' he said aloud peeking into the bag at the wads of cash tied securely and kept neat with cheap rubber bands. This was one of the biggest deals Max had made so far. He'd sold most of the stuff Hamza had given him to Frank and some to the Chelsea boys. Frank would cut the brown with some other shitty substance and sell it on to his people for twice the price he'd bought it at. Anyone who argued with Frank about the quality of the drugs he sold them – well they didn't if they valued their life. Max shuddered at the thought of what Frank was capable of and switched his thoughts to the amount of money he'd just got hold of and the two women he'd had in one day. Not bad going Max thought, not bad going at all. He couldn't wait to show Orghlaith the crisp bills and watch her eyes light up, a twinge of guilt about Saffanah and Alex fleeted through him but didn't stay.

Chapter 10

Orghlaith had come home to start cooking early hoping for all three of them to eat together. She was interrupted by Hamza. He'd come to see if Max had managed to sell the stuff to Frank yet, keen to get his cut as soon as possible and didn't trust Max too much when it came to money. He wouldn't trust Max too much with anything which is why he was surprised to see that Max's woman was made of good stuff. What the hell is she doing with him Hamza thought as he sipped the juice Orghlaith had made him. She sat opposite Hamza in the living room cupping her mug of tea and watching Erin decipher another new playmat, clapping her chubby little hands when the buttons she pressed made a beep sound. 'She's gorgeous,' Hamza said. 'How old is she now?'

'She will be three in July,' Orghlaith said proudly. She expected to feel ill at ease around Hamza, thinking he would be cold and somewhat creepy from her brief encounters with him before and knowing that him and his brothers were among the biggest drug smugglers and dealers in London. But, by contrast, he was not as she expected and surprised her by seeming genuinely interested in what she was about – asking what Orghlaith wanted to do when Erin went back to nursery – would she go back to Uni he had asked, and Hamza mentioned that his sister, Saffanah was studying for a law degree up North. Orghlaith was intelligent, witty, and clearly beautiful Hamza concluded. Her safe clothes seemed far too old for her – they didn't suit who she was. 'Oh Max said these looked really good,' she'd said. 'Oh Max bought me this bracelet – I used to wear awful rubber bangles and these great big crucifix necklaces - thought I was the next Madonna.' She laughed at herself. 'I even dyed my hair...' she had said, her gaze wondering off... 'I had long dark hair...' Orghlaith explained, thinking of her previous self. So Max had created her. Taken an intelligent woman with a child and a life in front of her and literally injected Orghlaith and her life with shit. You really are something Max, you really are Hamza thought. He didn't utter these words to Orghlaith – she probably knew deep down what the score was and who was he to start telling her what was what. He was hardly in a position to start giving out advice on morality or doing the right thing when he was sitting there waiting for his dirty money to arrive. But, he reasoned, I have made my choice to live this life – I haven't brought anyone else down with me. Max was wired wrong, so wrong.

The man himself walked through the door of his flat a little taken aback that Hamza was sitting far too comfortably on his leather sofa.

'Hey you,' Orghlaith said kissing Max and putting her arms around his neck.

'Hey gorgeous,' he hugged her back and couldn't hide the bag from Hamza as he placed it down near the other sofa. Hamza's eyes followed the plastic bag. Max hoped he could take a little more of the money but now that Hamza was here and had seen that Frank had paid up, Max knew he would have to give him at least half of what he had earned that day. He wasn't impressed.

'Ah, so that's what you're here for,' Orghlaith said smiling at Hamza.

'Well, just a second, take Erin into the bedroom sweetheart whilst I sort this out with Hamza. I won't be a minute,' Max said picking up Erin from her mat and handing her to Orghlaith as if she were a bad smell.

'Ok, well I've cooked dinner, it's in the oven so we'll eat when you're done.' Orghlaith said. She closed the bedroom door and pulled up the carpet and floorboard near the bed placing the tidy notes with the rubber bands on top of all the other bundles Max had given her in the past few months – she had over twelve thousand saved now – maybe even fifteen – she'd have to count it again. Floorboard put back and money in the safe place, Orghlaith held Erin's hands and let her jump up and down on the bed. Erin laughed and the more she jumped the more excited she got and laughed even more baring her few little teeth and her tonsils to Mum. She nearly lost her footing several times but of course Orghlaith was there in front of her holding tight to the little ones cherub-like hands so she could jump up and down once again safe in the knowledge that Mum would catch her if the little foot slipped again. Orghlaith laughed and giggled along with Erin; if you were to hear from the other side of the door you may have been mistaken in thinking there were a few children running riot in the master bedroom.

Max interrupted the girl's fun. 'Jesus Orghlaith, you couldn't make any more noise if you tried,' he seemed annoyed.

'What's wrong with you?' Orghlaith said irritated at his tone of voice towards them.

'I've just had to give Hamza half of what I made today. If he hadn't been here and seen the bag I could have slipped a few more thousand in to our pockets,' Max explained leaning against the arch of the bedroom door. 'Don't let anyone in who you don't know again. My contacts shouldn't come here unless they are invited,' Max said.

'Ok well I'm sorry, you never told me I couldn't answer the door to certain people did you?' Orghlaith said in a dry tone.

'Well now you know.' Max replied bluntly.

'Look, we lost some money, it's done. It won't happen again. Let's go eat. Shall we go eat Erin?' Orghlaith said trying to soften the situation. She didn't like it when Max was edgy or pissed off in this way – he made her feel like he could just go beserk at any moment or do something really crazy, even though he never had. He never had, but the look in his eye and the change in him when he was fired up over something made her feel that he could, possibly do something. She placed these thoughts on a mental white board and wiped the ones she couldn't deal with clean off, cleaned them from her mind and cleaned the idea that Max was capable of harming her or Erin. Of course he wasn't, don't be stupid. White board clear and dinner was served.

'How is it?' she asked. Orghlaith had cooked cottage pie which Erin hadn't had since living with Nanny D.

Erin was devouring hers and well on to demanding a second helping. 'Oh it's lovely, it is,' Max replied. 'Appetite is just flagging a bit. Thank you though,' Max said robotically. She wondered where his mind was. 'Shall we spend the day together tomorrow?' Max asked.

'That sounds like a great idea sweetheart. I'll organise Erin's things after we've eaten,' Orghlaith replied.

'Um, I thought it would be good for me and you to just spend some time... We can get someone to babysit,' he said.

'Well ok but who will babysit? I don't know anyone around here,' Orghlaith said, disappointed that they couldn't all go out together like a proper family, but pleased, nonetheless that Max wanted to spend time with just her. 'It might sound a little strange but maybe we could ask Hamza? He was really good with Erin today – he really was, and he doesn't seem like a bad guy other than the obvious. He seems pretty decent – you've known him for years haven't you?' Orghlaith said.

'Well, yeah, I mean he's pretty alright, and if you are ok with Erin staying with him that's fine by me,' Max said. Max wanted her all to himself. Seeing Hamza with her today made him rage with anger – laughing and talking with another man – it made him sick to his stomach. What was she thinking? He would have to shower Orghlaith with gifts and wine and dine her he thought, he would show her where her bread was buttered. Hamza could play nanny and stay home with Erin if he wanted to. At least he wouldn't be near Orghlaith. 'If not, we'll call up a childcare company in the morning or something,' Max had said.

Hamza agreed to look after Erin and arrived bright and early the next day. 'This is for you, not Max,' he said to Orghlaith whilst Max was in the shower. 'I don't know why someone like you is with someone like him.' The words were out of Hamza's mouth before he could stop himself.

Max came into the living-room before Orghlaith had a chance to reply. 'You ready to go gorgeous? Aren't you going to change out of that outfit first?' Max said to Orghlaith. 'I've left those beautiful trousers and that silk top on the bed for you, why don't you try them on?' Max said.

'Um ok,' Orghlaith didn't want to make a scene in front of Hamza so did as Max requested, but felt embarrassed at being told to change and, even worse, succumbing to his wishes so readily. Hamza observed quietly, taking in what he witnessed, baffled at how such a woman could be so influenced by anyone, let alone someone like Max. She seemed too bright to be that overwhelmed by the money – too bright and too much substance to stay with Max and put up with that kind of rubbish. Hamza couldn't make sense of the situation, or her. 'Erin's food is in here,' Orghlaith said, motioning to the fridge, showing Hamza the dozen or so plastic tubs labelled to indicate the contents. 'Don't give her too many sweets or biscuits, even if she gives you that cute little look of hers ok!' Orghlaith said laughing as she thought about Erin.

Hamza thought she would answer his question in the kitchen but she didn't. Instead, she showed him the mat Erin liked to play with that lay on the front room floor and where all her spare clothes and nappies were. 'She usually takes a nap around three but don't hold your breath – it doesn't always happen!' Orghlaith explained.

Hamza put his hand on Orghlaith's arm. 'She'll be safe with me Orghlaith, don't worry ok?' Hamza said in a way that made Orghlaith feel a reassurance she hadn't felt in a long time.

'Ok, I know, I'm sorry. It's just, I worry about her,' Orghlaith said, feeling bad that she may have offended Hamza.

'Of course you worry, she's your daughter, it's normal, but it's fine, she'll be well looked after – you go and enjoy your day out o.k.?' Hamza said.

'Thank you Hamza, thank you, I really appreciate this,' Orghlaith said. She picked up Erin and held her tight. 'You be a good girl for Hamza ok? Mummy won't be long. I'll be back later.' She smothered her in kisses and as Erin realised that Mummy was leaving she began to cry which made Orghlaith want to stay.

'Just go, go. She'll be fine,' Hamza said as he picked up the little bundle.

'Come on Orghlaith, come one, she'll be alright,' Max said, ushering her out of the door. 'She'll be fine ok?' Max affirmed. Max let Hamza know out of ear shot from Orghlaith that they wouldn't be back until the following day. Hamza nodded, and said it was fine. He didn't like Max much and barely knew Orghlaith but felt she was a decent woman and he didn't mind doing her a favour.

Orghlaith said goodbye to Hamza and Erin and left for her day with Max. Max said nothing to Erin as he left.

***

Orghlaith had changed from her fuschia pink woollen dress and boots to the outfit of plain black trousers and a silk top, both very expensive but as Orghlaith had looked in the mirror that day she didn't feel herself, she didn't feel great in these designer clothes as she thought she ought to. She was happy and sexy in the outfit she had chosen – and thought Max would really like it too, but he clearly hadn't. She sat in the chauffeur-driven car Max had hired for them and it felt good that it was just him and her. But the feeling that she had somehow lost herself these past few months kept nagging at her. She pushed it to the back of her mind, determined she would enjoy the day – grateful to have some quality time with Max. She loved him, she had become infatuated by him, bowled over by his charm and confidence, but she wondered if infatuation was not the same as love. As these thoughts teased around in Orghlaith's mind Max stroked her face and presented her with a large black velvet box tied with a blood-red ribbon. 'Do you remember the necklace I gave you when we first met?' he asked, 'Well, this one is better, so much better. I hope you like it.' He kissed her. 'Well open it then!' Max pushed.

Orghlaith untied the blood – red ribbon and carefully opened the clasped box. The diamonds sparkled on the necklace, each one shaped as a tear-drop with the smallest in rows at the top until the rows got bigger and bigger still. A huge diamond sat alone in the middle, demanding to be looked at above all of the rest. 'Max, it's breathtaking. I can't accept it... It must have cost a fortune...' Orghlaith said, shocked and overwhelmed, yet feeling like a Princess in a fairytale all at the same time.

'You're worth every penny,' Max said. 'And here are the earrings to match.' Max pulled out a smaller box, again, tied in the same fashion, and Orghlaith unclasped it to reveal dangly earrings to match the princess necklace.

'Max where am I ever going to wear these? We don't really go out to anywhere that I would be able to.'

'You can wear them tonight – when we go out tonight,' Max said.

'Ok, but where are we going?' Orghlaith asked.

'You'll see,' Max smiled at her.

'Max stop teasing me! Where are we going?!'

'It's a surprise,' Max said placing his hand on her thigh. 'But first, we will have to find you something to wear won't we?' Max's intention was to bring Orghlaith to pick a dress for the event he was taking her to that night but they took a pitstop to the place where they had first met – the cocktail bar with the leopard skin seating and the posh cocktails Orghlaith had enjoyed so much. It was like old times.

Two of Max's contacts were in the bar and came over to say hello. 'This is my wife, Orghlaith,' Max said to the two men.

Orghlaith didn't deny she was his wife even though they weren't married and thought it was quite sweet of Max to introduce her like that. 'Nice to meet you,' Orghlaith said, shaking their hands.

Max exchanged small talk with the tall blonde American guy Axel, and the other chubby one whose name Orghlaith couldn't remember. As the two men left the table Axel nodded at Orghlaith and said 'Well she is a beauty isn't she Max, well done, it's not often you find a woman with brains and beauty. You're a lucky man... Ok, well we'll meet for that drink next week Max.'

Orghlaith and Max stayed for a couple of hours and once they had finished their fourth cocktail it was on for lunch at an exclusive restaurant in MayFair. 'You go on and get in the car, I'm just going to have another word with Axel about the meeting next week.' Max said to Orghlaith.

'Oh ok, ok, well I'll see you in a minute,' Orghlaith said feeling quite tipsy at this point. She headed towards the Bentley car which had waited outside for them for several hours.

Max headed straight for Axel. 'Axel my good friend, fancy a quick bit of this in the men's?' Max showed Axel a glimpse of foil and immediately the American followed Max to the toilets to get his hands on the white stuff. Axel, eager to snort, was like a moth to a flame, and as his head bent towards the line of white powder on the sink Max grabbed his bleached hair, pulled his head back and smashed it against the edge of the porcelain sink. 'If you ever try it on with my wife again, if you talk to her or even look at her I will fucking kill you. Do you understand?' Max said in a calm, low tone. Max turned Axel to face him, blood dripping from the side of Axel's face who, being half pissed and half doped up, couldn't muster the strength to retaliate. Max clenched his fists and an uncontrollable anger raged inside him as he looked at the man who had dared to flirt with his wife. At this thought Max drew his arm back and swung it forward making a cracking sound as Max's bare knuckles smashed against Axel's nose. He threw him into the nearest toilet cubicle where Axel collapsed and slipped down into the space between the side of the toilet and the cubicle wall, his blood smearing the art deco tiles on his way. 'You don't fucking speak to Orghlaith. Ever!' were Max's final words to him as he stood in the cubicle doorway looking at Axel in disgust. Max washed his hands and the water turned pink from the blood that came off them. He splashed his face and hair with cold water, adjusted his shirt and returned to the car where Orghlaith was chatting away to the driver. 'Where have you been? You've got stuff down your shirt – what is that?' Orghlaith asked, pointing at the red marks on Max's shirt.

'Oh, you know my friend – that guy Axel who said hello to us, he only spilt his cocktail down my new shirt. We were just chatting, I didn't realise it had stained my shirt so much,' Max explained. He wondered how he hadn't noticed the faint specks of Axel's blood on his shirt, but was very impressed by his improvisation of the events which had led to his shirt being stained. 'Right, now to La Casa Blanca for lunch, it's near Burlington Street, Mayfair,' Max ordered the driver. 'Do you know where that is?' Max asked.

'Yes sir I do, don't worry,' The driver said politely.

'Thank you,' Orghlaith said to the driver, wondering where Max's manners had disappeared to.

'What are you saying thank you for?' Max asked her.

'Because it's polite,' Orghlaith said.

'It's his job Orghlaith, it's what I've paid him for today,' Max said.

'So because you have paid him that means you can't be polite?' She said in more of a whisper not wanting the driver to hear their conversation. 'Keep your voice down Max, the driver will hear.'

'You're so sweet sometimes,' Max said.

'Oh really,' Orghlaith replied smiling. Max did up the window so the driver couldn't see into the back and took out a small plastic bag. He showed Orghlaith. 'Max, don't, you know I can't.'

'It's just a bit of powder, just Charlie, nothing else. Pure stuff, I wouldn't give you anything but.' Max said. 'Do you remember when we first had some of this together? How good was that night? Wasn't it?' Max encouraged her. Fleeting flashbacks of the second night she ever spent with Max ran through her mind. With Orghlaith quite tipsy, little room was left for discipline or willpower and before she knew it she had allowed Max to rub his sugar coated fingers in her gums. He rubbed his own with the remaining white stuff, threw the empty bag on the floor and hastily undid his trousers as Orghlaith removed hers.

Twenty minutes later they arrived at La Casa Blanca managing to adjust their clothes and smooth down unruffled hair, unable to do much about their flustered faces. Max said

◆

114

thank you to the driver this time and requested him to pick them up in an hour or so.

After Tapas at La Casa Blanca Max took Orghlaith to pick a gown for the event they were going to that night. Orghlaith found herself amongst the most beautiful dresses she had ever seen, all hanging delicately, separated from one another lest they should cause damage to one another's perfection. The shop was a small boutique in Hampstead that Max knew well because of his Mother. 'She used to come here to get her dresses for the events my Father took her to,' Max explained. 'My Dad would rarely come so she would bring me instead and ask me what I thought of each of the many dresses she tried on.' Max drifted off for a few seconds. Orghlaith imagined Max's life of wonderful things growing up, his perfect family living a fairy tale. He didn't tell her that his Mother used to make him keep watch for his Father in the house while she had sex with his Father's best friend. When Max senior came in Max junior would have to knock on his Mother's bedroom door to warn her and the idiot in there with her. He cursed himself for letting her do that to him for so many years.

'Did she buy them or did she rent them?' Orghlaith asked wide-eyed, interrupting Max's thoughts.

'You can't rent them, you have to buy,' Max said smiling.

'Max, no. This is too much – it's far too expensive. Where are we going tonight anyway?' Orghlaith asked again.

'I'm taking you to a ball – it's a masquerade ball so you have to get a mask too. It's held every year by a friend of my parents – they won't be there but it's always been good fun so we must go – you'll love it,' Max said.

'A ball – really?!' Orghlaith said excitedly. 'I can't imagine you wearing a mask, Max,' she laughed, ruffling his hair slightly, 'You're too cool hey?' Orghlaith teased.

Orghlaith was 23 – an adult in most people's eyes, and even more so now that she was a Mother, but there was a big part of her that remained a little girl. She loved dressing up, painting her face and still danced around the flat to Wham and Madonna when Max was out doing business. This facet of Orghlaith's character only allows all things wonderful and feel-good in, ignoring the bad parts. She is just like the little boy or girl that refuses to listen to their parents who say they can't eat chocolate because it is bad for them, the little person reasons only by how good the chocolate tastes and how it makes them feel and so, if left to their own devices, will carry on devouring the chocolate for breakfast, lunch and dinner until someone steps in to explain that eating in such a way could be detrimental to their health.

Max watched Orghlaith try on umpteen dresses: long and black with no sleeves and a slit at the back; deep emerald that emphasised her eyes; silver-grey silk that clung to her slender shape and revealed her breasts a little too much for Max's liking, puffy dresses, long sleeved dresses, an ugly dress or two that made Orghlaith wince and many more besides. She had got used to the blonde bob she sported but looking in the mirror trying on the dresses, she wondered where the old Orghlaith with the long dark hair and fuller breasts had disappeared to. However, she finally found a dress that went well with the blonde bob. 'What about this one?' Orghlaith said about a red gown. She tried it on.

'That's the one,' Max said.

'Yep I think you're right, this is the one,' Orghlaith smiled. But then there was the dilemma of finding shoes to go with the stunning dress. The polite sales assistant who had been running around like a headless chicken bringing and returning dresses to Orghlaith in various sizes produced a spectacular pair of satin red pointy stilettos. 'God they're perfect,' Orghlaith said as she slipped them on her small feet. Orghlaith twirled in front of Max in the beautiful red dress, he looked at the stunning creature twirling in front of him touching her dress and checking herself in the mirror. He looked at her petite slender body, the halter neck front emphasising her perfectly rounded breasts and delicate collar bone. The dress was backless. Max gazed at her bare back, light olive in colour and smooth to the touch. How many times he had touched that back and pressed his hands into it as if he were to never let go. How intensely good had that felt, he never wanted anyone else to touch her or have her. Max tied up the halter neck a little tighter, making it into a small bow at the back at the nape of her neck.

'You are nearly ready. All you need now is the jewellery I bought you for the finishing touch,' Max said with his hands placed on her shoulders as they admired her reflection in the mirror.

'Thank you,' Orghlaith said and kissed Max. 'We're going for this one, and the shoes you chose. Thank you very much,' Orghlaith said to the sales assistant.

'Not a problem madam, you look stunning,' the sales assistant said smiling.

'Well it'll look better once my hair and make-up are done as well won't it,' Orghlaith said thinking out loud.

'You look perfect already,' Max said.

Chapter 11

Barrington Manor House was a huge Georgian Mansion on the outskirts of Surrey, England, and the ball was to be held in the main room downstairs. Max and Orghlaith were staying in the Executive suite on the fourth floor that overlooked acres of land, home to several horses that Orghlaith could see grazing from the window in the bathroom. With her hair in heated rollers and a towel wrapped around her she applied her foundation with a soft brush, the blush Max had bought her from Givenchy and smoked her eyes with a light grey eye shadow and black kohl eye liner on both lids. She slipped the red dress on and the matching shoes. Out came the rollers to reveal a mass of short wavy blonde hair. She checked herself in the mirror thinking she looked similar to Madonna in her Material Girl video.

Max knocked on the bathroom door. 'Are you ready?' he asked.

'I have your jewellery here, don't forget.'

Orghlaith opened the door. 'As if I could forget,' she said. Max's gaze led Orghlaith to think something was wrong. 'What's the matter? Don't you like it?' She asked, worried that she actually didn't look as wonderful as she thought she did.

'You look incredible,' Max said with absolute sincerity. He had said a lot of things he didn't mean to a lot of people in recent times, but this he meant. He put her jewellery on her and thus the finishing touches were in place. Orghlaith admired Max in his tuxedo with his hair gelled back and his freshly shaven tanned face.

They laughed at the masks they had both chosen; Max's mask was plain black with elastic attached either side so as to easily slip it on and off. Orghlaith's was far more glamorous – red to match the dress, trimmed with gold sequins and red and gold feathers. The mask, with its cat-like eyes covered her face only to her nose and left her lips exposed. It was attached to a long stick – like gold handle. Orghlaith amused herself by bringing the mask to her face and taking it away again and again, laughing and showing Max. 'I feel like we are in an old fashioned film!' Orghlaith said as they made their way down to the main hall.

'And does it feel good?' Max asked.

'Yes, yes it does. It feels amazing,' Orghlaith whispered to him and placed a delicate kiss on his cheek. They put their masks on and she linked her arm through his. The main room was full of masked people, men in their tuxedos and women in stunning dresses of all styles and colour, equally pleasing to the eye. Max lifted his mask to his forehead to let people know he was there, and let people know that the lady in red linked to his arm was his and not for the taking.

'Oh Max, how lovely to see you,' an older couple said. 'How are your parents? Enjoying America? I thought they would never leave England!'

Max introduced Orghlaith as his 'wife' to various characters around the room and many were quite taken with her. Eyes gazed over her wondering how the rebellious Max who had almost ruined his parents' reputation and family name had bagged himself such a woman. Perhaps he had bought her, one of his old University friends suggested, provoking laughter amongst the clique. The laughter soon stopped as Max approached the group of twenty somethings. 'Gentlemen.

Ladies,' he said. 'And how are we?' His tone was condescending to say the least and his presence clearly made the group feel slightly uneasy.

Orghlaith spoke to one of the men whilst Max was distracted by another young woman in the group who spoke out of earshot from the others 'Haven't given up the day job then Max?' the blonde said. 'Still a bastard,' she smiled.

'Ah, Susie, you can't still be holding it against me that I fucked you a few times and then got bored with you surely? You must move on. Honestly,' Max said grinning.

'You make me sick,' she replied. 'I'm going to get a drink.' Susie left and headed straight for the bar.

'Max, Max how are you dear?' a grey haired woman said kissing either side of Max's cheek. The grey haired woman, a well known Lady and her husband, a wealthy business tycoon, went to University with his Father.

'Hello, how nice to see you again,' Max said, not really interested in all this small talk rubbish but knew it would help to mingle in the right circles and show off his 'wife'. It would of course get back to Max senior and Max's Mother in America that he was doing well and had settled down etc. etc. and so they would keep the money going into his account and leave him and his other business well alone. 'I'm very well Julia... Yes I have several business ventures... Oh yes, they're doing very well indeed. Orghlaith and I are very happy... We have a daughter... Erin...'

Max talked the talk and did what he had to do to make his mark back in the circle and let everyone know he was a success – that he was no longer the rebellious, unhinged son of Angela and Max Gomez senior as had been his reputation since the sabotage of that law firm. The drink flowed, music blared and people let their hair down. Max was networking with his old associates and rather enjoying being centre of attention. Orghlaith had to mingle on her own for a great deal of it which she did with ease and people took to her well.

Max disappeared with a red-haired woman of around 35 for twenty minutes or so, they shared some of the white stuff in one of the unused rooms. He pulled at her bodice and she grabbed his tuxedo trousers in a drunken frenzy, Orghlaith totally oblivious as she spoke with the other guests downstairs. The pair emerged from the room and made their way back to the main room using separate stairs and entrants.

As Max re entered the main room he spotted Orghlaith surrounded by several men talking and laughing as one does at a party. Max felt the adrenalin pump through his body, his heart thumping against his chest so hard he imagined it could burst through the skin at any moment. He pummelled through the crowd with no 'excuse me' or 'sorry' for moving people out of the way in such an aggressive fashion. He grabbed Orghlaith's arm tight, pinching her skin. 'Excuse me gentlemen, may I have my wife back for a moment,' Max said smiling through gritted teeth.

'Max, Max what are you doing?' Orghlaith asked as she felt his grip tighten.

He dragged her through the main room and up to their suite. 'How dare you?! How dare you humiliate me like that?!' Max screamed at Orghlaith throwing her on the bed. 'Flirting with all of those men! Did you want to fuck them? You did didn't you!' Orghlaith sat up on the side of the bed but flew back immediately as Max's hand struck the side of her face. She cried out in pain and clasped her face with her hands.

'What are you doing?! What are you doing?' Orghlaith cried out to Max.

'You're a whore! You want those other men!' Max shouted at her.

'I was just talking to them Max! We were talking!' Orghlaith said tears streaming down her face. Her explanation fell on deaf ears. Max grabbed her hair and yanked her off the bed like a rag doll, dragging her across the floor into the bathroom. Orghlaith kicked and screamed. 'Get off me! Get the fuck off me!' She scratched at his face. He punched and kicked at her.

'Fucking bitch,' he yelled. Orghlaith gave up trying to fight back and lay curled up in a ball on the bathroom floor. 'You want those men? You think they're better then me? I'll fucking show you whose better. I'll – show – you – who's – better.' Max said undoing his trouser zip and spreading Orghlaith's legs ripping the red dress.

'Max no, Max. Max no!' Orghlaith's pleas for him to stop did nothing. She gave up and lay mute as his heavy body heaved on her up and down, up and down, up and down. The motion ended. Max lifted himself off her and walked into the other room doing up his zip breathing heavily. Orghlaith sat up curling her knees to her chest and cried. She didn't recognise the man who had just done that to her, she didn't know who he was. Orghlaith looked down at her dress and ripped it off, tearing at it frantically not wanting it anywhere near her skin.

She closed the bathroom door locking it with hands that wouldn't stop shaking. Orghlaith ran the shower until it was steaming hot and stayed in there for what seemed like forever washing and re washing herself. She got out of the shower, wrapped the towel around her and sat on the side of the bath. The one person she wished was there right now to cuddle her and tell her it was all going to be alright wasn't there. Her Mum wasn't there. She pulled the towel to her face that was aching from the blows and cried into it. 'Oh Mum,' she whispered into the towel.

Max poured himself another Jack Daniels straight and swallowed in one gulp. He sat on the sofa staring at nothing in particular, his thoughts muddled and incoherent. No words were exchanged between Max and Orghlaith that night as they both got into the same bed. She wanted him to sleep in the next room – anywhere but next to her, but he didn't. He got in to the king size bed and fell asleep. Orghlaith slept on the other side as far from him as she could making a massive space between the two of them. She lay still, memories and thoughts flooding her mind of things as they were before she met Max. She looked over at him, the light that cracked through the curtains shone across half of his face making him look frighteningly distorted. Orghlaith stared at the ceiling. She remembered reading about a volcano which had lay dormant on a remote island with no activity for over a hundred years. Local people thought it was harmless and so lived at the bottom of this silent beast without fear that it might cause them harm. One day, the volcano erupted, its lava consuming everything in sight. The people who lived below were burnt alive. Orghlaith looked across at Max again, sleeping soundly.

Orghlaith woke unable to open her right eye fully, she touched it gently and gritted her teeth at the pain. She looked in the bathroom mirror, shocked at what stared back at her. Orghlaith's eye and top lip were swollen and most of the right side of her face was now the colour purple. As much as she tried to mask the bruising with make-up it was still quite visible. She would have to hide behind her sunglasses for a while she thought. Max had ordered breakfast to the room with a huge bouquet of flowers for Orghlaith. 'I'm sorry, I'm so sorry,' he said as Orghlaith came out from the bathroom. He held out his arms for her to come to him. 'Please forgive me, forgive me Orghlaith, I'm so sorry. I truly am. I was jealous, so jealous when I saw you with those other men, I couldn't bear it. I couln't bear the thought of you being with them,' Max pleaded. He handed Orghlaith the flowers coyly as she hadn't reciprocated his arm gesture to hold her. 'Please accept them. Forgive me,' Max asked.

A different man stood before her to the one she had witnessed the previous night: soft, sad, almost pathetic. 'I don't think you realise what you did Max. You have hurt me so much... I don't even have the words,' Orghlaith said in a low tone. She took the flowers and placed them on the breakfast bar.

'I do, I do realise Orghlaith but I can't be without you. Don't leave me, you can't leave. Everything was so wonderful yesterday wasn't it? Before our fight, wasn't it? We can be wonderful together, we can. Just say you'll forgive me. I love you,' Max pleaded again. He walked towards her and put his arms around her. 'It won't happen again. I promise.' Max said.

Once upon a time Orghlaith would have slapped such a man, told him what she thought of him and left never to see him again blessing herself for the lucky escape and praising her Mother's good advice to 'never let any man lay a hand on you do ye hear?' Once is enough, Dympna would recite to Orghlaith – even if he says sorry, even if he says he loves you and he promises he won't do it again. But Dympna's words of wisdom were a distant voice in Orghlaith's mind as she let Max hold her and touch her softly and she held him back, making herself believe he was genuinely sorry and he had only behaved that way because he loved her so very much.

***

Hamza and Erin were playing with Erin's mini pink football, sitting opposite one another rolling the ball two and fro. Each time Hamza would say what a great player she was. 'Great football player! Great football player!' Erin would repeat laughing hysterically and clapping her little hands. She had seen

124

the men in different colour shirts play this game on television, Hamza was surprised at how quiet she was throughout the Chelsea v Millwall match the previous night smiling as he watched the little girl's eyes dart across the screen following the tiny specs on the television. The two had fallen asleep on the sofa, Erin finding a comfortable nook on the side of Hamza's chest to nestle into. Hamza rolled the ball to Erin once again when the door opened and in came Max and Orghlaith. Orghlaith wearing quite possibly the biggest sunglasses Hamza had ever seen.

Orghlaith hurried to pick up Erin, hugging her tight and kissing her over and over. 'Ooh Mummy has missed you. How has she been?' she asked Hamza.

'Oh it's been a pleasure to look after her Orghlaith, really. She's a little diamond. You should be proud. I think you have an aspiring footballer on your hands,' Hamza said laughing and explaining Erin's fixation for the football match they had watched together.

Erin was pleased to see her Mum nearly strangling her as she cuddled Orghlaith's neck. 'Ooh not so tight sweetheart,' Orghlaith laughed nervously. She was still wearing the sunglasses, and before she could stop her, Erin had took them off. Hamza couldn't hide the look of shock on his face. He looked at Max, already on the phone to a buyer, and then back at Orghlaith.

'Mummy has a sore eye,' Erin said, touching her Mother's face delicately with her stubby fingers covered in jam.

'Yes Mummy had a bit of an accident. Nothing to worry about,' Orghlaith said, hoping this would prevent Hamza from asking anymore questions. He didn't have to. He knew straight away what had happened.

Max went into the bedroom closing the door behind him. Erin made herself comfortable on the sofa with the new colouring book Orghlaith had bought her, content with her ham sandwich and the familiar presence of Mum being home.

Hamza took Orghliath by the arm into the kitchen. 'What the fuck did he do to you Orghlaith?' in an angry whisper.

'Please don't say anything,' she pleaded touching his arm.

'I'm gonna kill him. Fucking coward.'

'Don't do anything. Please, you'll make it worse. And anyway it's fine, we've sorted it out, please don't do anything Hamza. Please,' she said, her big brown eyes exuding a sadness he wanted to erase.

They heard the bedroom door open. Erin held up her colouring book to Max as he came into the front room 'Look look at my drawing,' she said smiling. The little girl frowned, confused as to why he had ignored her and walked straight into the kitchen.

Orghlaith was taking mugs out of the cupboard and Hamza pouring water into the kettle. 'Everything ok in here?' Max asked putting his arms around Orghlaith's waist.

'Oh yes, yep, fine. I was just showing Hamza the beautiful jewellery you bought me.' Orghlaith said glaring at Hamza, pleading for his co-operation.

'You have great taste Max.' Hamza said looking at Max.

'Yes I do have a knack for finding beautiful things.' He looked at Orghlaith and grinned.

Hamza restrained himself from fulfilling the fantasy unfolding in his mind which involved getting the iron poker from the front- room and beating Max about the head with it. He'd done that to guys like Max a million times before – men like him deserved it. The only thing that stopped him was Orghlaith, he didn't want to make things worse for her or push her away – not when they were getting so close. He had to leave before he did something to Max he might regret. 'I didn't realise that was the time, I better get off,' Hamza said.

'Leaving so soon?' Max asked.

Don't push me, don't push me Hamza thought, or you'll wind up dead Max I promise. Better get out of here, where's my jacket. Hamza got his black leather jacket and said goodbye to Erin giving her a big hug and kiss and admiring her artistic flare. He said goodbye to Orghlaith who was being hugged from behind by Max.

'See you Hamza.' Max said kissing Orghlaith's cheek and squeezing her tight. Hamza walked down the corridor towards the lifts rubbing his face. He stopped halfway putting his hands on the back of his head and looked up to the ceiling where the big chandelier hung, the crystal sparkling in his eyes. He let out a deep breath that felt as if it had been trapped in his lungs for a lifetime. Should he go back and sort Max out? What was he doing walking away? He'd done over plenty of scumbags in his time before, no big deal. But what would Orghlaith think if he did that? She'd think he was no different to Max and all those other guys he messed around with. And unless he got of rid of Max permanently she would always be in danger. If he got rid of Max that would bring more trouble to Orghlaith wouldn't it. I can't do that to her. He got in the lift and pressed G.

I may be living my life on the dark side, Hamza thought, as he walked down the empty high street, but how any man can do that to a woman is beyond me. God knows he'd seen grown men have their knees smashed to smithereens, bodies dismembered a few times for not paying up money or because the money from a deal had gone awol. But never had he seen or wanted to be part of such treatment to a woman. He had sisters and a Mother who were too precious to him to ever imagine doing that to any woman. Women *were* precious, untouchable and should be looked after he reasoned, especially one like Orghlaith. Her battered face ran through his mind a million times as he lay on his bed that night. He couldn't let Max get away with this. I have to do something.

Chapter 12

It had been six weeks since Max had attacked Orghlaith at the hotel, the bruising had taken nearly four weeks to leave her pretty face. The external bruising was of course superficial whilst the internal wound would nestle at the back of Orghlaith's mind. Hamza had taken to calling every day around 1.30pm, when Max was out, to check on Orghlaith and the little one. His phone calls gave her comfort and reassurance, something she wanted to feel from Max but probably never would.

'...I'll come over to see you and Erin maybe Wednesday, how's your... How are you healing?' he asked awkwardly.

'Oh yes yeah the bruising and swelling has really gone down, it was nothing anyway.'

'I know I ask all the time but Max... He hasn't done anything...You know nothing like that since?'

'Oh God no! No Hamza, honestly things have been fine, it really was a one off – he just get's so jealous, you know what he's like.' Orghlaith said in a high pitched tone.

'Ok, well you know I'm just looking out for you, in my family women are sacred and I don't want to see you hurt again or I might just have to step in.'

'Hamza I've got to go,' Orghlaith whispered. 'He's back.' She hung up. It had happened a few times when they'd been talking: Hamza would be mid flow in his sentence before hearing that dreaded flat tone noise indicating that Orghlaith could no longer speak because Max was home. But she never missed his phone call, she'd wait by the phone from 1.25pm eager to speak to Hamza and hear tales of his childhood throughout the many countries his family had lived in over the years. She had never been to Morocco - Hamza's birthplace, and imagined this distant land to be magical and mysterious with little towns made of white stone and markets selling wonderful exotic herbs and fruits. She daydreamed about escaping there.

***

'Orghlaith, Orghlaith I'm home, where are you?' Max called out, ready to rage if she had gone out without telling him.

Orghlaith came out of the bathroom with her hair wrapped in a towel. 'I'm here Max, I'm here, I was just having a bath, what's wrong?' Orghlaith asked.

'Oh nothing's wrong, I just thought you might be out – I couldn't hear Erin,' Max replied.

'She's having a very rare afternoon sleep so thought I'd soak in the bath for a bit,' Orghlaith said flipping her head upside down to towel dry her hair vigorously.

'Are you going anywhere nice?' Max asked knowing full well she knew no one apart from himself and Hamza.

'No, where would I be going?' Orghlaith replied wondering why Max asked her such a stupid question.

'Ok ok,' Max said. 'Well anyway I've just got this stuff from Tariq – it is meant to be absolutely fucking mind-blowing. Frank wants a cut tonight so I'm going to see him at the Jewel Bar and hopefully he'll take most of it off my hands,' Max said shaking the thick plastic bag grinning from ear to ear he put the bag of Big Harry on the front room table. He walked over to Orghlaith and pulled it off pressing himself against her, kissing her hard and running his fingers through her damp hair. He had tried on many occasions to have sex with her in the weeks following his assault but to no avail.

'I can't do this,' she'd said every time he'd grabbed her breast or crotch, Orghlaith flinching at his touch. 'You raped me.' She had shaken her head. 'How could you do that to me Max?'

How could I? He mocked silently. Because you're mine. Orghlaith was none the wiser to his skewed views as he continued to write her dozens of letters, apologising for his 'beastly' behaviour, declaring undying and eternal love and leaving bundles of cash in envelopes around the flat in the hope she would succumb and let him in. He seemed so sorry, so truly sorry. Max had enjoyed the chase but enough was enough, how much longer would he have to bloody wait until she got over it. He tried again and again recently, only for her to push him away; His fists clenched and his body shook, splashing his face with cold water and pushing his hair back breathing deeply attempting to compose himself after each rejection. But right here, right now he thought she might give in.

He stood back fumbling in his back pocket and pulled out a wrapped foil of the white, ravishing it open as if he were a child opening his last Christmas present and pressed his finger into it. 'Open your mouth,' he whispered to Orghlaith. She did what he said and let him rub the white stuff into her young pink gums. He did the same to his own. Frantically Max pulled at the buttons on his trousers ripping one off and finally getting them open. Orghlaith pulled him against her. She touched the bristle on his face, and breathed in as she caught the scent of his aftershave – he smelt good – a crisp, clean, fresh smell; She touched his bare chest with her palms before leaning against it with hers. She let him in, her head tilted back, eyes closed.

***

130

Frank was on his own in the Jewel Bar sipping on a straight whiskey in a booth in the VIP section. It was late afternoon so the Bar wasn't that busy. Max wanted to do a quick exchange without having to sit and talk for too long – Frank was full of it, full of himself and full of shit Max concluded. 'Max my friend, have a seat, have a seat and show old Frank what you got. One Bourbon and one Jack Daniels,' Frank shouted to the young bar man who nodded with deference.

'Thanks Frank,' Max said, surprised he remembered what Max drank.

'So this stuff is meant to be good yeah?' Frank said in his gruff east end accent.

'Absolutely, absolutely, brought in from Columbia by the same guys I used last time,' Max replied drinking his Jack Daniels.

'Yeah the last stuff was pretty good and I made a packet from it,' Frank said smiling and flashing several gold teeth.

'That's what I like to hear Frank,' Max said. Frank took half of what Max had and handed over the cash wrapped in a plastic bag. The women who were there at their previous meeting came and joined them and Frank insisted that Max stayed a little longer. Max accepted Frank's invitation which became more inviting with three women sitting at their table.

Orghlaith opened the door in the middle of cooking for herself and Erin to see the familiar face of Hamza. I brought you a present, he said, presenting a huge bouquet of brightly coloured flowers.

'Oh Hamza they're stunning! Come in, come in,' Orghlaith said taking the flowers. Orghlaith took the flowers and closed the front door.

Erin came waddling to see what the fuss was about. 'Pretty flowers Mummy, pretty flowers,' Erin said.

'Hello Erin,' Hamza said picking the little girl up. 'You get bigger every time I see you.' Hamza raised her above his head and Erin laughed as he brought her up and down catching her chubby belly firmly in his hands each time.

'It's just as well she hasn't eaten yet!' Orghlaith said laughing. Hamza placed Erin back down and she waddled off returning to her place on the floor of the front room scattered with colouring books and various crayons and pencils. 'She would spend hours drawing me pictures if I let her.' Orghlaith said to Hamza. He looked down at Erin who was scribbling away and back again at Orghlaith, he smiled. 'She's so cute. And you know it don't you?' He said to Erin. She laughed at him and continued with her masterpiece.

The two adults moved into the kitchen. 'How are things woth Max?' he asked gently.

'Good, yep good. Really good,' Orghlaith replied with her back to him as she put the lasagne dish in the oven. He admired her silhouette, although she could do with some more meat on her he thought. 'Drink?' she asked holding up a bottle of Vodka.

'Why not,' he smiled. He was freshly shaven wearing all black as usual; black trousers with precise crease down the front held up with a slim black belt and gold buckle. He rolled up his black shirt sleeves revealing a gold watch that looked good against his dark skin.

'Nice piece,' Orghlaith said nodding at his watch.

'Thank you,' he said. Flipping his wrist, he smiled and accepted his Vodka and Coke.

'For the drink or for the compliment?' Orghlaith asked. Oh shit, stop flirting Orghlaith, stop it she told herself. He put the Vodka and Coke on the kitchen side table and walked closer towards her.

'Look Orghlaith, why don't you leave him? Just leave him. Leave that bastard. I can help you.' Hamza said coming closer still, she was leaning against the breakfast bar.

'I can't... I... He's not a bastard really – he's not. I can't leave, I can't.' She took a large gulp of the Vodka mixer.

'But you can, you can, it is possible. I'll take you away to magical Morocco,' he smiled. She laughed. He came closer until the tip of his nose nearly met with hers. 'I've got enough money – more than enough to help you get away from him – as far away from him as you could get.'

She stepped away from his hold. 'I can't Hamza, I can't do that,' she said and put the Vodka glass in the sink. He nodded and didn't push any further but accepted Orghlaith's invitation to stay for dinner.

They laughed at Erin's attempts to put peas onto her fork without much success and managing to flick the little green vegetables everywhere else except into her mouth. 'She's a great kid,' Hamza said to Orghlaith.

'I know, I know, I'm lucky.'

The door opened and at that moment Hamza saw Orghlaith morph into someone else – her body and face tightened and she sat as if on the edge of a cliff anticipating a push from someone behind her. Max came through bold as brass and a little drunk after several more Jack Daniels with Frank. 'Hey you,' Orghlaith said getting up out of her seat to kiss him. Hamza's stomach flipped as he watched.

Max kissed her back his eyes darting towards Hamza. 'So what can I do for you Hamza?' Max said looking at him rather intensely.

'Oh nothing, I just swung by to check if the deal had gone alright with Frank and Orghlaith invited me for dinner. I haven't seen my little friend for a couple of weeks so thought I'd check how she was getting on too,' Hamza said ruffling Erin's giant mass of black hair.

'Ok, ok, well yes I saw Frank tonight – that's where I've just come from. He took half the gear so I've got to get rid of the other half. Tell Tariq I'll have his cut to him when I get rid of the other load,' Max said.

'Well he might want the money from the lot you sold to Frank upfront so you better give him a call and work it out yourselves. I wasn't involved in this one,' Hamza said, annoyed that Max spoke to him as if he were not worth his blue-blood breath. Your day will come to you, Hamza thought as he looked at Max. 'Well thank you so much for dinner, I better be off. Got to get home and call Saffannah – see if she is behaving at Uni,' Hamza said. 'Bye Erin, see you soon.' Hamza waved at the little one with most of her dinner over her face and hands. Erin waved back and smiled baring her tiny milk teeth. Hamza put his hand out to shake Max's hand, Max shook it briefly showing the handsome guy the door and getting him out of his house swiftly.

Erin, meanwhile, slid off her chair at the dinner table and resumed her place on the living room floor to colour in her Care Bear book unknowingly squishing bits of broken pencil into the cream rug with her chubby foot. Max turned to Orghlaith as she was clearing the plates away. 'What have I told you before? What have I told you about letting people who are just my contacts into the house? What did I say?' Max said clenching his fist.

'Max don't be silly, Hamza looked after Erin a couple of weeks ago – he's a bit more than just a contact if he's looking after our daughter.' Orghlaith replied.

'A bit more than a contact?' Max said getting closer to Orghlaith, gritting his teeth. 'A bit more than my contact to you is he? So you like him do you? Sitting here playing fucking happy families – you want him do you? Well do you!?' Max shouted grabbing Orghlaith's face and squeezing it as if it were malleable putty. 'You look ugly when I do that to your face,' he laughed. 'Bloody ugly.'

'Max get off! Get off me!' Orghlaith grabbed at his wrist desperately trying to wrench his hand from her face but it was like a solid piece of wood stuck there, immovable regardless of how much force she placed upon it with her two hands.

Erin started to cry and ran over to her Mum. 'Mummy, mummy, stop hurting Mummy,' Erin looked up at the man clasping her Mother.

Max let go of Orghlaith and for a brief second Orghlaith thought it was over. He swiped Erin from the floor and headed towards her bedroom dumping her on her bed slamming the door behind him. He turned towards Orghlaith. Erin's high-pitched cries echoed through the flat from behind her bedroom door. 'It's ok sweetheart, it's ok!' Orghlaith shouted out to the little girl who had wet herself.

The next thing Orghlaith remembered was waking up and Max sitting next to her, staring at her. She went to sit up on the bed and screamed in pain as if bolts of lightning had just shot through her entire body. 'You'll be fine, you'll be fine,' Max said stroking her hair.

Orghlaith staggered to her feet clutching her ribcage and not being able to stand up properly, her face throbbed and she could barely see out of her left eye. Max went to touch her hand and she pushed it away. 'Get away from me,' she said through swollen lips.

Her priority was Erin, she went straight to her room. Erin had fallen asleep on the pretty Princess bed with her old teddy bear that Nanny D had bought when she was first born. He had one eye and half of his foot was missing but Erin loved him. Orghlaith cried when she realised Max hadn't even bothered to change the little one's soiled nappy. 'Oh God Erin, what are we going to do?' Orghlaith whispered, shaking her head and stroking her little girl's hair.

Max came in to Erin's room. 'Is everything ok?' he asked in a sickly sweetly tone.

'No it's not fucking ok. She has shit and pissed herself – too scared to come out of her room and go to the toilet because of you – because of you Max,' Orghlaith said trying to be quiet in front of Erin, her words said to him through gritted teeth. She didn't know where she got the balls from to talk to Max this way after what he had done but it wasn't just Orghlaith he had hurt this time round – he had got to Erin too, and no one was about to do that to Orghlaith's daughter. Max left Orghlaith sitting on the edge of Erin's bed as she slept. Orghlaith heard him pick up his door keys and the front door of the flat opened and slammed shut, and he disappeared for the rest of the night.

Orghlaith changed a very sleepy Erin and the two fell asleep face to face in Erin's Princess bed. 'I love you Mummy,' Erin said comforted by her Mum's familiar smell. Erin touched her Mum's face gently and closed her eyes. Orghlaith was glad the room was dark and Erin hadn't woken up properly – she didn't want to have to explain why most of her face was now a blue-purple colour and distorted beyond recognition – yet again. That would have to wait until the morning when Erin would ask how Mummy had hurt herself so badly.

Hamza phoned at lunchtime the following day as usual around 1.30pm but today he felt as if he needed to check up on Orghlaith even more. She said she was really well, just feeding Erin lunch and sounded as if she were in good spirits which put Hamza at ease – he'd had a feeling that something would kick off between her and Max when he left last night and was pleased to hear her sounding good. He told Orghlaith he had to go up to Birmingham to sort out some money for his sister Saffanah and spend some time with her. 'Saffanah thinks money grows on trees sometimes honestly, and I'm paying her tuition fees and rent as well – it all adds up but I want her to do better than me you know? She's always had her head screwed on anyway...' Hamza said to Orghlaith.

'You're doing a good thing, it's nice to see you looking after your sister,' Orghlaith said, trying to sound as normal as possible despite her inflamed lips.

'Yeah, well it kind of balances out all the bad shit I've done you know – that there is some good in me...' Hamza trailed off.

'There is good in you Hamza,' Orghlaith said, gulping some water to wash down the painkillers. Hamza was leaving in the morning for a couple of weeks – taking a detour to visit another family member after Saffanah and then returning back to London. Orghlaith felt safe with him around. She was glad he was there and remembered feeling comfort in his being at the flat when she returned from the trip away with Max – he was so great with Erin too. He was the only other adult person she had contact with other than Max and would miss him.

'I'll take you out for dinner when I get back. We'll talk properly,' Hamza said.

'Yes we'll get together when you get back then,' she replied not wanting to sound as if they would be going on a date, although a part of her was pleased he had asked.

'I'll see you in a couple of weeks,' Hamza said, 'Look after yourself and the little one.'

Orghlaith smiled and looked over at Erin sitting on the sofa eating her ham sandwich. 'Oh I will, we'll be fine, I'll see you in a couple of weeks then.' Orghlaith wasn't sure who put the phone down first, but she found that she didn't really want to. She wished she had said 'Come round! Come round now and take me and Erin away from this – take us away from him.' But she didn't, the words didn't come. Max had a hold over Orghlaith as if he had morphed into a hard steel substance and moulded himself into a claw like shape that gripped tight around her and aggressively wedged itself deep underneath her skin cutting and tearin each time she moved against it's force. But it was so embedded now, so entrenched that if it were to be removed would leave bare a host of multiple wounds she would not know how to tend to, so better leave as it was.

Chapter 13

Winter 1989 was creeping in snatching the light evenings of autumn away replacing it with a bitter cold. Street lamps were turned on at 4.00pm and light jackets were replaced with heavy coats, scarves and gloves. Men and women who were used to commuting into the City had additional things to lug around with them on London transport – the hot flask to keep them warm, the long coat over the already uncomfortable suit and the umbrella lest they should get wet between leaving the station and walking to the office. For Dympna though, the past six months had blurred into one season, an extended, endless day that just repeated itself. Detective Paul Knight had pulled out all the stops to try to find Orghlaith and the little one but with no success. Three bodies of young women were found in that time but they were women belonging to another family who Paul Knight had to deliver the news to. In many ways he was pleased he didn't have to give that news to Dympna, but, although he would never say this to Dympna, he thought it was only a matter of time before Orghlaith's body turned up somewhere, and Erin's not far behind. So the investigation came to a halt when leads to the whereabouts of Dympna's girls fizzled away until the police had nothing to work with anymore. No one had seen or heard of the pretty twenty something or her daughter and police time and attention was needed on other cases.

Dympna hadn't been near the Church for three months, her crucifix and rosary beads gathered dust in the bottom drawer of the bedside cabinet. There were dark, square markings on the walls around the house where paintings had once hung of holy figures and decisive moments in Catholic religious history. They had been removed by Seamus on Dympna's request and were demoted to the attic to sit in the dark away from sight. Dympna had spent most of the six months confined to her bedroom, only venturing out to eat and drink and change her bedclothes. Her nightdresses became permanent attire regardless of what time of day it was. Her long dark hair hung loose and wild around her shoulders, gone were the days of wearing it in a tight bun or painting the graceful face she owned. She refused medication or counselling even though the medical team had persevered for her to have some form of therapy following the disappearance of her daughter and Granddaughter. Dympna's bloody mindedness shut out all of their advice. No amount of therapy or counselling can bring them back, she reasoned. I don't want it. So, as Dympna retreated into herself Seamus, Dooley and Mrs Wallis rallied round to support a woman they thought they would never see break. Paul Knight popped in now again, even after the investigation had finished to check she was ok, feeling a tremendous guilt that he had not found this woman's family dead or alive. She was an incredible woman, and he only wished he could do more. Seamus had pretty much let the boys take full run of the company back home and moved in to the spare room in Dympna's to look after and nurse her. He vowed to bring her back to life whatever it took. Finn and Conrad were coming to see Dympna in the next few weeks. It had been a couple of months since their last visit and Seamus hoped it would help her to have them near for a while. The boys and Seamus discussed bringing the Grandchildren over to see Nanny D but decided, given the fragile state she was in, to leave it this time round.

It was the not knowing that ate Dympna up, not knowing if Orghlaith and Erin were dead or alive – and if they were alive what state were they in? She imagined every day that Orghlaith would walk through that door with the little one in the pushchair and say it was all just a huge mistake. The front door would open and shut downstairs and it would be Seamus, Dooley or Mrs Wallis, Dympna would hear the footsteps coming up to her room and each time she would imagine it to be Orghlaith with Erin, but each time was a disappointment. Seamus had not seen such resignation and blankness in Dympna's face since the funeral of her family all those years ago. He had spent these months, along with Mrs Wallis and Dooley cooking for Dympna, cleaning her clothes and the house and keeping her company even though for the most part she barely spoke and often requested to be left alone. None of them would give up on her, all hoping that it was just a matter of time before she came back to life, that they would have the old D back. In the midst of all this, they all seemed to forget that Seamus was missing a daughter and a Granddaughter too. He cursed himself for not being there when Orghlaith was growing up, for making the most reckless decision of his life by leaving Orghlaith and Dympna for Ireland. He had lost out on years with Dympna, and a daughter who he had just lost all over again. Seamus didn't cry or get emotional in front of people – unless it was anger, which he had been taught was the only acceptable emotion for a man to express. But in the spare room of Dympna's house underneath the layers of sheets and candle-wick blankets he would cry freely on occasion, safe in the knowledge that no one could see his weakness.

Dympna was back in The Green again, 12 years old. She looks down at her bloody hands, her hands grow morbidly large and nausea overwhelms her body. The people come to knock on the door to take Dympna away, banging, banging and banging on the front door of the O'Meara house. Dympna picks up her

Dad's loaded rifle with the giant clown hands... 'Dad! Dad! Dad!' Dympna cried out. 'Dad!'

Seamus came quickly to Dympna's room and shook her gently. 'D, D...It's ok, you're having another nightmare, it's ok, it's ok,' Seamus whispered. He held her close and felt her back, drenched in sweat.

Dympna had come round realising where she was. 'Oh Jesus, I'm soaking,' she said wiping her forehead. She felt embarrassed that Seamus had seen her like this so many times over the past few months. The dreams – nightmares, had become more frequent and so vivid – too vivid and had woken them both up at all times in the night. 'I'll get changed.' Dympna said.

'Ok, I'll make us a pot of tea,' Seamus said touching her shoulder. He went downstairs and Dympna changed into a fresh nightdress. She splashed her face with cold water and as she looked up caught a glimpse of her face in the bathroom mirror. She looked at herself and cursed for not having these nightmares under control. She thought back to this particular nightmare with the people banging on the door and wondered what it meant – it felt so real but she couldn't make sense of it. She put her dressing gown on and went downstairs to meet Seamus in the kitchen.

They sat with hands clasped around their mugs of tea. 'D, if I say something, will you promise not to take it the wrong way? Please don't. Because you know I care for you. I love you for God's sake,' Seamus said.

'I know what you're going to say, you've said it before so you have, many a time,' Dympna said, 'but I'll hear it anyway.'

Seamus put his mug down and took hers from her. He placed his hands over hers. 'Look at me D. Look at me, you can't go on like this. The nightmares are happening for a reason – for different reasons and it's no good for you, it's no good for you D. Staying in that room...' Seamus continued, pointing upstairs, 'staying in that room all day with no light and not talking to a soul will only suck more life out from you. And I can't watch that happen anymore. I have let you deal with things your way these past few months but I need to tell you I think it's time to stop living like this. It's not right. I think you need to see a therapist or counsellor of some sort – you need to D,' Seamus said. He was worried how she might react but he couldn't let her carry on like this anymore. It was his responsibility to step in and pull her out from all of this, and if it meant her feeling angry or insulted by him for a bit then so be it.

To Seamus' surprise Dympna agreed with him. 'I have lost so much in me life Seamus, that when I lost two on top of it I gave up. I gave up trying. I gave up. I lost me family, you and the boys. Orghlaith and Erin were hope that life carried on – that it was worth going on for. And then they were gone too and now what do I have? But what you say is right. I probably need to see someone – a counsellor or some sort...' Dympna sighed and her sentence drifted off.

'You never lost me D, I was always there. And I'm here now. I'm here for good. We've got the boys and the grandchildren back home – a whole family is still here D.' Seamus said. 'And I want you. We've wasted 20 years and I'll not waste any more time, I want to be with you D, and I need you to come back from wherever it is you've been these past few months. I miss the girls too you know, it feels like I have lost Orghlaith all over again. I was just getting to know her and then she goes on me. We can cope with this together whatever may happen. I'm not going anywhere – not without you anyway,' Seamus said. He pulled his chair closer to hers and held her.

'It's the not knowing. I don't know where they are or what might have happened – all sorts of things have gone through me mind you know?' Dympna said, her eyes welling.

'Whatever happens I'm here. I'm here and we'll deal with it together. You don't have to feel like this on your own D,' Seamus said pulling her even closer towards him.

They sat in the kitchen until 6.30am talking about the kids and reminiscing about life when they were younger; Seamus teased Dympna about Dooley still fancying her and Dympna told Seamus he had a foul mouth at times. 'Don't sleep in the spare room Seamus,' Dympna said as they came upstairs. So Seamus slept next to D in her bed holding her for the next few hours. He had caught a glimpse of the old Dympna in those early hours and hoped that he would see more of it in time.

Chapter 14

Hamza's Father called to tell him his Mother was dying so he got on the first plane to Morocco to be by her side begging Orghlaith to come with him not wanting to leave her or Erin behind but she could not be persuaded. It had been weeks since she had seen him. She found herself hovering around the phone as the hands on the clock ticked closer to 1.30pm every day hoping Hamza would call at their usual time. He did call every few days from a pay phone several miles away so he could talk to her away from the prying ears of his large family. Their conversations were never without the muffled buzzing tone that made how far they were from each other even more pronounced.

'This is going to cost you a fortune Hamza...' she said.

'It's worth it just to hear your voice. I'm so sorry I had to leave, I'll be back soon.' He rubbed his coarse black stubble noting he would have to shave before he saw her again.

'Has Max been ok Orghlaith? – You should have come out here with me shouldn't you? I'm such an idiot for not making you come with me.'

'I wish I had Hamza, but it doesn't matter now, you'll be back soon...'

'Yes I will, and when I get back to London I'm coming to get you and Erin o.k.? I'm coming to get you.'

'I'd like that.'

'Have you got my letters? I've sent you three now?'

'No, I haven't received anything from you...'

'It's him isn't it – he's not letting you see the letters – he knows I'm here so probably figured out they were from me...'

'Hamza you can't send anymore, don't send anymore it'll... He'll go mad.'

'Are you sure he hasn't done anything Orghlaith?'

'No, nothing, he's been fine honestly, don't worry. When do you think you'll be back?'

'I'll get back on that plane as soon as I can.' Her heart sank, she went silent.

'Are you still there?' He asked. 'Yes, yeah I'm still here.' She replied sighing.

'I'll try and come home sooner I promise.' The beeping noise started. 'The phone card is running out, I'll call again in a couple of days ok? Send my love to Erin.'

'O.k., I will, don't forget to call!'

'Orghlaith I...' The phone line went dead.

She looked up and was startled as she caught Max's stern wide – eyed glare burning into her. She hadn't heard him come in. He held the disconnected phone wire in his hand that he had yanked out furiously and swung it round grinning with his hand in his pocket and head cocked to one side. She gulped. 'Max what are you doing?' she asked smiling. Had he been there all that time? Did he hear her conversation with Hamza? She would play dumb. 'I'm going to make some tea.' She got up.

He ran at her with the phone cable, Erin came out of her room. 'Get back in your room Erin, get back in your room,' Orghlaith tried to say to the frightened little one as calmly as she could.

'Mummmeee!' Erin cried out.

'Get in your room, do as Mummy says Erin. Now.' Max shouted.

Erin was silenced and retreated back to her room under the covers of her Princess bed. Max dropped the bag of brown he

146

was holding on the floor and grabbed Orghlaith's throat, tying the phone cable tight, tight and tighter. She wrestled with Max, her legs kicking, trying to gasp for breath but Max's grip too strong and tight. She was going to die, she was going to die. And then he let go. She desperately inhaled overcome that she could breathe again and ran to the other side of the glass table untangling the phone cable. He stood with his hands on his hips shaking his head, she knew this wasn't over yet. Erin opened the door of her room a little and peeked her head out. 'Erin go and play sweetheart, go and play, Mummy will come see you in a bit.' Orghlaith said. Erin looked up at the nasty man and shut her bedroom door.

Max ran at Orghlaith, a wild uncontrollable beast, veins protruding from his neck, eyes wide and glaring with rage, sweat beads on his brow as he threw her to the floor. Her head smashed against the corner of the glass table, cutting open at the side above her ear. 'You want him do you?! You think Hamza is your fucking knight in shining armour? After all I have done for you, I have loved you, loved you!' He kicked her then rolled on top of her. Here he was doing it again. She lost count of how many times this had happened and let him move her legs apart. She couldn't fight anymore. She couldn't. He heaved up and down with Orghlaith's head and neck crushed in his arms jerking up and down, trousers around his ankles holding on to Orghlaith as if she were a mere fixture with which to steady himself. Blood dripped from her nose and spurted from the cuts on her head, sporadically staining the cream rug with no apology.

Each time he had been sorry, so devastatingly sorry. Flowers delivered to the apartment by the dozen and rare gifts placed in secret places with notes scattered around for her to find. His loving words were so far from the beast that emerged on these occasions that she always forgave him, his 'sorry' said with such conviction and persuasion 'it won't happen again, I promise, I

love you.' There was no Dympna to whisper words of wisdom –
Orghlaith believed her Mother would not want to see her after all
of this time – Max had convinced her as such.

Her hand shook when she picked up the phone often dialling
Dympna's number until the last digit and then putting it down,
or sometimes she would hear D's voice or her Dad would answer
but she always hung up, not sure what they would say thinking
they had probably disowned her. After the assault on this
particular afternoon Max got up and left the flat leaving
Orghlaith lying on the apartment floor her blank gaze staring to
the ceiling, arms by her side as if she were playing dead lions.
Erin was still hiding in her bed. When Max had gone, Orghlaith
turned on her side into the foetus position, reduced to feeling as
if she were a helpless infant again unable to escape her
circumstances.

Her eyes trailed the front room – everything looked different
from this angle, she caught a glimpse of the brown paper bag
that was leaning against the sofa but her thoughts were
interrupted by Erin coming in and lying next to her Mum.
'Mummy... Mummy your face is bleeding,' Erin said with tears.
'Oh come here, I love you. Come here,' Orghlaith said. Erin
snuggled into Mum on the floor in a spoon shape and they lay
there for half an hour or so in silence.

Orghlaith made Erin some food despite her body and mind
throbbing with pain and Erin fell asleep not long after.
Orghlaith's eyes found themselves wandering to the brown paper
bag again. She had spent more than a year clean, the only thing
running through her veins was good healthy blood. But she
didn't want to fight it anymore, she wanted the pain to go away
and for life to be good again. For those few moments she forgot
everything as she pulled the brown from the paper bag and burnt
it in a large spoon until it became liquid. Max's drawers were full
of fresh needles. She sat back on the sofa looking at the beautiful

view of London and let the drug run through her until everything felt good again.

***

He had her now, Max had her. Oh, he loved how she called his name when she needed her fix, and only he could provide it for her. Only he could cure her nausea and stomach cramps that hurt as much as labour pains, only he could provide the sweet brown sugar that she now craved so much, that she had managed to defeat for so long. The little devil had wormed its way back in to Orghlaith's once young, healthy supple body through the diligent work of Max. Who else would she need now? Who else would give her what she wanted when she needed it and put her body and mind into a state of euphoria? Who else would clean up her diarrhoea when she was unable to control her bowels? Max. Both cure and cause. In the beginning Orghlaith functioned well and was able to play with Erin and even take her to the park. But those days became few and far between the more she ached for the next high. The feeling was all consuming physically and mentally, whilst pushing Erin on the swing or getting her dressed it was all Orghlaith thought about until eventually she could no longer do those things.

Orghlaith would change Erin's clothes every few days or wash her, but her inability to function and think properly meant Erin was often in soiled clothes and her small belly forever craving fullness. Max was out all day and would come home in the afternoon to feed Erin, often a sandwich or chips and Erin would wolf it down the same as a wild animal who hadn't been fed in days, grateful for anything thrown its way. Max would check to see that her Mother was still alive, providing Orghlaith with another hit of the brown. Orghlaith would be sitting in the spare room slumped against the wall already high or waiting for that next pin prick of unreal happiness to enter her blood. He loved the way she looked at him when the liquid first grabbed hold of her, as if he were the only one she needed and wanted – only he could make her feel like this. 'There you are darling, that's better isn't it?' Orghlaith could hear Max's distant voice in her state of semi-consciousness. Orghlaith detached further and further away from the harsh reality unfolding in that flat in Chelsea in 1989: that her four year old daughter had been forced to take on a ferrel-like existence in the absence of responsible adults or carers, scrabbling for food and figuring out ways to clean and look after herself.

Erin could often be found climbing on the unsteady stool to open the fridge door and to get to cupboards in the kitchen, nearly falling off and breaking her neck several times, her Mother in the next room oblivious to the risks her little one was experiencing on a daily basis. Whilst trying to wash her hands Erin had learnt the hard way that the blue sign indicated the 'Cold' tap and the red sign the 'Hot' tap scalding her thumb and a bit of her left hand; but once she realised her error through the unfortunate empirical test, Erin filled the sink, running both taps to provide luke warm water to wash her little hands as Mummy always said she should after going to the toilet and before eating. Erin had begun to store bread and jam in her room in the pink cupboard with the heart cut out so she wouldn't have to keep getting on the stool in the kitchen which scared her. In addition, Erin would keep half eaten biscuits and chocolate bars she would find that had been left lying on the living room table or had fallen down the creases of the sofas. Erin liked it when Mummy came out from the spare room sometimes and made tea and gave Erin milk and biscuits or when she ran her a bath. She missed her Mum but had neither the emotional or verbal capacity to express this, or indeed, anyone to express this to. Upon Max's entry to the flat Erin would scramble to her room away from the nasty man. Sometimes Max would leave the spare-room door unlocked and Erin would creep in to talk to Orghlaith or just sit and watch her.

One afternoon Erin made her regular visit to Mum in the horrible sparse room holding a cup of water with two hands walking slowly so as not to spill it. She placed it down next to her Mum in case she should get thirsty after all this sleeping she was doing. Orghlaith was semi conscious after Max had given her a pure hit not long before. She stroked Erin's face with half opened eyes. 'Thank you darling,' she slurred.

'That's ok Mummy. When are you going to wake up?' Orghlaith didn't answer, her head tipping backward, eyes closing. Erin left the room and returned minutes later with two pink hairclips and matching hairbrush she had taken from her doll set and Orghlaith's favourite lipstick. She gently combed Orghlaith's hair gripping the hair clips either side and then painted her lips. Erin kissed her Mum's cheek and hugged her. 'You have a rest Mummy.' She said and sat down beside her to begin work on her colouring book.

The capacity for survival in human beings – particularly children, is often underestimated yet at times when our innate capabilities are called upon they provide us with the survival tools we need. There is little room for rationality or lateral thinking, just a raw need to fill our stomachs and maintain the thing that keeps our organs intact – our body, clean and free from pain. It is only in the aftermath, when basic survival has done its job and we have kept our blood running and belly full that the psychological implications of our circumstances raise their ugly heads. Emotional and mental reasoning are, of course, fundamental elements to the human condition, though seem to be irrevocably lost or undeveloped in some of us.

Hamza stumbled out of the isolated grey shack he'd been held in wearing only his black trousers, torn and blood stained. All he could think about was her, that's what kept him going throughout all of this. He hadn't called Orghlaith since just after his Mother's funeral – before they had come for him. Hamza looked across the desolate dry land, squinting with his hand covering his forehead to block out the blazing Moroccan sun that was burning his eyes. He hadn't seen daylight for a month, his body a stone lighter and barely carrying him one step to the next, although where his steps were going he didn't know tripping over his bare feet dazed and disorientated. The three men, two white blonde guys holding guns and the cocky Moroccan holding the knife Hamza's body was too familiar with stood outside the shack in the distance; They laughed as they watched the beaten man, now with eight fingers instead of ten and partially sighted attempt to find his way back.

Chapter 15

Slowly but surely Dympna started to emerge from the cocoon that she had found herself in these past few months. Seamus waited patiently holding on to the little signs that she was coming back – and coming back to him. Her routine shower at 8.00am was followed by actually getting dressed rather than putting her nightgown on and retreating back underneath the bed covers. The wild hair found itself plaited and pulled back into a bun revealing a still beautiful face which she had begun to paint once again. The rouge blusher and red lipstick made a come back from their wilderness stay at the bottom of an old make up bag. Dympna checked herself in the mirror adjusting her blouse and tucking it slightly in to her pencil skirt. She looked at herself side to side and again from the front making small adjustments here and there, wiping her skirt down with the palms of her hands to press out any creases. Seamus had confided to Mrs Wallis and Dooley that he was sure she was getting better. They both agreed and all three of them hoped that the old Dympna would come back for good.

'Well you can stop talking about me now can't you...' Dympna said smiling as she came in to the kitchen that day. All three took a double take putting their mugs of tea down on the table simultaneously.

Seamus got up from the table so quickly the chair he was sitting on fell backwards, but he couldn't hide his joy seeing her standing there. He hugged her and kissed her forehead. 'How ye feeling?' he whispered in her ear.

'I'm better, much better, I'll not be staying in that bed any longer,' Dympna said, her words muffled as she spoke into Seamus' chest.

'Sit down, sit down, I'll make you a cup of tea,' Seamus said pulling out another chair. She sat with Dooley, Mrs Wallis and Seamus and they talked about as if nothing had changed.

'So how are the kids Maggie? I haven't seen them in so long so I haven't,' Dympna said, sipping her tea.

'Oh blimey, well Tom is doin' alright he's running the stall on the high street still, his Missus is pregnant with their fourth one...' Mrs Wallis trailed off.

'It's ok Maggie, life goes on, you can tell me all about your family it's absolutely fine.' Mrs Wallis looked at Seamus as if to ask his permission to carry on with this conversation – he shook his head.

'Dooley, tell Dympna about that woman you were trying it on with the other day... He's got himself a date D!' Seamus said as he made them ham sandwiches with the thick white bread Dympna loved from the bakers on the High Street.

'Oh Dympna, she's alainn, an absolute stunner so she is,' Dooley said biting into his sandwich. 'You make a great ham sandwich Seamus Killoughery, this bread is bledy good.'

'So when do we get to meet this lovely lady of yours then Mr McGuinness?' Dympna said smiling.

'Well Kitty...'

'Ah Kitty...' they all said.

'So you're on first name terms then eh Dooley you sly dog?' Seamus teased.

'Well of course of course. But ye know...' Dooley leaned forward with a cheeky look on his face and whispered 'ye know I was chatting up both her and the sister and I didn't realise for the life of me!' He laughed, slapping his knee and making a 'click click' with his tongue against his teeth. 'I still have the charm so I do, ah yes.'

'There's Mr bleedin' love machine over there,' Maggie said setting them all off into fits of laughter.

'Are ye's taking the Michael out of me eh? Ye feckers,' Dooley said laughing. 'Ye bledy feckers!'

It was so good to see her laugh, to see that flame back in her eyes Seamus thought as he watched Dympna in the kitchen that day. He knew Erin and Orghlaith were on her mind but he didn't want to talk about it with Maggie and Dooley there – not yet anyway, let her find her feet first he thought.

No one knew what jolted Dympna back from her abyss and no one asked either. Mrs Wallis and Dooley left around six that evening and Dooley shook Seamus' hand. 'You're a lucky man, you really are. I'll pop in during the week to see how she is if that's ok.' Seamus knew how right Dooley was. And to think that if he hadn't come back to her she may well have fallen into Dooley's arms – the thought made Seamus feel nauseous. He closed the door and went into the living room to find Dympna sat in her old chair sipping her tea.

'So what were you two gassing about at the door?' Dympna asked smiling. 'Like a pair of old women at times aren't ye?'

Seamus laughed at her teasing him, how he had missed the banter between the two of them. 'Well I may be like an old woman – but you are one, how old are you now madam?!' Seamus said winking. The chemistry between these two was as strong now as it was 30 years before, not whithered or worn but sharp, intense and incapable of being tamed.

Seamus watched the resurrection of Dympna in the following weeks, surely and steadily she would do a little bit more each day – go to the supermarket maybe, clean the kitchen or trim the hedge in the front garden. Dympna couldn't bring herself to go into Erin's room – which of course was Orghlaith's bedroom as a little girl too. It had stayed the same since Orghlaith took Erin, Dympna making strict instructions for no one to go anywhere near it – not even to dust or clean. She didn't want it touched. Seamus, Dooley and Mrs Wallis accepted Dympna's wishes and so the room remained. What Dympna hadn't divulged to Seamus or anyone else for that matter was her intention to hire Paul Knight privately and get him to find Orghlaith and Erin. What did they think that she had forgotten about the girls? That she would just sit tight now she was feeling better and hope they would miraculously turn up? Would she shite. She'd spent long enough wallowing in her mind and in her own loss – and Dympna cursed herself for not pulling herself together sooner and giving in too easily. She should have been thinking of ways to find them and bring them back home where they belonged. Whilst peeling carrots in the kitchen one evening Dympna resolved that if the police couldn't or wouldn't find Orghlaith and Erin then she sure as hell would. She would put posters across London, adverts in the 'Missing' section of the paper... Whatever it took. She cut her thumb with the sharp knife as her thoughts wandered from what she was doing. Dympna also decided to go back to the cleaning agency as she wrapped her thumb with a bit of old rag. She needed to work, the strong work ethic of her family ran through her veins, and it had never left her. Whatever jobs she had done over the years – factory work when she first came to England, office work or cleaning, she was never late, never took unnecessary time off, and worked hard. She was about to apply this work ethic into getting her girls back, whatever it took she would find them.

Dympna went to the printers with two photos of Orghlaith and Erin, one of them together and one of them separately.

Hello Marian, how are ye my love,' she said putting the photos on the desk top.

'Ah Dympna I haven't seen you in ages, it's lovely to see you!' The red haired Marian said as she came from behind the desk and gave Dympna a hug. 'Maggie said you wasn't well, how you feelin' now love?'

'Oh yes, yes I'm much better and I need a favour...' Marian looked at the photos.

'How many do you need?' 'Well I have £150.00 to spare – how many can I get copied of both for that?' Dympna asked. 'I tell you what D, I'll do it for free. You've been through enough trying to find them.'

'Oh Marian I couldn't ask you to do that, honestly I couldn't.'

'Listen, leave them with me and I'll make sure they're all ready by tomorrow afternoon ok? I'll do you a big batch and let me know when you're putting them out – I'll give you a hand too ok?'

'Marian you're too kind, really. That's so kind of ye.'

'Come on, how long have we known each other for? It's nothing Dympna, really.' Dympna hugged Marian once more.

'Thanks so much.'

'You'll find 'em D, mark my words you'll find them.' Marian said smiling and picking up the photos. Dympna left feeling as if she were one step closer to finding her girls. 'I got Marian to print up posters of the girls. I picked them up today.' Dympna said to Seamus as they lay in bed together.

'I know, I saw the boxes in the spare room D.'

'Well, what do you think?'

'I think if you feel it is going to help to find the girls then it's a good idea. It's just so soon after you getting yourself better, I don't want you getting ill again,' Seamus said turning to her and stroking her face.

'I'll get ill if I don't do something about it. I know they're out there Seamus, and I have to find them before he does something to them – I've a gut feeling that for as long as she is near him she'll be in danger and so will Erin. If Orghlaith is back on the drugs there is just no thinking about what might happen.'

'We'll find them D, we'll find them I promise.'

'Will you help put the posters up?' Dympna asked putting her fingers in between his.

'That's a silly question, of course I'll help, we're in this together ok? Come here.' Seamus held her tight, pulling her petite frame into his stocky body where she felt safe. He pulled her chin towards him and kissed her feeling her warm body.

'You are a cheeky beggar Seamus Killoughery,' she smiled. 'May I remind you we're not spring chickens anymore.'

'Now that's true, but that doesn't matter does it?' The light from the street lamp outside their room strayed through the opening in the curtain so she could see the outline of his body kneeling on the bed as he pulled his shirt off.

'We shouldn't be doing this,' Dympna whispered. 'I feel like I should be out there now, doing something, looking for them or putting the posters up... something.'

'We don't have to do this D, if you're not ready.' Seamus lay next to her.

'I want to.' Dympna whispered back.

Chapter 16

Dympna picked up three cleaning jobs a week and was into her second week of work when the cleaning agency rang to offer her another job in Chelsea. Because of the location, the rate went up so Dympna would be putting a few more pounds in her pocket if they decided to keep her on.

'Apparently, some wealthy man needs a cleaner twice a week and the agency have asked me to do the job.' Dympna said to Seamus over breakfast.

'Well that's great news D, but are you ever going to stop working? You know I've enough money in the bank for you not to work don't you?' Seamus said. But he knew Dympna was too proud to say yes. He thought it was a good idea that she was working for now so she could keep her mind occupied and not focus so much on what had happened with Orghlaith and Erin. Seamus knew that every time the phone went D hoped it would be Orghlaith's voice on the other end or Paul Knight with some sort of news. Her face would light up at the phone ringing but the light would fade in the same instance once she realised it wasn't the voice she so desperately wanted to hear. Seamus was on the phone to Finn talking about the company's finances. Dympna managed to have a quick chat with Finn before handing the phone back to Seamus and leaving to collect the keys for her new job – it was good to hear Finn's voice.

'I'll be home this afternoon,' Dympna whispered in Seamus' ear and kissed him goodbye. It was early October and the cold morning air hit Dympna as she left the warm house and headed up towards Kilburn High Street. It was bitter but the fresh air was heaven to Dympna after spending so long cooped up in one room – and cooped up in her own mind. She walked along the High Street noting the barrow boys setting up their fruit and veg stalls and Mothers doing the school run. She saw a poster of Madonna drive by on a double decker bus and immediately thought of Orghlaith. She smiled at the memory of her free spirited daughter and walked into the cleaning agency to collect the keys for the job in Chelsea.

Dympna arrived at the mansion flats with some of her own cleaning detergents, but most were always supplied by the client. Dympna was used to working in well-to-do places for people who had too much money and not enough sense to spend it wisely so the block of luxury flats didn't overwhelm her. She got to the second floor and walked down the corridor towards number 8b. The lock was a bit stiff but after a while of trying Dympna managed to unlock the door and let herself in. Her senses were knocked sideways – it was a beautiful flat but a stale smell lingered and Dympna winced at the idea of having to clean whatever it was that was making it smell so bad. Why were wealthy people so bloody dirty? She thought. The flat, in spite of the rancid stink was exquisite with a panoramic view overlooking London that would make the birds jealous. Dympna placed the keys down on the breakfast bar and walked over to the windows to get a look across the city. The sky was grey and it looked like it was going to start pelting with rain anytime soon, London looked sad – tragic. A beautiful city with its grand buildings and unique history yet cursed with the ugliest grey weather that often distorted its beauty.

Dympna shook herself out of her thoughts and headed towards the kitchen cupboards to hunt down the cleaning agents she would need. There were a couple of bottles of floor cleaner and a bottle of surface wipe stuff. 'Bejesus, do they not clean in this house...' Dympna said aloud shaking the bottle. 'Well, it's just as well I brought some of me own eh.' She went to her bag of cleaning products and began taking out her polish, bleach and cloths ready to give the posh flat a well needed spring clean. The smell was still bothering Dympna and she wondered where it was coming from – eager to clean up whatever it was that was making her want to put a peg on her nose. How could the people living here live with that stench she wondered? As Dympna was sorting through what she needed and where she was going to start she heard a faint noise from the bedroom. It sounded like a cat... She thought she was hearing things at first but then it came again. And again. Dympna put the giant bottle of bleach down on the kitchen tableside and walked to the bedroom only for the noise to become louder and clearer. As she looked over the bed to the cupboard in the wall, she saw a huge metal pole had been slotted through the handles to stop whatever was inside the cupboard from coming out. Dympna heard the crying sound again – but she realised this wasn't the sound of a cat. It was a child. 'Jesus, Jesus!' Dympna said. The child must have heard her voice because it started to cry more, making Dympna even more anxious. 'Mummy, Mummy,' the little voice cried out. What is going on here, Dympna thought. D grabbed the metal bar that was jammed through the handles of the cupboard and tried to force it to the other side. It wouldn't come out, and all the time the child kept crying and crying and calling for its Mother. 'I'm coming little one, I'm coming, don't worry, we'll get you out,' Dympna called back becoming more anxious as she couldn't budge the bar. She stood up and used the heel of her foot to kick the bar through, kicking it and kicking it until it started to move. One final kick and the bar succumbed to Dympna's force sliding to the other side allowing the cupboard doors to open slightly and bang against the frame. A shrill cry came from inside again.

Dympna pulled the cupboard doors open but the light was dim and she couldn't see much – where was the little one? Then Dympna saw a little foot move in the dark... the child had wedged itself to the right and to the very end of the cupboard. The cupboard, it turned out, ran parallel to the length of the room so was long and deep but awkward for anyone of adult size to get inside. Dympna placed her head inside and called softly for the little thing to come to her but realised after several attempts that the child didn't trust Dympna. The cupboard smelt of urine and excrement; who could do this, Dympna wondered, immediately thinking of Erin and what state she could be in this very moment. D manouvered her body into the claustrophobic space lying on her stomach shuffling herself forward with her arms and elbows like an army trooper on a mission.

'Come on,' Dympna whispered. 'Come on it's ok, I won't hurt you my little darling.' D felt around in the badly lit space and reached out an arm slowly, towards what she thought was a little foot. It was. Dympna held onto the child with one arm pulling it awkwardly towards her until she had a firm grip and was able to shuffle backwards and get them both out of the wretched space. Dympna put the child through the entrance first and then got herself through. As soon as Dympna saw the child in the daylight she realised that the beautiful little girl with black hair covered in her own waste was her Granddaughter.

'Erin! Erin! Oh Jesus! Jesus!' Dympna picked her up and held her tight covering herself in the muck but she didn't care, her eyes streaming, overwhelmed by the gem she had just discovered in the cupboard. But the feelings were mixed. Dympna didn't know where Orghlaith was. Was she still alive? Erin started to cry, touching her Nan's face hesitantly as if she were someone she knew once upon a time.

'Nanny, Nanny.'

'Yes it's me my little chicken, oh Erin I've missed ye. I've missed ye.'

Erin needed cleaning and to be fed straight away. Dympna bathed Erin, noting all the kids bathtoys lying around. She made it quick wanting to get Erin fed as soon as she could. She wrapped her in the fluffy white towel.

'Is that better yes? Shall we get you some food?' Dympna asked Erin while towel drying her hair.

Erin nodded, still seeming slightly disorientated and hesitant with Dympna.

'It's ok me darling, it's ok, Nanny's here now,' Dympna raided the kitchen cupboards and found a loaf of bread and strawberry jam so made Erin several sandwiches cutting them into small squares. Dympna wondered if Orghlaith had lived here, was she still living here? Oh please, please let nothing have happened to her. While Erin sat on the sofa and devoured her food Dympna began to frantically search the house – not knowing quite what she was searching for – anything – anything that might give her the clues to where Orghlaith might be. She searched the living room – under the sofas, pulling the cushions out, going through paperwork, opening drawers. Nothing. There was little in the bathroom other than expensive products and make-up everywhere. She opened a door to what she thought was a cupboard but realised, after switching the light on, that behind it was a long, narrow corridor leading to what looked like another door at the end. The smell that had lingered throughout the flat was now intoxicating and the closer Dympna came to the end of the corridor the more her senses were overwhelmed to the point she could have been physically sick.

She was hesitant in opening the door, covering her mouth and nose with her scarf, taking a breath as she opened it. Her eyes scanned the room and Dympna felt as if she were watching a film, that this was somehow not real life. The blonde woman lie face down in her own vomit on the dirty stained mattress, arms and legs sprawled as if she were sleeping. 'Jesus,' Dympna said aloud, stepping further into the room seeing the other body lying on his side his head flopped to the side covered by his hair. She saw a syringe hanging from a protruding vein in his right arm. 'Oh God. Oh God.' Dympna didn't know what to do edging closer towards the blonde, knowing she was probably gone already, but she couldn't just leave them like this. Again, Dympna was back in The Green 12 years old and not knowing what to do. Flashbacks of her Father hanging from the beam of the barnhouse and her brothers limp bodies on the floor came flooding back as she bent down and turned the body of the blonde over onto her front. The next moment happened in slow motion as the blonde hair fell away from the face it covered and Dympna recognised the dark brown eyes that glared back her and the light olive complexion. 'No!'No! God No!' Dympna screamed out. She laid Orghlaith on her back and placed her hands over Orghlaith's heart pumping, pumping eventually thumping Orghlaith's chest with her fist out of sheer desperation to resuscitate her daughter. She dragged Orghlaith's body through the tiny corridor into the living room and tried again pumping, pumping and then mouth to mouth. Orghlaith didn't respond. Dympna called for an ambulance with one hand whilst keeping the other pressing on Orghlaith's chest trying again and again. 'Don't leave me Orghlaith. Don't go please don't go.' Erin could hear Dympna's cries from the other room and began to cry out for Mum.

The ambulance and police sirens outside the luxury flats in Chelsea were deafening. Paramedics came rushing through the door, one male two female. One female took care of Dympna, the other two surrounded Orghlaith so Dympna could barely see her. 'Please, please help her. She's my daughter. Please...' There was nothing they could do. Orghlaith was gone.

'I'm sorry. I'm so sorry.' The female paramedic said to Dympna.

Dympna pushed her out of the way and held on to Orghlaith's limp body kissing her forehead and cradling her as if she were a tiny baby. What did he do to you, what did he do Dympna thought as she stroked Orghlaith's blonde hair. 'I loved you. I loved you so much. Why didn't you come back? Why?'

At that point the man from the room was being carried out on a stretcher. It was Max. Dympna couldn't believe her eyes. She hadn't even paid him any attention once she realised it was Orghlaith on that mattress. Jesus, you did this, you did this. Dympna's inner thoughts came out as she shouted frantically at the medics 'What are you doing with him?! What are you doing? You can't save him – he killed my daughter! He killed her! You bastard!' Dympna grabbed at the blanket covering Max pulling it off him dragging the oxygen mask with it. 'You killed her! You took her from me!' Dympna cried.

'Can someone get her out of here please. This lady is in shock,' said a police officer.

'Let him die! Let him die!' Dympna cried out as Max was taken out of the flat towards the ambulance waiting downstairs.

Dympna held her face in her hands. A familiar voice made her look up. It was Paul Knight. 'D, I'm so sorry. I came as soon as I got the call.' He placed his arm around her shoulders. 'I'm sorry D I really am, I don't know what else to say,' Paul said looking around him.

'We need to speak to her,' a police officer said to Paul as if Dympna couldn't hear him.

'Not now ok, not now. I'll deal with it – I said I'll deal with it ok?' Paul said getting rid of the insensitive officer.

'Come on D, we need to get you and the little one out of here.'

Chapter 17

Orghlaith's body lie in the handmade coffin in the living room. Dympna took a flannel and washed her face and arms delicately kissing her cheeks and forehead. Her usual light olive skin was a shade of grey. Dympna placed the Crucifix her Mother had given her on Orghlaith's chest and Rosary beads through her fingers, stroking Orghlaith's arms and holding her heavy hand for a minute, looking intently at her daughter. A sick empty feeling overwhelmed her and she nearly fainted.

'D, come here, sit down a minute D, sit down.' Mrs Wallis said, catching Dympna and bringing her gently to the armchair. Mrs Wallis' sisters Annie and Josephine were helping with the Wake, Annie was a make-up artist and had been asked to paint Orghlaith's face in preparation.

'I'll make her look lovely Dympna, don't you worry.' Annie said pulling out her brushes from the big black and white vanity case she had brought with her. She leant over the coffin.

'Be careful with her – just be careful.' Dympna said, not knowing what she meant only that she felt as if no one should be touching Orghlaith other than her, but she thought it was right to have this done, Orghlaith would have wanted it.

After a few minutes Dympna shook herself and wiped her eyes with her tissue, 'Right, right I have to get the candles lighted and we need to lay the food and drink out on the table... People will be coming shortly, yes yes.' She placed candles on top of the mantleplace, on the cabinets, on the window sill, and at the bottom of the fireplace, 'Can you pass me those matches please Maggie?' she asked. The house was silent other than the unpacking of the food and cutlery in the kitchen and the scratching of the match against the matchbox each time Dympna lit another candle.

Seamus came through the door holding bags of shopping and Erin on his hip. He had explained to Erin on their trip to the high street that Mummy would be in the house when she got home, Erin had asked if she would be able to watch a video with her.

'No, my lovely, we have to send Mummy to see the Angels in Heaven, but first of all we need to celebrate her life here before she goes,' Seamus had said to a confused little girl.

'I will give her a video to take to heaven Grandad,' Erin replied.

When they came in Dympna was covering the mirror in the hall with a blanket and had turned the other smaller mirrors to face the wall before stopping the clocks in the house. 'Is Mummy here Nanny?' Erin asked.

Dympna looked at Seamus and back at Erin. 'Yes, she is, she's in the front – room, would you like to see her?' Dympna asked putting Erin's little hand in hers. Erin didn't reply and followed her Nan into the living room, Annie had just finished painting Orghlaith's face. Dympna picked Erin up to see Orghlaith in the coffin who looked as if she were sleeping peacefully to young Erin, her cheeks a blushed pink courtesy of Annie's paintbrush.

'Would you like to say a prayer for Mammy?' Dympna asked.

Erin nodded. 'Yes Nanny,' she whispered.

'Ok my little chicken, we'll say a prayer for Mummy together then yes?' Dympna replied.

Erin put her hands together and closed her eyes, Dympna watched the little girl. Erin opened her eyes and looked into the coffin. 'Can I go into the other room now Nanny?'

'Yes, yes of course you can, go and help Granddad in the kitchen with the food.' Dympna said putting Erin down and fluffing her hair.

Dooley arrived around four that afternoon. He took his hat off as he made his way inside, the front door left ajar, and into the front room 'Hello Maggie.' He whispered to Mrs Wallis who had taken on the role of protector as she sat next to the coffin under strict instructions from Seamus and Dympna that Orghlaith's body should not be left unattended at any point during the Wake.

'Hi Dooley, good to see you,' she whispered back.

He knelt beside the coffin and recited a short prayer for the woman who had lost her life too young. 'May you rest in peace Orghlaith,' he finished crossing himself once again. 'Where are D and Seamus?' he asked Maggie.

'Dympna is in the kitchen preparing the last of the food, she's been preparing all day. I think Seamus is getting Erin changed into her little dress.' Maggie said quietly

Dooley went into the kitchen where there were a few neighbours he recognised talking in hushed voices and offering their condolences to Dympna. 'Hello D, I'm sorry for your loss, I truly am.' Dooley said. Dympna nodded, her eyes welling again though she managed to hold the tears from rolling down for the umpteenth time that day.

'Help yourself Dooley, make sure you get a drink and some food.' Dympna said pointing to the huge spread covering every inch of the dining room table: Quiche, ham sandwiches, cheese sandwiches, tuna sandwiches, sausages, bacon, ham, jelly, plates of cup cakes and more besides were laid out on beautiful blue and white china plates for those who attended the wake to help themselves and pay their respects to Orghlaith. The small house in Kilburn soon filled with neighbours and several of Dympna's old friends had flown from Ireland when they had heard the terrible news. The English neighbours found the idea of a body in the house rather odd but respected the old tradition all the same.

Erin stayed in the kitchen wearing her white embroidered dress especially for Mummy and made a space on the dining table for her colouring book and pencil tin, eating the sandwiches Nanny had given her swinging her legs and wondering how far away the Angels lived from Kilburn. Dympna kept checking on Erin, hugging her and asking if she was ok, placing her on her knee in between talking to the visitors and cooking more food. She kissed Erin on the cheek as she sat on her Nanny's lap. 'We're going to miss Mummy aren't we my chicken?' Dympna whispered.

Erin looked up. 'Yes,' she nodded. 'Don't cry Nanny.' She wiped Dympna's face. 'Mummy is with the Angels.' Erin said.

Finn and Con arrived around six thirty. 'Hello Mam, come here.' Finn had said.

'Oh Finn!' Dympna cried as he hugged her.

Con was next to hold his Mum. 'I wish I had known her better Mam,' he said.

'So do I Con, so do I,' she said.

Seamus hugged his two sons', his mind saturated with unlimited thoughts of regret.

'How are ye Dad?' Finn asked.

Seamus shook his head and his eyes filled. Finn put his arms around his Father and whispered. 'It'll be ok Dad, we'll all pull together, we'll get through it.'

'Thanks son, thanks.'

Several hours passed with more visitors coming in to pay their respects. 'Come on, time for your bed madam.' Seamus said coming into the kitchen.

'Yes, I think it's time you went to bed.' Dympna said passing Erin over to her Grandad. Seamus took the sleepy little girl upstairs.

'You come too Nanny' Erin said gently tugging Dympna's skirt.

Dympna handed a full plate of food and a whiskey to Evelyn (the neighbour from two streets away she'd known for years) and said 'You help yourself to more if you like.'

'Oh no, that's fine thank you Dympna, you get the little one to bed, but do come and find me when you come back down now won't you.' Evelyn touched Dympna's arm with her free hand, her other hand holding the plate and balancing the glass of whiskey. 'She was a lovely young woman Dympna, I'm so sorry.'

Dympna nodded accepting Evelyn's kind words for Orghlaith and followed behind Seamus and Erin as he carried the little one up the stairs. Dympna got her nappy out preparing for any mishaps that may happen during the night. The bed wetting had become more frequent recently. Seamus pulled her Disney pyjama top over Erin, her head getting stuck before the cotton gave in and let her little head and mass of black hair pop out of the opening.

'Come here and get ye nappy on then,' Dympna said and patted Erin's bed. Erin clambered up next to Dympna put her nappy on.

'Can you stay here Nanny and Grandad, until I go to sleep?' Erin asked.

Dympna looked at Seamus. 'Of course we will. Let's get your pyjamas on first and then get into bed.' After putting her bottoms on Erin snuggled underneath her duvet cover, her wide innocent eyes staring at Dympna and Seamus as if she had a thousand questions to ask.

'You know Mummy will be safe and happy in Heaven don't you?' Dympna said holding Erin's hand.

'But Mummy is downstairs,' Erin replied frowning.

'But her soul is with the Angels.' Seamus said kneeling down next to the bed and holding Erin's hand. 'Do you remember what I told you about our souls?' he asked.

Erin nodded. Dympna lay one side of Erin and Seamus the other with leg on the floor to hold himself steady as all three of them couldn't fit on the small bed but Erin had insisted they both stayed with her. They did, and stroked her hair and held her hand until she fell asleep. They gently made their way off the bed and crept outside careful not to wake her.

Seamus held Dympna in the landing. 'It'll be alright do ye hear? It'll be alright?' He said and cupped her face with his hands, his eyes staring directly into hers. She nodded and half smiled and they returned to the Wake downstairs.

The loud wailing and muffled sobs from Dympna and the other Irish women filled the front room. Dympna had explained to Maggie earlier in the day that this was called keening. Maggie had heard of Wakes before, but this was the first she had ever been to and thought it was a much more personal way to send someone off, although apparently not many people did this anymore. She comforted her close friend as Dympna mourned her daughter, rubbing her back and passing her tissues. Several more neighbours entered the house, saying a brief prayer at the coffin and offering kind words to Dympna, Seamus and their sons.

Maggie led Dympna into the kitchen leaving the role of protector of the coffin to her sister Annie. Dooley took Seamus into the kitchen and motioned for Finn and Con to follow. 'Come on everyone, this is a Wake, everyone into the kitchen for a drink.' Dooley announced quietly yet with a firm tone. The visitors ate and drank in the kitchen and listened to Finn and Con recite their tales of chasing Orghlaith across the farm when she came to stay with them. Finn swigged his glass of whiskey.

'We were all much younger, Orghlaith must have been about ten when she came over to stay on our farm, and she was such a city girl wasn't she Con?' Finn nudged his brother.

'Oh aye yes, and we ran after her across the field and she fell in a load of mud, she was not happy and ignored us for two hours telling us what dreadful brothers we were.'

The mourners listened and laughed at Finn's accounts of his childhood experiences with Orghlaith.

Con was next. 'I remember Mam calling Dad to tell him Orghliath had dyed streaks of her hair pink and had tied it up with strips of rag from her good sheets. Orghlaith was unique, an individual, I admired her spirit,' Con said, gulping down the last of his wine and looking at the floor.

'And do you remember at her communion when she set fire to her dress, oh I was so cross so I was, but I admit I did laugh at the sheer boldness she had even at that age,' Dympna said pouring another whiskey.

More funny stories circulated and they all laughed at Orghlaith's cheeky bold habits as a child, and cheered her individual and warm nature as an adult.

'Let's raise our glasses,' Dooley said, lifting his glass to the air. 'A toast to Orghlaith.'

'To Orghlaith,' they all said.

They all returned to the front – room and huddled around the corpse while Seamus recited the Rosary prayer.

'God, Creator and Redeemer of all the faithful, grant to the souls of your servants and handmaids the forgiveness of all their sins. Through our devout prayers may they obtain the pardon which they have always desired. We ask this through Christ our Lord. Amen.'

The prayers were repeated by everyone. Seamus finished with, 'Lord, hear our prayers; in your mercy, bring us to your place of peace and light the soul of your servant Orghlaith, whom you have summoned from this world. Call her to be numbered in the fellowship of your saints. We ask this through Christ our Lord. Amen.'

The visitors began to leave around midnight offering their condolences once again and making their way home in what had turned into a stormy night with heavy rain pounding London town. Dympna, Seamus, Finn, Con, Dooley and Mrs Wallis sat into the early hours drinking whiskey telling more tales from Orghlaith's short lived life, crying one moment and laughing the next, the conversation diverting at times though always returning to Orghlaith.

***

It had been six weeks since Orghlaith's wake and burial. Christmas was only a couple of weeks away. Neither Dympna nor Seamus felt like celebrating anything but they made an effort to make Erin's first Christmas with them as good and normal as they possibly could. Erin helped her Granddad decorate the tree in all sorts of multi-coloured baubles and tinsel – Dympna left them to it, whilst she cooked the meal for that evening. Finn and Conrad were visiting for a few days and were due in London that afternoon so Dympna was cooking for them, Dooley and Mrs Wallis.

The busy schedule kept Dympna's mind occupied but Orghlaith was always in her thoughts, and every time she looked at Erin she was reminded of Orghlaith. How could she not be? Erin was the spit of her Mum, masses of black hair, dark brown eyes and a light olive complexion. She wondered if she hadn't put Orghlaith back into rehab would things be different, could she have just made Orghlaith go cold turkey at home – maybe she'd still be alive now. Dympna lost count of all the times she thought about the different things she could have done or not done, said or not said to stop Orghlaith from getting mixed up in all the drugs and with a character as lowly as Max.

'Granddad Seamus! You put it on wrong way!' Dympna could hear Erin saying in the front room. 'Pink one! Only pink one!' she said.

'We can't just have pink! What about the other colours? They might feel left out!?' Seamus replied to the little one who was refusing to put any other colour tinsel on the tree.

Dympna remembered Orghlaith at Christmas time when she was a little girl, always curious asking question after question about why we celebrated it and talking to Dympna endlessly while she cooked.

'Mind you don't burn yourself Orghlaith... Don't get so close to the cooker.' Dympna remembered saying to her. One day Orghlaith burnt her little finger when she touched the hot pan. Orghlaith didn't go near the cooker for a good while after that. Dympna smiled at the memories as she placed the last spud in the pot, a tear rolled down and she wiped it away with the dishcloth tucked in her apron.

'Right Seamus, the potatoes are on, the meat is in the oven, can you cut the veg I've left on the side whilst I go and pick up some stuffing for the chicken?' Dympna said untying her apron.

The boys arrived that afternoon, booked themselves into their hotel and made their way over to Dympna's around five. They had flown over weeks before for the funeral but wanted to see Seamus and Dympna again before having Christmas with their wives and kids back home.

'Hello Mam, hello.'

'Oh it's so good to see you boys again, it really is,' Dympna said hugging her sons, although having to hug them more at waist level now as they towered above her both being nearly six foot tall. 'I don't know where you get that height from, really I don't – your Dad isn't that tall and I'm a short little beggar!'

Seamus was pleased to see his sons too. He'd missed them. 'Come here and give your old man a hug,' Seamus said to Conrad as Conrad offered his hand out to shake, 'I'm not your business partner, I'm ye Father, now give us a hug!' Conrad smiled at his Dad and followed his instructions to hug him instead of shaking his hand. Conrad wasn't sure why Seamus had become more tactile in recent times but thought Orghlaith's death and Seamus' lack of affection towards her growing up had pricked at Seamus' conscience. Finn and Con were equally surprised at their Father's hugging and touching of their Mother – something they didn't see much of – even when they were together. But now Seamus was openly touching D on the shoulder or placing his hand over hers without looking uncomfortable, and D would let his hand rest there. Finn and Con were happy that their parents had found one another again but were not sure where it would lead seeing as Seamus couldn't bear London and had built his life in Ireland and Dympna was hellbent on not returning to the place that had cast a permanent shadow over her life. There would come a point, the boys had both concluded when one would have to decide if they would compromise and if they couldn't then they would be right back where they were all those years ago having to part once again.

Dooley arrived that evening in his new grey suit with yellow shirt and pink tie accompanied by very shiny black brogue style shoes.

'Boys you've met Dooley,' Dympna said.

'Oh yes Mam, how are ye Dooley?' Conrad said, shaking his hand.

'I'm grand, I'm grand, and how are you boys getting on?'

Whilst Conrad struck up conversation with Dooley, Finn whispered to his Mother, 'Does he dress like that all the time Mam? Bejesus, you wouldn't miss him walking down the street would ye?'

'Oh he's a lovely man Finn, now don't be teasing him,' Dympna replied smiling.

'I'm sure he's lovely, but my eyes are going funny just looking at the shirt and tie!' Finn joked.

'Now stop your teasing young man and help me put this food on the table,' Dympna said.

Dooley certainly knew how to liven up the place without even saying a word Dympna thought smiling to herself as she carried a huge dish of runner beans to the dining table. Mrs Wallis arrived soon after Dooley, her cockney accent sounding foreign amongst the Irish tongues but with a voice that managed to extend itself well, having raised 16 children altogether, she was well able to make herself heard.

'Don't just stand there having a whiskey you cheeky beggars help Dympna lay the table – come on!' Mrs Wallis ordered the boys. She had an air of authority about her that many just seemed to succumb to, her plump shape and large bosoms had a dominating presence which Mrs Wallis used to her advantage whenever she could.

'How are you D?' Mrs Wallis said as she set the cutlery next to the place mats.

'Don't be doing that Maggie, I can do that, you go and get a drink,' Dympna said, avoiding Mrs Wallis' question.

'I will go and get a drink, I asked how you were though D?' Mrs Wallis replied.

'I'm ok, I'm ok. I miss her you know, I miss her. I'm so glad I have me little one back but there's not a day go by I don't think of Orghlaith, not a day.' Dympna said putting out the china plates decorated delicately in white and blue.

'That's to be expected D. You know I'm still here ok love?' Mrs Wallis said.

'Thank you Maggie, thank you, you've been so great these past few months, I would have been at a loss without you here,' Dympna said touching Mrs Wallis' arm.

'It's what friends are for D. Now let me call the boys in from the front room before they get too drunk to eat.'

Dooley, Mrs Wallis, Finn, Conrad, Seamus, Dympna and Erin sat around the old wooden table barely visible as it was covered with dishes of food, dressings, sauces and several bottles of wine.

'Dympna this looks amazing,' Dooley said.

'Yes it does Mam, it looks grand, really it does,' Finn agreed.

'Well stop your gassing and start eating before it goes cold,' Dympna said.

Everyone waited for Dympna to say grace as she had done for many years but it didn't come, Seamus broke the awkward silence. 'Finn, can you pass the lamb over?' Finn passed the plate full of sliced lamb to his Dad and everyone else took this as their cue to dig in to the feast laid in front of them. The conversation diverted in all areas that evening and, as always found itself on the topic of politics. In the previous year, 1988, three IRA members were shot by the SAS in Gibraltar; at their funerals, a Michael Stone killed three people. In a separate bomb attack eight British soldiers were killed in Northern Ireland which led to British Government banning the voices of Sinn Fein members from broadcasts.

Finn addressed the table 'I wonder when the British Government will let Sinn Fein broadcast again. I think it's a disgrace they have disallowed it. People have to listen to the shite that the British Government are always spouting. A democratic Government should allow all voices to be heard.'

'Democratic Governments have every right to put a silence on people who are terrorists. Murderers should have no right to freedom of speech Finn. No right at all,' Dympna said firmly.

'But Mam, they have a right to what they believe in surely? And they should be allowed to access media to express that right if they want to,' Finn pressed, enjoying the political debate.

'Finn, everyone has a right to what they believe in and to express that, but what rights should they have if they are taking away the right of others to live? Where is all this murdering going to get us? Life is too precious Finn, you should know that after we just buried your sister,' Dympna said firmly.

'I'm sorry Mam, I didn't mean it like that,' Finn said, now feeling that his comments were completely reckless given what had happened.

'I know you didn't Finn, I know. But say if Orghlaith was taken like that – if someone had murdered her for the sake of their political beliefs – it would make you feel differently I'm sure,' Dympna said.

'Well now listen, we don't need to be talking about the political state of home right now, let's enjoy a toast. We'll toast to all of us here, and more importantly to Orghlaith, God rest her soul,' Dooley said easing the tone.

The sound of glasses being chinked filled the small, cosy dining room and Finn apologised to his Mum once again but Dympna knew he had not meant anything malicious in his words.

'Don't worry, I understand my love, when you look at it from another perspective things can look very different,' Dympna said. She kissed Finn on the cheek and ruffled his hair as if he were ten years old again.

Erin became restless after finishing her dinner swinging her legs and pulling on her Grandad's check shirt so he put his drink on the table, leaned to the side and brought the little girl sit on his lap. 'Come here to ye Grandad – now what's the matter with you little one? Are ye not getting enough attention is that what it is eh?' Erin nestled into Grandads chest as he chatted to the other adults, twiddling with the buttons on his shirt and examining his large hands though this didn't last long as she spotted the shiny desert spoon with its delicately patterned handle lying on the dining table. She reached across, picking up the spoon and proceeded to use it as a replacement drumstick drumming away on her Grandads knees. There was only so much Seamus' poor knees could take before they began to feel numb. Distraction was the key so he offered Erin a piece of chocolate and as she reached for it Seamus took the spoon from her other hand, Erin too busy filling her mouth with the delightful Cadbury square to notice her drumstick being carefully manoeuvred from her grip.

'Nothing like a bit of bribery eh Seamus,' Mrs Wallis said laughing at Seamus' tactics to get the spoon away from Erin.

Seamus laughed. 'Me knee was killing me – but we might have a drummer in our family yet!' Seamus said stroking Erin's black hair. Thoughts of Orghlaith as a little girl danced around in Seamus' head as he looked at Erin – almost a replica of her Mum.

'We need to take you to the bathroom to clean away that mess eh?' Seamus said. The chocolate had managed to go everywhere else but Erin's mouth and bits of potato and a half eaten runner bean had also managed to find a home in her hair. 'Are ye saving it for later?' Seamus said to Erin laughing. Erin laughed not because of her Granddad's bad joke but because she was squeezing Seamus' face together and smearing chocolate over him too which she found very amusing – as did the rest of the guests at the table.

'I think you'll need a quick wash while you're up there too Seamus,' Dympna said laughing. Seamus took Erin to the bathroom and Erin's hysterical giggling could still be heard from the dining room.

As Seamus was cleaning Erin and sorting out her pyjamas upstairs the doorbell went. It was around seven in the evening, 'Who else has your Nanny invited over eh?' Seamus said to Erin as he popped her pink top on.

'Don't know,' Erin said shrugging her shoulders and turning her palms upwards – something she had seen adults do on television when they weren't sure about something.

Seamus laughed at her interpretation of adult expression. Seamus could hear voices in the hall and by the sound of Dympna's tone he knew something wasn't quite right so he picked Erin up and went downstairs into the front room, the others still eating in the dining-room.

Finn came out 'Is everything ok, Da?' he asked Seamus.

'I don't know son, I'm going to find out, can you take Erin for a minute?'

Finn took Erin into the dining room and Seamus entered the front room not recognising the man or woman sitting down. Worry was etched across Dympna's face.

'Is everything ok, D?' Seamus asked not liking the feel of this situation. The skinny rat-faced woman sat on the edge of the sofa in a beige suit with an air of superiority about her, whilst the chubby balding man with glasses sat rather uncomfortably on Dympna's armchair.

'They're from social services Seamus,' D explained. 'This is my husband Seamus.' D said.

'Hi, I'm Bernadette and this is my colleague Collin. We have just come round to discuss the situation regarding your Granddaughter Erin,' Bernadette explained.

'What about her?' Seamus asked. 'It's seven o clock on a Friday evening, what could you possibly want to discuss at such a time?' Seamus said. Seamus and D both had a shared fear and contempt for anyone from, or remotely linked with social services. Both had experienced the care system as kids and neither one had a good word to say about those experiences.

Bernadette had been in enough hostile situations throughout her career so wasn't surprised at Seamus' response although a little intimidated by the stocky Irish man that stood before her. Bernadette cleared her throat before answering Seamus. 'I do apologise for the untimely visit Mr...'

'Mr Killoughery,' Seamus said.

'Mr Killoughery. We were running slightly late – London transport was not kind to us today.'

'Are you not supposed to call or arrange a meeting or something?' Seamus asked again, rather infuriated at their sheer front of just turning up unannounced like this.

Bernadette ignored Seamus' question. 'We were alerted of your situation and would like to just have a chat with you and make a report before seeing where it is best to place Erin now that her Mother has passed away,' Bernadette explained.

'There isn't a "*situation*" so what do you mean where is it best to place Erin? She's staying with me – with us. I have raised her since she was born all throughout my daughters' addiction and through rehab – I've only just got her back and there is no question of where she will be staying or who will be her guardians,' Dympna said.

'I don't believe this,' Seamus said shaking his head. 'We have only just buried our daughter and you turn up doing this?'

Seamus and Dympna couldn't quite believe what they were hearing.

'We understand you are her Grandparents and social services always try to keep families together in all instances but we have to make sure it is in the best interest of the child,' Bernadette said in a rather condescending tone.

'Of course it is in Erin's best interest to stay with us – we're her Grandparents! She belongs with us! Get out of my house! Get out!' It was too much for Dympna, her eyes started to well.

'I'm going to speak to my wife in private for a minute if that's ok? Come on D, let's have a chat outside,' Seamus said and took Dympna into the kitchen out of earshot of Bernadette and Collinearshot. 'Listen D, I know what you're thinking – that they're going to take her, but they haven't a leg to stand on, we're a good family and she belongs with us. Let them do their report and write their silly notes and they'll leave us alone.'

'How can they justify this? How can they just turn up out of nowhere and question our capability to look after Erin? I can't believe it, I just can't,' Dympna said.

Seamus held D tight. She took Seamus' advice and allowed them to do what they needed to do. They looked around the house checking its suitability and introduced themselves to the guests sat around the table – all bewildered at why social services were here now. Bernadette kept scribbling furiously on her pad the whole way through with Collin following her around as if he were a desperate old hound dog begging for leftover treats. He irritated Seamus more than the woman did.

Bernadette fired questions at both Seamus and Dympna about how they would financially support Erin and more personal questions about Orghlaith and her drug use often making Dympna feel that she had been a bad Mother and couldn't possibly be any good in raising Erin.

'And I just wanted to ask you about your illness this year Mrs O'Meara. You were in hospital for a short period for mental health reasons – is that correct?' asked Bernadette.

'What? That is private and confidential – how did you get that information? I was not hospitalised, but yes I became ill after my daughter disappeared taking my Granddaughter with her,' Dympna explained, shocked at the information this social worker had managed to obtain.

'Yes, I understand it was very difficult for you, especially at your age. How old are you both now?' Bernadette pressed.

'I am 55 and Seamus is 56. What has this got to do with anything?' Dympna asked.

'We need to make sure we have all the accurate information on the carers of the children on our books Mrs O'Meara. And finally, can I ask why you have different surnames? Are you divorced? Seperated?'

'Right, that is enough.' Seamus said. He picked Bernadette up by her arm and physically removed her from the house, opening the front-door and pushing the rat-faced woman into the rain. Collin got up and left not wanting to be man handled by Seamus.

'You have done yourself no favours Mr Killoughery. My colleagues from the department will be in touch.' Bernadette said pulling her ruffled jacket straight attempting to gain the composure she had lost via Seamus.

Collin mumbled something along the lines of 'thank you for your time.'

Dympna stood in the doorway. 'Let me ask you this, where were you people when you were really needed? When my daughter was in rehab? When she went missing? Where were you then?' Dympna asked shaking.

'We were not aware of your case Mrs O'Meara.' Bernadette said bluntly.

'No, of course you weren't.' Dympna turned and leaned against the door looking at Seamus.

Seamus looked at her. 'It'll be alright D, it'll be alright I promise.'

Dympna wasn't so sure and the two returned to the guests in the dining room.

'Everything ok?' Conrad asked holding Erin.

'Oh yes, yes everything is fine,' Seamus replied.

Erin was sleepy and irritable so while Dympna put her to bed Seamus filled them all in on what had happened.

'It's just procedure, of course they will leave Erin with you and Dympna. Who else would she go to?!' Mrs Wallis asked in complete disbelief.

Chapter 18

March 1st 1990 was the first hearing. Seamus and Dympna sat behind one desk with their notes laid out in front. Bernadette and Collin sat next to them with two chunky files and a set of notes on their table. On the bench behind Bernadette and Collin was a blonde woman probably in her thirties and a grey haired man – they looked like a couple. Dympna and Seamus both presumed they were more social workers. The Judge entered, Dympna slightly relieved that it was a woman – she may show more sympathy than a man would – at least that's what Dympna hoped. All people present stood to the call of 'all rise' and sat at the Judge's indication.

The Judge cleared her throat and peered into her glasses which hovered near the tip of her nose as she examined the papers in her hand. 'We are here today to discuss who shall take responsibility for the child in question, that child being Erin O'Meara, Granddaughter of Mrs O'Meara and Mr Killoughery. Now before we begin are you Mr Killoughery and Mrs O'Meara still happy to represent yourselves?' The Judge asked staring down at the rest of the court from her chair.

'We are your Honour,' Seamus said standing up to address her.

'Very well, right, well let us not delay the matter. I understand that both Mr Killoughery and Mrs O' Meara would like full guardianship over Erin. Is that correct?'

'It is your Honour,' Seamus replied.

185

'Ok, and Miss Bernadette Stone and Mr Collin West of North London Social Services are presenting the move to place Erin into Foster Care, is this correct?'

'Yes it is your Honour.' Bernadette replied.

'Ok, Miss Stone, well as you might know I am a firm believer in trying to keep families together in these type of circumstances so I am keen to hear your case as to why the young child should not be placed with her Grandparents. Please do proceed,' the Judge said to Bernadette.

Dympna and Seamus' eyes remained fixed upon the rat-faced social worker as she presented her case for Erin's removal from their care. Seamus squeezed Dympna's hand, a we're going to be alright squeeze.

'In the first instance I would like to draw the attention of the Court to the home environment of Mrs O'Meara and Mr Killoughery, where Erin has been residing on and off since her birth and would continue to live if she stayed in their care. I refer to their address 55 Terence Road, Kilburn, London. Over the course of several visits to the home we noted that it was unsuitable in many ways including dirty dishes piled in the sink, a generally unclean and hazardous environment with clothes everywhere and, more notably, bottles of alcohol well within reach of Erin,' Bernadette explained.

'What, how dare you!' Dympna shouted across the table. 'How can you tell such lies?!' Dympna said. Seamus was equally shocked at the fabricated account given by Bernadette at no hesitation – she continued with her assault.

'Secondly your Honour, I would like to draw attention to the age of them.'

The Judge interrupted, 'I presume by 'them' you mean Mr Killoughery and Mrs O'Meara. Please be respectful in my Court Miss Stone and address the other members by their names.' The Judge frowned.

'Sorry your Honour,' Bernadette continued. 'As I was saying, the age of Mr Killoughery and Mrs O'Meara is significant given that they are in their mid and late fifties and Erin is just turning five this year. It is questionable whether people of such an age should be given full time responsibility of a child so young. It has various implications. In addition, and something which I think should be seriously considered by the court is that Mr Killoughery and Mrs O'Meara have lived apart for well over 15 years with Mr Killoughery raising their sons in Ireland, and Mrs O'Meara raising their daughter in England. They now want to be formal guardians of Erin when they were unable to raise their own children together. My final point is with regards to Mrs O'Meara's fragile mental state following the disappearance of her daughter and granddaughter with her daughter Orghlaith passing away only several months ago. Subsequently myself and my colleagues do not feel that Mrs O'Meara is, at least at this time, in the right mindset to take on full responsibility of a young child. Given these facts, we put the case forward that Erin should be placed with foster carers, Ben and Jill Thomas, who have fostered several children from our services in the past with a view to Erin eventually being adopted,' Bernadette pointed to the couple sitting behind her.

Dympna and Seamus couldn't believe that these people had actually come along to court – as if Bernadette and Co. already knew that this was a done deal. Tears filled the eyes of both grandparents.

Dympna, who had been standing fell into her seat and crumpled, her shoulders slacking, head bent forward as if the last gasp of life had suddenly been wrenched from her. 'We've lost her, we've lost her,' Dympna said not really addressing the statement to anyone in particular.

Seamus remained standing, knowing that it was now that he needed to be strong, he needed to be the rock. He made the mistake of leaving Dympna and Orghlaith in London all those years ago and he wasn't about to let her down again when she needed him the most. So Seamus cleared his throat, and with the Judge's approval, he began his argument in a desperate bid to keep their Granddaughter. He wasn't a lawyer and neither had he ever made any form of speech in a court of law, but he knew what the truth was, so that's exactly how he told it.

'When my wife and I moved to England over 25 years ago, finding work was near to impossible, especially with an accent like mine, I might as well have lost me legs. We had two boys, Finn and Conrad, and Orghlaith our daughter, who passed away in December just gone. All my wife and I wanted was the best for our family and we thought London would give us an opportunity to do that. Dympna's family were...' Seamus looked at Dympna to get approval for him to say what had happened out loud.

She knew what he wanted so she nodded and stroked his arm. 'It's ok, it's ok,' she whispered.

Seamus carried on. 'Ah hem, hem, sorry... My wife's family were murdered in our home town in Ireland when she was a girl and as soon as we could move to England we did – I wanted to make her happy and so we left for England when our children were still in nappies. However, all I had ever known was the farm business – I knew no different and though I tried relentlessly I couldn't make a decent living in London. The kids were getting older and I wanted the best for my family and the only way I knew I could make that happen was to go back home and start building a business. It was a different generation – a different era...' Seamus paused looking down at the table in front of him as he laid bare his story, dredging up uncomfortable feelings he hadn't dealt with. He continued. 'I took my sons with me so they could learn a trade, to set them up for their future. It turned out eventually I made enough money to help put all three of them through University. I left Orghlaith with Dympna – thinking, or more probably convincing myself that a young girl would need her Mother more than her father and the boys needed me more. I realise what a huge mistake I made, but I thought, at the time, I was doing the right thing and eventually things would somehow sort themselves out. Dympna's family had been murdered and following that she experienced things in the care home too horrendous to repeat in this court room so I understood completely that after all she had been through in The Green she couldn't bring herself to come back. And so we lived. For the 16 years or so after that, our family saw each other only every other month and I missed Dympna and Orghlaith for every day I couldn't be there as they did me and the boys.' Seamus took his gaze away from the Judge for a second and looked straight at Miss Stone though she couldn't hold eye contact with him. Unashamed tears streamed down Seamus' handsome face. He wiped his cheeks with his large rough hand, the salt taste of his tears catching his lips. He took a breath and continued. 'The picture painted by Miss Stone is not as it seems, our love for our children – and each other, runs deeper than you can possibly imagine and it is the same with our Granddaughter. My wife looked after Erin whilst Orghlaith attended University only wanting the best for them both, hoping that Orghlaith could still get an education despite becoming a Mother so young – that's how much she loved and still loves her children. When Orghlaith became addicted to drugs it was my wife and eventually both of us who looked after Erin and tried to support Orghlaith throughout her rehabilitation. Dympna did become very ill after our daughter's disappearance and experienced depressive symptoms after Orghlaith's death, but I think any decent, normal human being would have broken down too had they gone through all that my wife has in recent months. To add insult to injury we have had absolutely no support from social services at all, and yet now, when we finally have Erin safe and sound and she is settled back with us, you want to take her away from the people who love her in a way that nobody else can? Where were you Miss Stone – you and your colleagues when this all started?' Seamus glared at the social worker. 'And now you step in and tell us you think Erin should be looked after by strangers? As for your complete and utter distortion of the truth about a dirty house and alcohol bottles and such nonsense, I don't know how you live with yourself spinning such a yarn of lies in a court of law.'

Dympna pulled at Seamus' arm as she could feel him begin to lose his composure and his temper about to explode out in to the court room which was definitely not what they needed. The Judge asked the court room to settle.

'I'd just like to say one more thing if I could your honour,' Seamus asked.

'Ok very well Mr Killoughery,' The Judge said nodding.

'My wife and I haven't come here today with knowledge of the law or of how to win a court case, or which things we ought to say to prove we are the right people to look after Erin. This isn't about barristers making a good case for us – because we are the case. We are good parents and have been good grandparents, and that should be enough.' Seamus felt exhausted by this point, feeling as if he had said all he could possibly say and divulged the most painful parts of their lives in order to convince the Judge.

The Judge called the court to attention. After a brief break for half an hour or so the opposing groups were called back into the courtroom and this was the Judges conclusion.

'It seems clear how much you both love Erin and indeed your other children, and that all of you have been through a great deal of emotional stress and upheaval in your lives. I sympathise with you and the situation you have found yourselves in. However, your relationship has clearly not been stable with an unorthodox set up for your children which included an extended separation between yourselves and one another. If that were to happen again it would no doubt have a significant impact upon Erin and place pressure on whichever one of you would be left to raise Erin alone as in previous circumstances. The mental stability of Mrs O'Meara as outlined by Miss Stone is also of concern to me with regards to how that might impact upon Erin now and in the future. I must make a judgement based on what is right for the child and in this instance the court rules that Erin O'eara be placed into the care of Ben and Jill Thomas as recommended by Miss Stone and Collin West on behalf of North London Social Services.'

Dympna couldn't breathe and placed her hand on her chest as if to magically put the oxygen back in that had been rapidly drained out of her as the Judge said those last words. 'That Erin O'Meara be placed into the care of Ben and Jill Thomas...' That was all Dympna heard, and it kept playing in her head, and the more it played the tighter her chest felt. 'That Erin O'Meara be placed into the care of Ben and Jill Thomas...'

Seamus looked at Dympna and saw how pale she looked. 'Your Honour, I think my wife needs a moment – can we have a moment outside, please?'

The Judge agreed and told them to take their time and come back when Dympna felt better. Seamus poured Dympna some water and escorted her outside with the clerk ushering them to the doors of the courtroom. As soon as they were outside Dympna took in a long deep breath.

'Try to calm down D or you'll have a full on panic attack...' Seamus said rubbing her back.

Once she had calmed down and got herself back Seamus held her with both arms and kissed the crown of her head. 'You ready to go back in?' he whispered. Dympna nodded and they returned to the courtroom where Dympna thought she may just suffocate.

The Judge granted Seamus and Dympna access to Erin – twice a week and two weekend visits a month. They would have Erin for this weekend before delivering her into the care of Jill and Ben Thomas on Monday. The case was over, and everyone left the courtroom. As Seamus and Dympna walked through the court halls towards the lift they passed Collin and Bernadette.

'You pleased with yourselves are ye? You call yourselves bloody care workers? Care workers my arse, you don't know your arse from your elbow. This isn't over.' Seamus shouted at the two.

The foster carer Ben tried to calm Seamus 'Look Mr Killoughery, Jill and I would want nothing but the best for Erin' – but Seamus didn't want to hear it, the stout Irish man pushed Ben away as if he were an irritating fly.

'We have nothing to say to you,' Seamus said looking at Ben and Jill. Dympna held onto Seamus, her arm linked in his.

Mrs Wallis had been looking after Erin while Dympna and Seamus attended court that day. 'She's been an absolute star, haven't you my little darlin',' boomed Mrs Wallis as they walked through the door. But she knew what the verdict was as soon as she saw Dympna's face.

'Have you been crying Nanny D? What's the matter Nanny?' Erin said standing in the hallway looking up at her Grandma.

'Oh come here me little mite, come here.' Dympna bent down and picked up Erin, holding her tight and smothering her with kisses.

Seamus explained to Mrs Wallis in the kitchen what had happened.

Mrs Wallis cried. 'I can't believe it, I can't believe it Seamus. Those bloody people – they don't know anything.'

Seamus and Dympna watched Erin sleep peacefully that night with her door slightly ajar, the little girl stirred a little and pulled the ugly teddy she adored closer to her chest. Dympna sighed heavily and Seamus stood behind her placing his hands on D's shoulders.

The weekend came and went – seeming to fly quicker than any other. Dympna and Seamus took Erin to the cemetery where Orghlaith was buried in south west London and Erin said a little prayer to her Mum and crossed herself 'Father, Sons and my holy spritz' Erin said aloud.

Seamus and Dympna looked at each other and laughed at her interpretation of this – they were shortly told off by the little girl who told Nanny and Grandad that it was 'Wude to laugh at peoples'. Although Dympna still hadn't fully returned to the Church, she didn't want her own confusion with her religion to affect what she thought was Erin's need to have something to believe in. Erin did believe in God and she believed that Mummy was with the Angels and that Orghlaith was in a special place.

The three went to PizzaHut – Erin was amazed at the 'PizzaHut IceCream Factory' where you could custom make your own ice cream. She insisted on having 3 scoops (one of each flavour – strawberry, chocolate and vanilla) and topping it up with hundreds and thousands, jelly sweets, smarties and strawberry sauce. Seamus and Erin returned to the table and Dympna laughed at the sight of the little tot attempting to eat the mountain of ice cream.

'I'll give it a few more mouthfuls and your belly will be too full to eat anymore.' Dympna said to Erin.

'I'm gonna eat it all Nanny D,' Erin said shovelling a load into her little mouth while the toppings fell off onto the table unable to fit into Erin's mouth alongside the mammoth mound of ice cream.

'Why did you get her so much Seamus?' Dympna asked smiling at him.

'Well, whatever she doesn't finish I'll eat...' Seamus said putting his spoon in to steal a bit of the ice cream.

Erin told him off and said for her Grandad to go and get his own ice cream and they all laughed.

After only a few more mouthfuls and still a mass of ice cream to work through Erin could eat no more. 'My belly is full,' Erin said rubbing her little round stomach.

'I'm not surprised!' said Dympna smiling across the table at her Granddaughter. 'Ye eyes are bigger than your belly aren't they?!'

When the three returned home later that Saturday afternoon, Dympna and Seamus attempted to explain to Erin what was going to happen on Monday – and all the days thereafter.

'But why do I have to stay with strangers, Nanny? I want to stay with you and Grandad...' Erin's voice started to crack and her chin wobbled as she began to make sense of the situation. 'I don't want to say goodbye again, not again.' Erin said, sitting on Nanny's knee and hugging Dympna for dear life.

'Now we won't be saying goodbye. What will happen is this: you will stay with Ben and Jill for a few days and then with Nanny and Grandad on the other days ok, my little darlin'? That's all, you will still have your room here and all your toys and Grandad and I will always be here too.' Dympna kissed Erin repeatedly on her forehead and held her tighter stroking her hair. 'Did you hear what Nanny said sweetheart?' Dympna asked Erin as she hadn't responded to what she had said choosing to nestle her face upon Dympna's chest.

Erin lifted her head and eventually replied 'Yes Nanny,' but didn't say anything more. She just put her small arms around Dympna's waist and hugged her as tight as she could – it made

Dympna want to pack up all their things and leave the country with Erin and Seamus there and then.

Seamus interrupted the idea Dympna was flirting with as he came in to the living room. 'Now shall we get you in your pyjamas and then we can watch the video you picked today?' Seamus said to Erin. She had chosen her favourite film – Jungle Book, which Erin had seen at least five times before but insisted on watching again. Erin's 'bestest' part of the film is when King Louis the ape sings the famous lyrics 'I wanna be like you – ooh, I wanna talk like you, walk like you...' and dances around as if he's had a few too many. As soon as the ape would appear on screen to the excited sounds of the saxophone and drums Erin would spring from her seat and sing along at the top of her voice encouraging Dympna and Seamus to lose their inhibitions and join in the fun too – which of course they always did. And so the three of them would dance and sing as if they were all King Louis' disciples – Dympna and Seamus forgetting they were grown-ups in those care-free moments and Erin enjoying the playful innocence that childhood should encompass.

Dympna looked at Erin's small red suitcase sitting in the hallway that Monday morning as she came down the stairs. She could hear Erin laughing with Seamus in the kitchen over breakfast, she sat down on the middle step of the stairs facing the front door running through ways in which they could leave yet again – imagining that when Ben and Jill got here they would find only an empty house and would return home without Erin. Seamus came out into the hallway. 'D... oh D come here,' Seamus said as he knelt on the step below her. 'Listen to me,' he whispered. 'We'll get hold of the best bloody barrister we can find and we will fight to get her back do ye hear me D? We lost Orghlaith, we're not losing that little one right?' He cupped Dympna's face in his hands. 'It's not over D. Today is going to be hard but it's not over. We'll appeal, we're going to appeal.

Now don't let Erin see you like this, come on, come and get some food in you,' Seamus said.

His words and touch made Dympna feel better – she had questioned whether she had any more fight left in her, but when Dympna looked at Erin the resilient woman knew she would have to fight every corner to try and get her Granddaughter back.

Ben and Jill arrived at 11.00am. Seamus sat on one side of the living room with Erin, Dympna standing, and Ben and Jill sat awkwardly on the sofa opposite. After an exchange of irrelevant niceties – the grey weather in London and the unreliability of London Transport the awkward conversation moved onto the agreed terms and conditions as laid out by the Judge's ruling in court (two weekly visits and two weekend visits a month for Seamus and Dympna.)

Dympna took Erin out of the room when the finer details were being discussed telling Ben and Jill this wasn't a conversation for her ears – she didn't need to hear it. They didn't argue with the firm woman. After a short while the inevitable came and Erin turned to Nanny D 'When am I coming back home Nanny? Grandad?' Erin looked at them both for an answer.

'I can't do this Seamus.' Dympna said, and left the room running up the stairs.

'Mrs O' Meara!' Jill shouted out.

'Please, just leave her for now, my wife is finding this really difficult,' Seamus said.

'I know, I know,' Jill said tucking her blonde hair behind her ears. 'Well we really ought to be going... Would you like to see your new room Erin?' Jill said softly and put her hand out for Erin to hold. Erin hesitantly reached up to Jill's hand and followed her and the other adults into the hallway.

'I'll wait in the car,' Ben said and took Erin's suitcase.

'When am I coming back Grandad?' Erin asked again. She peered up at her Grandad who, at her height, seemed to tower feet above her.

He bent down and picked Erin up, her arms draped around his neck and head on his shoulder. 'You'll be back in a few days me darlin', not long and you'll be back I promise.'

Erin looked at her Grandad's face touching his bristle. 'Why are you cyring Grandad?'

'Oh because I love ye so much that's why. I love you so much and I know you are going to be a good girl for Ben and Jill aren't you?' Seamus said.

'Yes Grandad,' Erin replied, nodding. Seamus put her down.

'I don't want to go with you – I want to stay with Nanny and Grandad,' Erin said frowning at Jill, hiding behind her Grandad's leg.

Jill reached her hand out to the little girl. 'Come on Erin, it's ok, you will be able to see Nanny and Grandad all of the time I promise. We have a special surprise for you in your new bedroom.' Jill coaxed.

'I don't care, I don't want a new bedroom,' Erin said solemnly.

Jill tucked her neatly cut bob behind her ears and bent down so she was the same height as Erin, balancing on the balls of her feet. 'You'll have lots of fun with the other children – we have a playroom full of toys and colouring pens and pads - you like colouring don't you?' Jill pursued.

'Only colouring at Nan and Grandads house,' Erin said defiantly, still frowning.

Jill stood up and reached her hand out again. 'Come on Erin, we have to go now.'

Seamus sighed and picked Erin up once again, his eyes red and swollen. 'You have to go with Jill for now my darling, just for a little while ok? You'll still see Nanny and Grandad and come to stay.' Erin could detect the tremor in Seamus' voice, he didn't want her to see him upset again, but she knew he was.

'I don't want to go Grandad.' Erin rested her head on his shoulder. He put her head towards his and squeezed tight.

'I know, I know,' he whispered. 'But you'll be back here with Nanny and Grandad before you can say Jungle Book. And do you know Jill and Ben have got lots of fun things in their house – even a big pond in the backyard with lots of fish.'

Erin shook her head and cried. Seamus put her down and put her coat on. Jill took her hand.

'Grandad,' Erin said looking up at him.

'I'll see you soon me darlin.' He bent down once more to kiss her cheeks either side. He looked at Jill. 'Can you call us when you get back – just let us know how she is.'

'Of course I will, of course.' Jill smiled awkwardly.

Jill and Erin walked up the pathway towards the car where Ben had been waiting. Seamus looked on from the doorway, Erin's brown eyes staring back at him. He felt helpless. If Erin would have looked up from the car she would have seen that Dympna had watched her too, saw her red duffle coat get in their car and watched them drive away.

Chapter 19

Erin's new room had been decorated by Jill and Ben in bright primary colours and a freshly polished wooden floor. The pinewood bunk bed in the corner of the room had a desk attached to it, home to fun colouring pads and chunky pens and pencils neatly arranged by Jill. Erin's huge bedroom window looked over a 60ft long garden with a swing, trampoline, latest trendy toys ordered from a French toy maker and a pond at the end of it with all sorts of odd looking fish. When Dympna and Seamus visited this child's haven Dympna thought Erin would never want to come back to them after living in such a wonderful home with three floors and an attic especially for dress-up and painting activities only.

'How can we compete with this Seamus?' Dympna had asked him when they left the "perfect" house. Jill and Ben had two other children – Amy, six who they had recently adopted and Mark, 10, who they were fostering. Erin played with both children harmoniously and was generally well behaved but despite being with Jill and Ben for three months she still had not settled properly. The days Erin visited Nan and Granddad she had done all sorts of things to stop herself from being dropped back at Jill and Ben's home. Erin had locked herself in the bathroom on numerous occasions, only being coaxed out when Seamus said he would tell the policemen that she was being very naughty. Erin didn't want to get in trouble with the police so eventually, after two hours of negotiation with the cheeky little one, she turned the key in the lock and Seamus was able to drop her back, having to explain to Jill what had happened since they were so late. Other ploys to delay her return home would be the stomach ache which suddenly started as soon as Dympna said Erin had to put her shoes on to go home, or pretending to be asleep thinking that Nanny and Grandad would just let her stay over.

Of course Seamus and Dympna never wanted to bring her back, and both loved the fact that Erin wanted to stay with them, but they were under obligation to return Erin back to her foster parents, which they always did. Dympna and Seamus had actually struck up a good rapport with Jill and Ben – they were a nice, decent couple, both teachers who loved their jobs and loved kids, but there was always going to be a slight tension between the foster parents and Dympna and Seamus, because Jill and Ben had their precious gem, and the Irish couple hadn't stopped wanting Erin back, not for a moment. When you love someone – whatever that relationship may be, and they are taken away to be looked after and cared for by someone else, to live another life which partly or wholly cuts you out, it often highlights the strength and magnitude of your love and the unlimited lengths one would endeavour to bring them back home.

Dympna and Seamus fully recognised what was being asked of them by some sort of invisible force, to keep going, keep working at it, to tap into every resource they had to get her back.

They did. Dympna took on three additional cleaning jobs, against Seamus' wishes, but there was no stopping her. Seamus rented out some office space to a local businessman back home for extra income and got Finn and Conrad to extend the exporting of their home-made cider to France and Italy and two other companies in London. The purpose of all of this was to raise funds to obtain a cream of the crop solicitor and any lawyer fees that would inevitably fire a hole in the finances. Dympna and Seamus spent hundreds acquiring solicitor's advice and hours searching in the library grappling with the English legal system – its unnecessary jargon and frustrating ambiguity making it even harder to find what their rights as grandparents were. They were getting nowhere fast feeling as though they were banging their heads against a brick wall – until the pair stumbled across successful lawyer Harvey Dench in an unlikely place.

Dench was an east end wide boy with a strict Italian Mother to whom he was grateful for inheriting her good looks and articulate brain. She taught her son the art of a well developed argument informed by a love of Plato and Socrates. Dench's sponge like brain absorbed his Mother's lessons, as did he absorb his Father's sharp thinking, eye for detail and 'gift of the gab' making him the best jewel thief among his peers. Dench was a product of this unusual combination: he had an analytical mind, bright as anything with the common sense some academic minds might lack and a soft heart inside a large hard body. Perhaps an unlikely description of your average lawyer – but he wasn't average, he was a rare find. Dench took an instant like to Dympna and Seamus in the cafe that evening as he finished off his gravy and peas and listened to the rest of their story. He empathised with the decent Irish couple and informed the Grandparents he would take on their case representing them for less than half his usual price. On any other night Dench would have walked past the cafe and headed home but he was starving and fancied something warm and stodgy despite it being the middle of June. Seamus and Dympna hadn't eaten all day and neither wanted to cook so here they were, and they sat until closing time drinking builders' tea in Styrofoam cups talking to the intriguing Mr Dench.

Dympna and Seamus liked the young barrister, he had fire in his belly and a passion to do what was right. The three of them spent many an evening since that first meeting in the cafe huddled around the dining room table discussing their case. Harvey explained that if they were granted something called a Residence Order it would give them total parental responsibility and they would receive an allowance from social services to help them financially, but from the people he had spoken to Seamus and Dympna had only a small chance of financial help from social services. But Seamus and Dympna were not interested in what money they might or might not be entitled to.

'I don't want anything from the bloody state. Nothing. We'll support Erin ourselves,' Seamus said proudly. 'I have a thriving business back home and savings in the bank and Dympna and I both work so it'll be fine.'

Seamus and Dympna hadn't realised there was so much to consider. All they wanted to do was take care of their Grandchild and make sure she was going to be looked after properly - why was this so difficult? Harvey finished off his cup of tea. 'Thanks for dinner Dympna, I'll call you when you get back from Ireland' Harvey kissed Dympna and shook Seamus' hand, gathered up the bulk of paperwork and headed to his BMW.

Chapter 20

Dympna had agreed to visit The Green for the weekend. Seamus wanted to go back home having had enough of London. He hoped that coming back home might help Dympna to face her fear and remind her how good life could be. He'd missed home. It was July now and The Green always looked so beautiful in the summer, green fields for miles and unspoilt landmarks decorated with bold coloured flowers. Seamus imagined himself back there again, with all of his family together – could it happen? Could he make that come true?

They flew in to Cork airport. It took about an hour and a half to get to The Green. Dympna forgot how stunning home was as the cab weaved in and out of country lanes, beautiful remote houses planted here and there tucked away behind masses of trees so you could just about see them. The Old Post Office was still there and Mrs O'Brien was still here too! – Dympna couldn't believe it, she was as old as Ireland itself ,Dympna thought smiling. They drove up a hill and as they got to the peak Dympna could see for miles what looked like a patchwork quilt of finely crafted green and yellow squares with brown specks in some and white in the other – horses and sheep Dympna concluded. The smell was familiar – fresh and unique to The Green – clean and wholesome, so different to Kilburn. But the familiar smell also brought back memories of her family – it seemed like yesterday that they were taken from her and then social services had come to place Dympna in care when Aunty

Garbo died. The rest of the O'Meara family had already left The Green dispersing across the globe leaving Dympna at the mercy of the care system. Oh but before then life was good – running freely in the fields with her brothers, helping her Dad on the farm, eating the food they had cultivated themselves. What a wonderful life it had been – even if it was short-lived. Although in her fifties now, the memories were clear and sharp as if she'd only just experienced them: the smell of her Mother's cooking, her Mother's sweet light Irish voice, the scent of her Dad when he picked her up and hugged her and of her room up in the top of the farmhouse – fragrant old wood and fresh air. The cab drove on bumping up and down over the hilly lanes and uneven roads.

Dympna could see across several fields and on top of the hill was her old home – the place where her family were... Though it was a fair distance away she could see that part of the brickwork had come away at the side – it now looked much like an old ruin. Seamus realised she had seen it and held her hand. 'You ok?' he whispered.

'I'm fine, I'm fine,' Dympna said smiling at him.

'Do you remember that over there?' Seamus asked with a cheeky glint in his eyes trying to divert her thoughts. Dympna looked to a shed that now housed horses.

'Wasn't that old Jimmy's workshop?!' Dympna said laughing.

'Oh yes, and didn't we have fun in there Dympna O'Meara!' Seamus said kissing her on the cheek.

'Seamus you are terrible don't you know!' Dympna put her hand over her mouth covering a shy smile as Seamus nudged her memory back to their courting days. They were two kids in the care system who had stumbled across one another finding themselves instantly intrigued by the other and thereafter the two were joined at the hip, planning escape from the mouldy walls of their care homes anticipating a better future.

Dympna and Seamus stayed in a hotel not far from Finn's house – they didn't want to impose on their children so thought a hotel would be best. There was to be a dinner party at Conrad's house at 7.30 that evening, so after a quick respite at the hotel with a shower and change of clothes Dympna and Seamus headed to see their sons.

Finn answered the door with his youngest daughter in his arms. 'Mam! Da, Good to see you! Come in come in!'

Conrad came up behind Finn. 'Where did you find these pair of tinkers?' They all laughed and Conrad hugged his parents, both boys pleased that the two of them were not only together, but back home. Finn looked at Conrad and smiled.

'Nanny D! Nanny D!' Finn's two daughters and Conrad's two sons came crashing through all of the adults to see their Grandparents.

'Oh haven't ye grown!' Dympna said as she hugged them all individually.

Finn had given Niamh, now over a year old to Seamus so he had to say hello to the other grandkids whilst holding the little one. 'Let me get you a drink Maam.' Conrad said. She indulged herself with a glass of creamy Irish whiskey – known to most people as Baileys, but this was homemade stuff – stronger and creamier and all the better for it.

'Oh this is lovely, thank you me darling,' Dympna said.

Conrad sat next to his Mum. 'It's so great to have you here Maam, it really is. I know it must be hard for you? Are you feeling ok?' he asked, putting his hand on top of his Mum's noting how tiny her hands were.

Conrad was just like Seamus, around five foot nine with a stocky build and the same light colouring, he had inherited his Father's piercing green eyes and reddish hair with golden blonde specks that went lighter in the summer sun. She had never noticed that his hands were the same as Seamus' too, thick and strong workers hands, with a few light freckles sprinkled across them.

'I'm ok son, I'm ok, it's lovely to see you all, you, Finn, the Grandkids... I feel much better than I expected. Seeing the old house – you know my parent's house was... Well, it was hard on the old mind, but I think your Father was right when he said I needed to face these things ye know?' Dympna explained to her son. She had never spoken openly to her sons about how she felt or what affected her, Conrad was glad she had confided in him.

Dympna got chatting with Ria, Finn's wife, and Tatum, Conrad's wife, discussing all sorts of things – in particular the ups and downs of being a Mother.

'Oh you never stop being a Mother – even when they're in their thirties you worry about them terrible all the same as if they were still little ones,' Dympna explained.

'Oh yes Motherhood is for life that's for sure,' Tatum agreed.

The women's conversation was interrupted as Conrad and Finn moved the tables out of the way in the large living-room to make way for the local band.

There were still a few other guests floating around and the civilised dinner party was turned on its head as old Irish instruments were pulled from their cases and filled the room with a sound so enchanting you couldn't help but tap your feet: the old man with his moustache and red nose caused by too much whiskey sat in his seat and began to tap the Bodhran with the white drumstick setting the pace for the other musicians; the young boy strummed the Mandolin guitar and the other two men came in with a violin and fiddle. The woman in her late twenties with masses of red hair sang above the instruments bringing all the guests to their feet at the sweet sound of her voice. Before she knew it Dympna was up dancing wildly with Seamus, Finn grabbed hold of Ria and Conrad had Niamh dancing in her little dress. The other guests filled the living room floor, dancing and clapping. A few songs later and Jerry, one of Conrad's workmates started singing the song 'Molly Malone', an old Irish classic. Of course everyone knew the words as their Mothers and Grand Mothers had sung it a thousand times over so all belted out the song as harmoniously as they possibly could though not doing too well due to the amount of alcohol all had consumed, but nevertheless singing loud and proud. So in the large house on the edge of The Green that summer evening there was a noisy party where Dympna let her hair down, literally, as it fell out of the tight plaited bun and hung loose around her shoulders, her shoes thrown to the side as she sang and danced following Seamus' lead. It had been a long time since Dympna had done this and even longer since Seamus had seen the worry and anxiousness totally disappear from her face. The music played until the early hours and the drink kept flowing, it wasn't what Dympna had expected on her first return to The Green after all these years but that wasn't a bad thing.

Dympna and Seamus slept in Finn's spare room when they all eventually went to bed at around five in the morning. Finn was the first up to see to Niamh who woke only three hours after he had nodded off; Ria was sound asleep and Finn didn't want to wake her so he changed Niamh's nappy and checked in on his other two girls Alaina and Ciara. They had separate bedrooms but often slept in the one bed together one cuddling the other, Finn smiled as he watched the little fair haired girls sleep soundly. Conrad and Tatum had slept on the sofa bed in Finn's living room with their sons Daley and Senan enjoying the comfort of sleeping in between their parents. Heavy heads and sleepy eyes were prominent features on all of them that morning as their livers attempted to churn out the overload of alcohol consumption. Stomachs craved grease and salt to cure what they were all officially suffering from – a very bad hangover. The smell of egg and bacon and slightly burnt toast filtered through

Finn's large five bedroom house and the whole family sat down to enjoy the breakfast put together by Dympna, Tatum and Finn – the only ones who were up early. Dympna sat near the end of the table next to the sliding doors which Finn had left open, the sun beamed into the room and Dympna could see the acres of land owned by her husband and the two boys stretching for miles. She peered around the table as everyone tucked in: her husband, her sons and their wives and her five grandchildren together again.

Seamus squeezed her hand. 'Isn't this great?' he said.

'It is, it is,' Dympna replied, and she kissed him right there in front of everyone. The boys were still getting used to their parents displaying affection so openly to one another but both were agreed it was a good thing.

'Would you put each other down?!' Conrad said teasing them, 'You're like a pair of teenagers so ye are!' The family laughed, the children joining in laughing at Nanny and Grandad having a little kiss.

The kids ran outside as the grown-ups cleared away the plates and cups. Dympna caught sight of Ciara, Alaina, Daley and Senan running across the land at the back of the house playing 'It' and chasing one another. She imagined Erin running with them too in her little vest and shorts with not a care in the world laughing with her cousins and surrounded by the family.

'Erin would love it here,' Seamus whispered as he came up behind her. He put his arms around her waist, he felt good.

'I was just thinking that ye know. She'd love it so she would, away from that city, ah it would be grand. I have been so scared to come back here,' Dympna said, shaking her head.

'Do you think maybe you were too proud to come back too?' Seamus asked.

'I don't know, maybe. Too proud to say I missed you and wanted to come back. Maybe I used what happened with me family to hide behind a little,' Dympna said, surprised at her admission and saddened that pride in her younger days had forfeited the happiness of herself and the people she loved.

'I was too proud as well D. Too proud to ask you back after I got me self settled here. I thought you wouldn't want to know, and I was too scared you'd reject me. I felt an idiot for leaving you in London. I didn't think you'd ever come back after that,' Seamus explained.

They stood in silence for a while watching the kids play in the fields, Tatum and Ria shouting out for them to 'not go past the hill!' 'We need to still see you do ye hear me? Don't go past that hill?' Tatum reiterated. If the children went past the big hill and onto the other side they would be out of sight so the rule was not to go beyond that point. The kids co-operated with the adult's requests and remained in view of the grown-ups.

The one thing Dympna knew she needed to do while she was here was return to the farmhouse where her parents and brothers were killed. It was a fear she would have to face, although she wasn't quite sure what going there would accomplish. Would it give her answers? Would it make her ask more questions? Would it just make everything worse? Whatever it was going to be she had to know, she had to do it. That afternoon Dympna left the others and made her way back to her old home.

Dympna walked through the old path she used as a child – no one else knew about this path other than her family – it was a short cut to their house through a narrow lane with stone walls either side covered in moss and weeds. She got to the end of the lane where the walls stopped and opened the old gate hanging on for dear life by rusty hinges that hadn't been changed in years. The gate led into an overgrown and unkempt field – she barely recognised it. Remains of the horse sheds stood timidly as if a gust of wind would take them to their knees in an instant. She made her way towards the house, the only sound was the whistling of the gentle breeze through the long blades of green grass. Dympna's footsteps got slower as she approached, her stomach churning as the image of the boys falling into this exact field exploded across her mind. Though it was a summer afternoon, it could easily have been a winter evening for all the light that was shut out of Dympna at that moment, her body covered in goose pimples. She stopped in front of the house looking up to her old room at the top.

It was a large house through default in that it was originally built to house cattle but Dympna's Dad had converted it. The front door was made of solid oak with thick black beams of iron driven across vertically and horizontally giving it a medieval look. She took a deep breath, closed her eyes and opened the door. The front door led straight into the open dining room – the table where her Mother's body had been laid was still there. She stroked the table slowly with her fingers – dust gathering on the tips. As the dust was wiped away it revealed faint marks of blood stain; Dympna pulled her hand away quickly and gasped for breath. 'Oh Mam.' She looked up at the beam where her Father's body had hung, and back down to the floor where her brothers' bodies had lain all that time ago.

The house was covered in thick dirt and cobwebs and the windows smothered so heavily with dust and grime it shut out any light that may have strayed upon it. Dympna crept around like a timid cat as if she were trying not to disturb anyone, treading carefully, avoiding bumping into or touching anything else. The door to the basement caught her eye – she couldn't go near it. She went upstairs looking at the door of her parent's bedroom and the door to her brothers' bedrooms but not entering. She went up another two flights of stairs to reach what used to be her room and hesitated but then pushed the door slightly, and a little more again – it creaked, a creaking sound which seemed impossibly loud in this silent place. The door opened into Dympna's childhood bedroom, her bed in the corner adjacent to the windows, and the white chest of drawers with the pretty mirror she loved so much sitting on top of it. She couldn't believe this stuff was still here. Why hadn't anyone done anything with the property? It was over forty years since... She sat on her bed and picked up a doll that was propped up against the headboard, this was the doll her Nanny D had given her – a red haired doll with freckles and a black velvet dress. The material had taken a battering over the years – worn and thin, grey where it was once white but all in all Dympna's favourite doll was doing quite well considering her age. Dympna sighed and looked around. She wiped the window clean with her palm and looked across the fields. The sun set just behind the hills the other side of The Green, its orange-red colour penetrating through the blue and purple sky. And there she was back again running across that field with Kian and Donal towards the horse sheds to help muck it out. She could hear her Mother's voice shouting behind her 'Don't be late in for ye tea D! And don't come back home too filthy do ye hear?!' 'Yes Maam! Bye!' Dympna would shout back then running faster to catch up with her brothers. Dympna smiled. She wandered around the house a little longer. She found old family photographs in the living room – though there weren't many, and put them in her handbag.

D left the house closing the heavy door behind her. Various stories circulated after her parents and brothers were murdered – that it was a political killing intended to provoke the IRA, that someone had a vengeance towards her Father for doing so well, and another rumour that it was her Mother's lover that had gone mad and killed them all – Dympna only surviving because she had been hidden. Although the IRA were not sure that this was a political killing the notes left on the bodies of the O'Meara family generated even more tension between the Protestant and

211

Catholic communities furthering the divide and made worse with the murders being so brutal. Dympna shook her head at the capability people had to do such cruel things. She left the farmhouse and walked across the fields with a weight lifted from her mind though this puzzled her as she had no more answers than she did before she came here. But she did feel as if she had finally gained a certain peace with what had happened all those years ago.

Chapter 21

After the weekend spent with their family Dympna and Seamus left for London early Monday morning ready to go back to Kilburn and make further preparations for their appeal. Erin was coming over that evening and Seamus and Dympna couldn't wait to see her.

'I'm glad I came with you,' Dympna said to Seamus in the cab as they waved to their family through the back window.

'I'm so happy you came D, I really am. Above all I think it was really brave of you to go back there to the house, I know how tough that was, but you seem better for it so you do,' Seamus said stroking her hair.

'I am, I am. I was surprised at me own reaction but what a heavy weight has come off my shoulders. Apart from that it is still beautiful here, absolutely beautiful and full of good memories,' Dympna said smiling.

'Good memories are sometimes mixed with bad ones Dympna – I suppose that's life you know?' Seamus said. She nodded in agreement as he pulled her next to him.

Jill dropped Erin off around 6.00pm at Dympna's that evening. 'Nanny!' Erin hugged her Nan as she opened the door to the excited little girl desperate to see Nan and Grandad.

'Oh hello me little chicken,' Dympna said scooping Erin up and smothering her with kisses. It had only been a few days since Erin had stayed over but the days they didn't see her felt like weeks, it had felt even longer for Erin. Hours feel like days and days seem like forever for children, especially when they are desperate to see someone or something – like when it is only three days until Christmas Day yet children will cry out 'three days! – That's ages away! I can't wait that long' Whereas the grown-ups will know that three days really isn't too long and Christmas Day will come and go in a flash, the children will spend that interim period counting down the hours and minutes until they can tear open the pretty wrapping of their presents and devour the chocolates from their selection boxes. That was how Erin felt in between the days she couldn't see Dympna and Seamus, asking Jill and Ben what day could she see Nanny and Granddad next and how long until Erin could go back home, and would she be able to stay the weekend with them. Erin would pencil in her pink Princess diary (locked tight with the heart shaped padlock) the days and weekends that she'd be able to get to her presents. Of course these presents weren't wrapped up in pretty paper or moulded by Fisher Price or Disney, but were real and tangible and better than any gift Erin could have received in the shape of D and Seamus. Each time Erin ran through the door in Kilburn a huge smile would spread across her face, her cheeks would glow and Erin would forget how long it had felt since her last visit savouring the time with them which always went too quickly of course – even for the two adults.

Erin gave a cheeky smile to her Grandad as they walked to school that morning talking incessantly about what it would be like to live in the Jungle like Mowgli. Her smile was currently missing two top front teeth and a new adult tooth was sprouting through her bottom gums. She had acquired three pounds from the tooth fairy for each one she had lost. Skipping along holding her Grandads hand, he could hardly believe it was the same child from the night before. She had been terrified from yet another nightmare, wetting the bed and shaking furiously bless her. Seamus and Dympna had calmed her down and changed her into some dry clothes before Seamus carried her tired little body into their bed. She eventually fell asleep in between Nan and Grandad with the ugly teddy she couldn't do without.

'I think she needs to see someone D,' Seamus had whispered as he gently manuovered himself into the bed.

'I know, I know. But I don't want them to use this against us ye know? What if they use this in the courtcase and blame us – you know what they're like.'

'Mmm.. but she needs to see someone – a child psychologist or something. We should speak to Jill and Ben?'

'You're right.' Dympna replied sighing, thoughts of being in court again running through her mind, feelings of worry penetrating every part of her.

'You can't blame yourself D, she's been through a lot and something like this was bound to happen, it would have come out in one way or another and that's not your fault do ye hear me D?' Dympna nodded her head. He placed his arm over Erin reaching for Dympna's hand. He squeezed tight. 'Don't you worry - we'll get through this.'

Seamus waved Erin off into school and she ran off into the crowd of red and grey uniforms. 'Bye Granddad, see you on Wednesday!' Erin chirped excitedly. Seamus hurried back home for a meeting with Harvey.

Harvey was already at the house sifting through paperwork when Seamus returned. 'Hello Seamus, hi, good to see you fella.' Harvey's cockney accent and slang popped up now and again, Seamus liked the sincerity in that Dench hadn't felt the need to stray far from his origins just because he was a lawyer. Harvey must have been surrounded by other lawyers who spoke the Queen's English Seamus thought, but Dench had made it to the top of his field by obviously being damn good at his job without sacrificing his identity or where he had come from; Seamus identified with the savvy lawyer in many ways making it easy for the two men to get on well. Harvey needed to know if Seamus and Dympna had made their decision about the Residence Order. Seamus and Dympna were not interested in getting any money – they didn't want any interference from social services ever again if they could help it. 'If we get Erin back I want nothing from those fecks, they have brought us too much trouble and god forbid they were to take her again from us, it would put me in the grave so it would,' Dympna explained. Seamus agreed, more from the point of view that he was too proud to take money from anyone – he would support his family whatever it took. 'Ok, so we are going for a Residence Order right?' Harvey confirmed. Seamus and Dympna nodded.

'There's something else Harvey,' Seamus said glancing at Dympna.

'Yep sure, what is it?' Harvey said sipping his coffee and organising his paperwork on the dining room table. Seamus paused. 'Look, whatever it is, you can tell me alright? It's all in confidence. You're my clients. And besides, I happen to like you both.' He smiled.

'It's Erin,' D hesitated. 'She... She's started to have these terrible nightmares and is wetting the bed and getting so upset.' Dympna's eyes were welling. 'We...I'm scared they're going to use this Harvey, that they'll use it against us in the court case.' Dympna shook her head and looked to the ceiling. No use looking up to Him, she thought and looked back at Harvey. He could see the desperation in Dympna's eyes.

'Listen to me Dympna, you have nothing to worry about this time round do you hear me? This isn't your fault. If, and I say if, they even dare to use this against us in court then I'll come back at them twofold, but they won't, it's completely irrelevant to whether you and Seamus are fit to look after Erin. She saw a lot go on in that flat and it's not surprising this is happening now. I'm no expert on child psychology but what happened has obviously affected her and it's coming out now.' Harvey leaned against the kitchen worktop as Seamus comforted Dympna. ' But you can't blame yourselves. And you're going to get your granddaughter back, I give you my word.' The lawyer said firmly.

It would be another 8 months before Dympna, Seamus and Erin would discover their fate. Harvey wanted a particular Judge – Ms Lillian Ellis (renowned for her no-nonsense yet often sympathetic approach) with whom Dench had worked with in the past. His gut feeling told him he needed her – and that's who he was holding out for. He had done some background research and noted that she herself had brought up her Grandchildren so may show some private empathy – even if this were not to be displayed in the courtroom. Consequently, they couldn't get a hearing with her until March 1991 which Dympna and Seamus were naturally anxious about but trusted Harvey's judgement and so agreed that they would be patient and brave the tide for the next few months. It also gave Harvey the opportunity to take advantage of the amount of time they had to make it a watertight case. Dench wasted no time, keen to bring this one home for the grandparents he had come to admire so dearly and, of course, Erin. As part of the preparation Dench organised for Seamus and Dympna to undergo psychological evaluations to ascertain their suitability as parents. The results, as predicted by Harvey, indicated that Seamus and D were both of sound mind and were well-adjusted, well-rounded people who in addition, appeared to have a very happy and healthy relationship. Dench didn't organise this because he doubted whether Seamus or Dympna were capable of being good parents or not, or whether they were clinically sane. On the contrary, he did it because he knew the evaluation would state that they were both of sound mind and well-adjusted – of course they were, you only had to be in their company for a few minutes to establish that. But Dench knew that in a court of law he needed proof of this sanity, of their

217

capability to be good parents – it required solid concrete evidence so that's what he got. The evaluations were conducted by one psychiatrist and two psychologists – all well respected and established in their field and willing to testify that Seamus and Dympna were more than capable of taking on parental responsibility of Erin.

Of course presenting this notion to Dympna and Seamus was no easy task for Harvey – he had anticipated that the two of them would be very offended at his suggestion of being psychologically evaluated but he needed them to do it. 'Ah now Harvey ye can't be serious! A bledy psychiatrist and a psychologist! Bejesus, is this what everyone goes through when they have children is it? If only they did do this we'd have less bad parents and less dead and neglected children in the world, eh?' Dympna said. She wasn't angry at Harvey, she could see what his point was, but frustrated at what she had to go through. Seamus was equally shocked and secretly terrified of anyone with 'Doctor' before their name especially those qualified to assess mind and behaviour, Seamus referred to such people as 'quacks' or 'shrinks' and, though happy to undergo their questions for the sake of Erin, would have preferred to never have to speak to one in his life. As well as the evaluations, which were conducted over a period of three months, the Grandparents also had to put up with social worker visits which were every six weeks or so – more checking to see if they were suitable. At least this time the two social workers – Ann and Jake were pretty decent, polite and friendly which made all the difference.

However difficult the Grandparents found all of the intrusion into their lives, nothing matched how hard it was to see Erin being cared for by strangers: that it was they who were dropping off and picking her up from school, cooking her tea and playing with her or checking her homework. Sure, Dympna and Seamus got to do this twice a week and she still stayed over every other weekend – but it just wasn't the same. Each time Jill picked Erin up from Dympna's or was dropped back Erin cried, knowing she was going to miss her Grandparents and not see them again for another few days. The weekends without Erin left Dympna feeling empty and the little one wondering what Nan and Granddad were up to. Even when Jill and Ben took her to Rococo Theme Park for the day and they went on all the rides and ate loads of sweets and candy floss, she still pined after Nan and Granddad. 'Granddad would have loved this cake,' she would say. 'Nanny D would never have got on this ride!' Erin would pipe up. Jill would look at Ben and Ben at Jill, wondering if and when this child would ever settle in with them – they wanted her to so much and hoped to adopt her eventually – she was perfect for them. The thing is, she belonged somewhere else.

Chapter 22

The months went on until it grew dark again, winter 1990 drawing in and the shops prematurely pushing Christmas (as they did every year). Adverts for My Little Pony and the latest Fisher Price kitchen (pots and pans included) going out on air at a calculated seven in the morning to catch the kids while they were eating breakfast or getting ready for school. At which time the kids would point at the television set and say something along the lines of 'I'd like that for Christmas...Oh and that... Oh, and that one too.' Realising that it was not only one advert but many with various enticing toys and games ready to be purchased 'Right now! Get it in time for Christmas!' Erin was explaining to Dooley one evening, as he sat with Seamus and Dympna having his tea that she would like the doll that she could put make up on. She pointed to the doll in the catalogue which only had a head with huge blonde hair and a blank face ready to be painted with any of the colours provided in the palette.

'Well I'm sure you'll get some lovely presents this year me darling,' Dooley said smiling at Erin.

'Where are you going for Christmas Dooley?' Erin asked.

Well, I have a little plan so I do...' Dooley said with a glint in his eye.

'Ah bejesus Dooley, what are you up to? You'll be spending it with us so you will as ye did last year,' Dympna said.

'Ah, well actually, I won't D, because, well, I'll be spending it with me girlfriend,' Dooley said beaming from ear to ear.

'Oh and who is this girlfriend?' Seamus asked.

'Well, I've told her to pop in to meet you two around now if you's don't mind – I'd love you to meet her, oh she's just grand so she is, and has asked me to spend Christmas with her in America – that's where she lives now,' Dooley explained.

The doorbell went at Dympna's and sure enough it was Dooley's girlfriend as he had anticipated, though Seamus and Dympna were not prepared for what they saw next: a very tanned woman with big white candy floss hair – who looked much like the doll in the catalogue appeared in Dympna's front room escorted by Dooley's hand on her bottom.

'Everyone, I'd like you to meet Kitty,' Dooley said gesturing to Kitty as if she were the magician's helper. Seamus shook her hand.

'Pleasure to meet ye Kitty.' Seamus said wondering where Dooley may have met her.

Dympna offered Kitty a seat and a cup of tea and noted the patent pink six inch heels Kitty was sporting – I'd break me neck trying to walk in those Dympna thought smiling to herself. Dympna cooked dinner for them all and both her and Seamus noted how besotted Kitty and Dooley were with one another. Kitty explained over dinner that they had met in the Harpers Tap Pub and Dooley had kindly offered to buy her and her sister a drink. Dympna laughed out loud at this (not meaning to offend Kitty) at the vision of Dooley attempting to chat up two sisters.

'Well you've obviously got the charm Dooley so ye have,' Seamus said laughing.

'Well, if Kitty likes the Dooley charm that's enough for me.'

Kitty put her hand on top of Dooley's revealing long manicured nails painted a light pink colour, her gold jewellery jingling everywhere as Kitty moved her arm and looked at Dooley as if they were teenagers again. Dooley reciprocated her gaze and it seemed he had finally found what he had been searching for – a female version of himself.

'Ah they seem happy don't they,' Dympna said to Seamus that evening.

'Ah they do, they do. It's good to see he's found someone D. They're a good match that's for sure,' Seamus said laughing. Dympna smiled as she lay on Seamus' chest.

'I think you should have your hair done like that D – what do you think?' Seamus said.

'Oh aye yes I think I will, and maybe you could ask to borrow Dooley's green shirt and the pink tie,' Dympna replied laughing.

'No, he's a good man, he's a good man,' Dympna said, feeling a bit bad for teasing Dooley's dress sense.

'Oh he is D that's for sure. When you were ill he was here one hundred percent, he's got a heart of gold so he has, a genuine fellow and that's rare to find you know,' Seamus said as he stroked D's hair.

'There is someone else who is a rare find too says I,' Dympna said looking up at Seamus.

'Oh is that right? And who might that be then?' Seamus replied smiling.

'Well, he is a rare find, but he's also a pain in the back side at times and leaves the potato peelings in the sink which drives me mad, but other than that...' Dympna said, not finishing her sentence and kissing Seamus.

'Well I must be a rare find to get this sort of attention from Dympna O'Meara eh?!'

The romantic moment between Seamus and D was cut short by the telephone ringing. 'Leave it D, come here.' Seamus said.

'What if it's Jill or Ben?' D replied getting out of bed. She answered the upstairs telephone. 'Hello?... Yes... Right Ok, ok we'll be over right away,' Dympna said.

As soon as Seamus heard this he leapt from the bed. 'What's wrong?' Seamus asked.

'We have to go to Jill and Ben's right away,' Dympna said.

It was gone midnight when the couple got to Jill and Ben's house. Erin was half asleep and disorientated lying on the leather sofa with her blanket.

'I found her by the side of the bed shouting and crying and absolutely covered in sweat. She's wet the bed too,' Jill explained.

Dympna could see the poor woman was upset.

'She wouldn't stop asking for you two, shouting hysterically to see you and that's why I called, I'm so sorry, I know it's late and it's not what we would normally do but in this case I could see she just needed you.'

Erin slumped over Seamus' shoulder, her arms draped around him and head nestled in the side of his neck.

'That's the most calm I have seen her these past two hours,' Jill said nodding at the little girl.

'Has this happened with you before?' Jill asked.

'It's happened twice,' Dympna said. 'We were going to raise it with you but it seems we have been beaten to it.'

'Yes, we have had the same problem – but only in the past two weeks, I thought it would settle but think it is to do with what she went through when she was...' Dympna looked down to the wooden floor.

'It's not your fault Mrs O'Meara,' Jill said warmly and rubbed her arm.

'Well I can't help but feel that it is.'

'D, come on don't be saying such rubbish. I think what we are all agreed on is that she will need to see someone. We will speak to Ann and Jake about it' Seamus said.

'Oh yes, they will have to know, they will probably put us in touch with someone who can help her. We have had children before with similar problems, and they are usually referred to a child psychologist.' Jill explained rubbing Erin's back. 'Would you like to take her home for the night?' she asked the grandparents.

'Really?' Dympna replied.

'Yes, I think she's been through enough bless her, and she only seems to want you two right now,' Jill said sighing. She was breaking protocol, but all she wanted was for the little girl that she had come to love to be happy, and it seemed that was only by being with the people who couldn't have her . It was clear to Jill how much they cared, and how dedicated they were to Erin – nothing like the picture painted in the court room all those months ago. Perhaps she wasn't in the right place after all Jill concluded as she packed Erin's overnight bag.

***

After several meetings with social services, Erin started to see child psychologist Deborah Jennings. Deborah concluded that Erin was suffering from Post Traumatic Stress Disorder and so embarked on a series of sessions with Erin in the hope that the little girl could recover from the damage inflicted in her short lifetime. Erin liked Deborah and enjoyed playing with the toys in her office and talking to Deborah about her dolls house and pink diary that she wouldn't let anyone else see.

'Why don't you let anyone else see it Erin?'

'It's Private,' Erin said, crossing her arms in the chair.

'Ok well we all have things that are private so that's ok. You don't have to show anyone.' Deborah explained.

After a short pause of silence, Erin said 'I draw and write things in my diary. I have a picture of me and Mummy with Nanny D too in there.'

It was the breakthrough Deborah had been working towards – that Erin would come to trust someone outside of Seamus and

Dympna and, after eleven sessions with the strong willed little girl Deborah had finally gained Erin's trust and was able to speak to her about what had happened in the flat in Chelsea all those months ago.

It took many more sessions and even more determination from Deborah and her colleagues to help Erin's nightmares stop and to curb the bed wetting with both eventually subsiding by the time the court case came around in March 1991. Erin could sleep soundly, and was proud that she no longer needed to wear a nappy to bed anymore. 'No more nappies!' she cried out, putting them in the kitchen bin. Erin's cautiousness with strangers was still apparent but she was able to function well away from the safety net of her Nan and Granddad, i.e. with Jill and Ben. Dympna was over the moon with Erin's progress but felt guilty for worrying that this might help social services with their case to keep Erin with Jill and Ben. Dympna just wanted her back home for good.

Chapter 23

A few days before the court case, Dympna visited Orghlaith's grave by herself – she usually went with Seamus and Erin, but this time felt she needed to go alone. Seamus had dropped her off in the car, and as Dympna made her way through the numerous headstones in the peaceful cemetery she noticed a man standing near Orghlaith's grave and then, as she came closer, she realised he was standing over Orghlaith's grave, putting flowers on top and then staring with his hands in his pockets. Dympna hastily walked over wondering what on earth he was doing, ready to give him a piece of her mind.

'Can I help you?' Dympna said abruptly. 'This is my daughter's grave,' she said.

'Oh, I didn't mean to offend you, you must be Orghlaith's Mother,' the man said.

'Yes, yes I am. Who are you?' Dympna asked, still suspicious at who he was and what he was doing here.

'My name is Hamza, I was a very close friend of your daughters. I went away for a while and when I came back I was told by... I was told that she was dead.' Hamza's eyes welled.

Dympna wasn't quite sure what to say or do. She put her hand on his shoulder.

'How is Erin?' he asked, wiping his face attempting to compose himself a little.

'Oh she's well, she's well, but there have been some complications...' Dympna said. He seemed like a nice fellow,

Dympna thought. She took the dead flowers away and replaced them with fresh ones – bright, multi-coloured flowers.

'Orghlaith would have hated anything else,' Dympna said. She said a prayer for Orghlaith and after a few moments both of them standing in silence thinking of their loved one, Dympna asked if Hamza would like to join her for a coffee. He agreed. The two filled each other in on what had happened – Hamza told Dympna about Max, trying to soften the edges so as not to upset Dympna too much. Dympna explained how she had found Orghlaith and the battle they were now facing to get Erin back. Hamza was brutally honest about his past – the drugs, the money and the things he had been involved in.

'But now, now I have lost someone I truly loved through the very drugs myself and my brothers would bring into the country. I didn't directly supply Orghlaith with drugs, but I might as well have done. So after I found out, I left it all behind – I haven't been near the drugs or those people ever since. I just can't believe she's gone,' Hamza said shaking his head staring into his coffee mug.

'Neither can I,' Dympna replied sighing.

'Well at least Max got what he deserved,' Hamza said.

'Did he?' Dympna asked remembering Max being carried out on a stretcher while Orghlaith lay dead.

'Oh yes he did. He was working for an east end gangster – Frank... can't remember his surname. Anyway, to cut a long story short Max tried to rip Frank off and had upset one of his associates – some American guy, so Frank had his guys sort Max out. Apparently his body was never found, but everyone knows Frank got to him,' Hamza explained.

'Jesus, what sort of people was Orghlaith mixed up with?' Dympna said.

'She wasn't mixed up with them Mrs O'Meara, honestly, that world was Max's world – not hers,' Hamza said, although he could never understand, and now never would know why someone like Orghlaith – bright, beautiful and loving could end up with a character like Max and injecting herself with that shit, it just didn't make sense to Hamza. Dympna and Hamza went their separate ways after the meeting in the coffee shop, both wondering what might have happened had it been Hamza she had met and not Max, perhaps she would still be alive. Hamza never forgave himself for going away, and as he walked down the High Street in south London he couldn't stop thinking about what Dympna had relayed to him about Orghlaith and what Max did to her and Erin.

It is often hard to believe that one human being can inflict such intense pain on another without a second thought, as if all feeling and sentient emotion has been ripped out vicously – replaced only with a blank space longing – aching to be filled in some way but never would be. The blank space in Max only grew until there was a void and he no longer felt anything for anyone. Hamza only wished Max was still alive somewhere so he could act out his revenge in the form of a slow and painful torture, but, of course, Frank had got there first and Max was no more.

Chapter 24

Seamus and Dympna arrived at the courthouse half an hour early, meeting Harvey in the main hall.

'We're gonna get her back, don't you worry, we're gonna go in there and Erin is coming back home, I promise,' Dench said. He wasn't sure what he would do if he couldn't win this for them so he pushed that thought to the back of his mind and focused on how he was going to nail this.

Dympna spotted Erin first holding Jill's hand as they walked through the court doors with Ben not far behind. Erin came running up to Nan and Grandad straight away. 'Nanny! Grandad! Am I coming home with you today?!' Erin said excitedly hoping she would be able to go back and live with her grandparents.

'We'll have to see what the Judge says me little chicken. Harvey has to talk to the Judge and then we will have to wait for the decision ok?' Dympna said, not wanting to get Erin's hopes up, or, indeed, her own.

'Well I'll have to pray then won't I Nanny?' Erin said. 'Can I go and sit over there for a minute?' Erin asked. She was pointing to a round marble bench with a huge fake plant placed inside it.

'Ok sweetheart but we're going in to the courtroom in a minute alright?' Dympna said, taking Erin's coat as she ran off. Erin sat on the edge of the marble bench and put her small hands together, closed her eyes and prayed for God to let her go back home to Nanny and Grandad. She told Him upstairs that she really liked Jill and Ben – they were really nice people and she really liked playing with their children but she loved Nanny and Grandad very much and would prefer to live with them.

'What is she doing over there?' Seamus asked laughing at Erin praying in the middle of the courthouse.

'Oh, I think she's having a little chat with the man up there.' Dympna said pointing to the ceiling and smiling.

Jill and Ben walked over to say hello to the determined Grandparents. 'How are you feeling Dympna?' Jill said softly.

'Oh you know, nervous, I only want what is best for Erin.' Dympna said sighing.

Jill put her hand on Dympna's arm. 'I know you do Dympna, I've seen how close you all are over these past few months. She adores you,' Jill said.

'We adore her,' Dympna replied looking over at Erin now sitting with Seamus on a nearby bench. Dympna went over to see Seamus and Erin, Harvey had struck up conversation with Jill and Ben. Dympna's body stiffened as she saw the two social workers Bernadette and Collin come through the main doors. Seamus looked at Dympna, she looked at him, both feeling an uncontrollable rage inside knowing that these people were the very reason they had been separated from Erin and may never be able to have her with them again. It had been months since they had seen the rat-faced Bernadette and her fat little side kick Collin who was stuffing the remains of a jam doughnut into his mouth washed down with his take away coffee. The urge to go over and tell Bernadette exactly what she thought of her was overwhelming for Dympna but Harvey got to her just in time.

'Don't even think about it D, don't. It will not make the case look good for us if you go at her all guns a-blazing ok? Let me do the work in that courtroom alright?' Harvey gave Dympna a hug and reiterated for her not to worry, he didn't tell Dympna he had a trick up his sleeve which he hoped would cement the Judge's decision in their favour as the empathic lawyer didn't want his clients to be disappointed if he couldn't win this for them, but he wholeheartedly hoped he could. It was one of the few cases Harvey had worked on where he had become emotionally attached but Dench maintained his professional composure to the end.

The social services team were not representing themselves this time, instead had hired lawyer Karen Thicke from the reputable Hudson – Gibbs Law Firm. Thicke was blunt and cold in her approach going straight for the jugular as she presented her case. 'It is difficult to see why we are here again when it is clear that the original decision to place Erin into foster care was the correct one based on these facts...' Thicke reiterated what Bernadette had stated the first time round about Dympna's mental instability and the unorthodox relationship between Seamus and Dympna. Dympna shook her head and Seamus sighed, bowing his head as they listened to a woman who didn't know the two deem them unfit to be Erin's carers. Thicke continued in her assault using Bernadette's paperwork to refer to for evidence that Dympna's house was unsuitable to bring up a child in. 'It was clearly stated that the house was filthy and Erin had access to bottles of alcohol. Given that their eldest daughter was also a drug and alcohol addict and that the two could not look after their own children and were unable to maintain their own relationship it seems only logical and fair that Erin remain with Jill and Ben in an environment which is stable and with parents who are young enough to be there as Erin gets older.'

Thicke took no prisoners using what she could to paint the bleakest picture of the two Grandparents to the point that it crossed Dympna's mind that perhaps she wasn't good enough to look after Erin, or young enough, and that perhaps Erin was better off in that big perfect house with Jill and Ben after all. Seamus held her hand as they sat next to Harvey on the front table. 'Don't worry,' Harvey had whispered into Dympna's ear, and he winked.

'Well Mr Dench, it is good to see you back in the Family Court again, although given the argument just given I hope you can present a better one as to why I should allow your clients to resume care of their granddaughter,' the Judge said. The Judge was Lillian Ellis, 60 years old, and one of the few women to make it as far as becoming a Judge. Lillian and Harvey had met several times over the years and had a mutual respect for one another's passion for justice.

'Your Honour,' Harvey began, getting up from his seat and taking control of the court room in an instant. 'Yes, it is true that my clients have had what some may call an unorthodox relationship over the years, and that, not until their later lives have they rekindled their love and a relationship which is as strong as the love for their children and for Erin. What has been repeatedly overlooked are the lengths Seamus and Dympna have both gone to for their children and for their Grandchild. Here are two people who sacrificed their own wants and needs for their children – a man who brought his sons to another country because he believed he could give them a better life, and a woman who looked after her Granddaughter and worked all the hours God sent so her daughter, who has now passed away, could go to University and get an education. When Seamus' and Dympna's daughter Orghlaith became ill, Seamus left his home and his work behind to come back to London to be there for Dympna and Orghlaith. They supported their daughter throughout her drug rehabilitation and had months when they didn't know if Erin and Orghlaith were dead or alive. Unfortunately Orghlaith died in tragic circumstances and the two Grandparents thought nothing about taking their Grandaughter into their care – it wasn't even a question, it was a given for them. When I met this couple I found that between them they had spent large amounts of time and money between the original court case and now, trying to find ways and means to get their Granddaughter back. They have had to cope with the death of their daughter, their own complex relationship, which, although unorthodox to the outside, is full of love and a respect between two people that is rare to find. Despite these personal obstacles they have persevered in an effort to get Erin back and have shown nothing but dedication and devotion to Erin. They have been through rigorous assessments by psychologists and psychiatrists who have all stated that they are more than capable of taking responsibility of Erin. I refer to the reports 1a and 2b your honour.'

'Yes I have read the reports Mr Dench, thank you, and am happy with that evidence,' Ellis said peering down from her chair across the court.

'However, all of this is irrelevant isn't it? Isn't it? It is irrelevant if we do not take the wishes and needs of the child into account which should be at the very core of this case, so I would like to ask Erin how she feels about where she would like to live,' Harvey finished.

Erin was asked if she would like to stay in her seat next to Jill or if she would like to sit in the box. 'I would like to sit in the box so I can see my Nanny and Granddad,' Erin said in a rather grown up manner.

'You can bring your doll with you,' Harvey said softly and held Erin's hand escorting her to the box.

Erin looked so small in the huge chair, holding on to her doll as if it were a lifeline. 'Do you know why you are here today Erin?' Harvey asked.

'Yes,' Erin said now feeling a little shy in front of all the adult's eyes fixated on the little one.

'And why is that?' Harvey said smiling at her.

'Because Nanny and Granddad want to look after me all the time like a proper Mum and Dad but they are not allowed to so they have to ask the Judge to let me come back home,' Erin replied pushing her black hair out of her eyes and clutching her doll.

'And what would you like to do Erin? Where would you like to live?' Harvey asked.

'Well, I like Jill and Ben, and I like their trampoline in the garden and playing with the other boys and girls but I... I don't want to hurt their feelings, but I would like to live with my Nanny and Granddad all of the time,' Erin said fidgeting in her chair.

The Judge looked down at the little girl with the red bow in her pony tail and matching red dress and shoes. 'Do you think Nanny and Grandad are good at looking after you Erin?' Harvey asked.

'Oh yes!' Erin said beaming. 'We do loads of good things together – Granddad and Nanny dance to Jungle Book with me all the time when I visit, and give me lots of cuddles,' Erin said. The innocence of Erin's answer and untainted words put a smile on everyone's face in the court room – well, everyone except Bernadette who seemed to be physiologically incapable of smiling.

Thicke was offered the opportunity to ask Erin questions but she didn't take it resolving in her mind that the case was already won: the rapport between Grandparents and Grandchild illuminated across the courtroom, visible for all to see as Erin looked at them from the box smiling, wondering when she would be able to go home with Nanny and Granddad for good. It didn't take long for the Judge to come back from her chambers with the answer. Seamus and Dympna sat in silence, hands interlocked tight, palms sweating. Harvey was equally nervous – was Erin coming home? How could he look Dympna and Seamus in the eye if he were to fail today? Waiting for Erin had felt like a lifetime for Dympna, each time she had reached for her the little girl ran through Dympna's fingers as if she were a slippery substance, Dympna just grasping her only for Erin to be gone again leaving behind a residue of memories. But now, here she was, within reach, ready to be a permanent fixture in their lives if Judge Ellis would permit it.

Judge Ellis had become a Judge through sheer hard work and competing against the male dominated world that law firms incorporated. She had won her justified position through working within the law citing evidence for and against but never forgetting what was moral and good where the law could often be ambiguous and downright useless. It was these types of cases where human judgement and gut instinct would come into play and Judges would set precedence with their decisions in unique cases.

The evidence was clearly in favour of the Grandparents, but it was also Ellis' gut instinct and moral belief that children should be with the people who they want to be with, who they love to be with and who can look after them and care for them properly. There was no doubt in Ellis' mind that Seamus and Dympna were the right people for the job – the evidence pointed to that, as did Erin's testimony and the fact that these Grandparents had done so much for each other and for their Grandchild.

Judge Ellis stated this as her reason for placing Erin back into the care of her Grandparents whereby they would take full parental responsibility for her. It took a few moments for the Judges words to sink in, but when they did Seamus and Dympna leapt from their seats and hugged each other and then hugged Harvey.

There wasn't a dry eye in that courtroom. Dympna ran to the other side of the courtroom where Erin was sitting who hadn't realised what the Judge had said.

'You're coming home, you're coming home me little chicken. Oh, you're too big for me to lift up these days!' Dympna cried. Erin jumped from her seat to give her Nan a huge hug.

Seamus was next over, scooping Erin up in his big arms. 'Can I come home right now, today Granddad?' Erin asked.

'Well I don't see why not me darling,' Seamus said kissing her and hugging her tight.

'Granddad you're crying,' Erin said.

'Yes I am, I am,' Seamus said.

Erin held on to her Granddad's neck. 'I'm so glad I'm coming to live with you Grandad,' Erin kissed his cheek. They all left the courtroom and Dympna and Seamus spoke to Jill and Ben in the foyer while Harvey kept Erin occupied playing I Spy.

'I'm pleased for you Dympna, truly I am. I know how much you love her, and she clearly loves you and wants to be with you – that has never changed in the whole time she has lived with Ben and I.'

Dympna asked if they could pick up Erin's things over the weekend, Jill agreed saying Sunday would be better for them. Jill and Ben said goodbye to Erin, hugging her and telling the little girl to be good for Nanny and Granddad. Erin nodded and waved as her two temporary parents left the building.

Bernadette and Collin were nowhere to be seen making a swift exit after the case not wanting to be anywhere near the people they had referred to as the 'crazy Irish couple'.

Thicke shook Harvey's hand, congratulating him and left to meet another client. 'Another client, another day,' she sighed, and left. Dench was saddened at Thicke's lack of enthusiasm for her job, perhaps not realising that what she did impacted so greatly on people's lives. Perhaps she had become disillusioned, disheartened, who knows, Harvey thought, but at that moment he no longer cared because he had just managed to win a case for three very special people, it was a feeling that he had never experienced whilst practising business law. No amount of money could buy what he saw when Seamus, Dympna and Erin were together.

'Let's get out of here,' Harvey said to the elated couple and Erin. So that's what they did.

It was a bright, fresh spring day and Seamus, Dympna, Erin and Harvey sat in a cosy restaurant in the City of London, eating, drinking and celebrating.

'Am I allowed that chocolate cake Granddad?' Erin asked cheekily once she'd finished her pizza.

'Well, seeing as it is a special day, I think I shall order that same cake so we'll order two eh!?' Seamus said laughing.

'I think a bottle of champagne is well needed too – my treat.' Harvey said.

'Oh no Harvey, you've done enough, we'll get this. Really,' Seamus said.

'Listen, I haven't worked all me life in this game not to splash out a little if I want to alright – you two deserve it. Seriously, I'll get this,' Harvey said smiling, ordering the most expensive bottle of champagne on the menu.

Later that evening, Dooley arrived with Kitty and Mrs Wallis came round for more celebrations with Dympna, Seamus and Erin.

'I'm so pleased for ye Dympna, I am,' Dooley said hugging her.

'I knew you'd get her in the end,' said Mrs Wallis.

'Oh Maggie, I'm just glad I've got her and we can get on with our life you know?' Dympna said smiling as she looked at Erin sitting on Seamus' knee.

Seamus placed Erin on the sofa, picked up his glass of champagne and stood up 'I have an announcement to make,' Seamus said 'so everyone raise your glass. Dympna and I are going to renew our wedding vows – the ones we made all those years ago, so she will no longer be calling herself Mrs O'Meara, but she'll be a Killoughery.' Seamus walked over to his wife kissed her and chinked her glass against his.

'Oh yey! Can I be your bridesmaid Nanny!' Erin asked excitedly clapping her hands. 'I'm going to be a bridesmaid! I'm going to be a bridesmaid!' Erin shouted. She ran to get the catalogue to hunt down a dress for the big day.

The adults laughed at her innocent enthusiasm. 'It will be a little while yet Erin, you've plenty of time to choose a dress,' Dooley said to her. But Erin was too busy putting little star markings next to the dresses she liked.

'Congratulations Seamus, I couldn't be happier for you,' Dooley said, shaking Seamus' hand, 'It's about time you two had some good luck.'

'Oh tell me about it Dooley, tell me about it. So what now for you and Kitty Mr Casanova?!' Seamus asked Dooley.

'Well, she's going back to Boston, and I'm going with her,' Dooley explained.

'Really?! Well, if it makes you happy you go for it, when are you planning to leave?' Seamus asked.

'Two weeks, I've got a dual nationality passport so there'll be no problems with me living there or any of that Visa complication ye know?' Dooley replied.

'Bejesus, watch out Boston here comes Dooley McGuinness!' Seamus said laughing.

'Ah the Boston women'll love me sure they will – though I can't let Kitty hear me say that or she'll skin me alive!' Dooley and Seamus chuckled like two school boys.

The women were in the kitchen sat around the old wooden table. Kitty filled Dympna and Mrs Wallis in on her plans to leave with Dooley for Boston.

'I think it'll do him the world of good Kitty, you're just what Dooley needs, I'm so happy for ye both so I am.' Dympna said touching Kitty's very tanned hand affectionately.

'Dooley will be missed that's for sure, he's been a great friend to me he really has, and to Seamus since he's been over here but he needs to be happy and he is certainly happy with you Kitty, he's smitten with ye!'

Kitty blushed, clearly relishing the notion that Dooley felt like that for her. Two peas in a pod is how Seamus had described the two love birds.

'Bejesus wait 'til it's been a few years and you'll be murderin' him eh!' Dympna had said a few days before.

'Irish men are charmers but so much bledy trouble aren't ye Seamus?' Dympna winked at her husband, he took her banter on the chin and enjoyed that they could still flirt with one another after all these years.

'Yes he's a great man.' Kitty replied.

'So what now for you and Seamus D?' Mrs Wallis asked.

Dympna told Kitty and Mrs Wallis of her plans to move back to The Green for good with Seamus and Erin. 'I think it's time to go back Maggie ye know? It really does feel like the right thing to do.' Dympna said sipping her wine.

'Well, I'm pleased for you my love, I am, but I'll miss having me tough old Irish cookie living round the corner... Where else am I gonna get a good cuppa tea and ham sandwich from?' Mrs Wallis put her hand on Dympna's and D saw the old cockney woman's eyes fill...

'Oh no, don't you start Maggie or you'll get me going aswell.' Dympna said wiping her eyes.

'Come here and give me a bledy hug.' Dympna gave Mrs Wallis a hug and knew how much she would miss her, especially as they had grown much closer in recent times, but leaving

London was something Dympna knew she had to do and should have done sooner.

Seamus interrupted the chatter in the kitchen, entering with a bottle of champagne in one hand and Erin on his hip. Dooley following behind. Seamus popped the bottle and poured everyone a drink. 'I'd just like to say can we take this moment to feel blessed for the good news today... That Erin has come back home, and is where she should be. And to our dear daughter Orghlaith, to remember her, God rest her soul. You're always with us Orghlaith, and we'll do our best by Erin, we'll never to forget you. Raise your glasses. A toast to Orghlaith and Erin,' Seamus said lifting his glass in front of him.

'To Orghlaith and Erin,' they all said simultaneously.

'To Orghlaith and Erin!' Erin shouted and held out her plastic cup of squash.

Seamus and Dympna looked at one another and at that moment both felt a bitter sweet flow of emotions – that they had conquered in getting Erin, but had been defeated in losing Orghlaith. Mrs Wallis put her arm around Dympna. 'Come on you, no more crying.'

Two weeks later, Dooley left for Boston with Kitty. 'You've been a great friend Dooley,' Dympna said as she hugged him.

'So have you D, you're a fine woman so ye are. You keep in touch do ye hear? And come and visit us,' Dooley replied.

'Oh we will visit – of course we will, now you behave yourself out there ok – you've got ye self a nice woman now.' Dympna said smiling. Dooley laughed.

'I'll be looking after Kitty don't you worry about that.'

Dympna said goodbye to Kitty and Seamus shook Dooley's hand. 'Look after her won't you now Seamus.' Dooley said.

'Oh I will, I will, I won't be letting her go again.' Seamus replied rubbing D's back.

Dooley scooped Erin up and gave her a tight squeeze and a kiss on the cheek. 'You be a good girl for Nanny D and Grandad do ye hear? And come and visit me in America!' Dooley said before he and Kitty left to go through security at Heathrow Airport waving to Dympna, Seamus and Erin until they had fully disappeared to the other side amongst the sea of travellers.

Three weeks later Dympna, Seamus and Erin began packing their things into boxes preparing for their move to Ireland. Erin was helping Grandad sellotape the boxes shut downstairs in the living room whilst Dympna was now sorting through the drawers in her bedroom. She found old skirts and tights she hadn't worn for years and put them in the pile of clothes ready to take to the charity shop. She reached to the back of the drawer to pull out some more middle clothes and her hand touched something soft and velvet. She reached in further, gripping it and pulling it from underneath everything to reveal a black velvet pouch that she knew contained her rosary beads, the beads she had discarded all those months ago but not quite managed to rid of completely. She pulled the strings apart to open the pouch and slipped the beads out onto her hand. Dympna rubbed the Crucifix attached with her thumb and forefinger and held the precious object up before her. An impulsive thought made Dympna reach for her coat lying on the bed, she put her coat on and the beads in her pocket.

'I'm just popping to get some more cleaning detergent for the kitchen.' She said hurriedly to Seamus, popping her head around the front – room door.

'Ye not trying to get out of packing up these boxes are ye D?' Seamus said winking at her.

'Now would I do that Seamus Killoughery?' Dympna replied smiling. He saw the rosary beads hanging over her pocket and realised she wasn't going to get cleaning detergent after all.

'Take as long as you need D,' he said.

'Thanks, I'll be home soon,' Dympna replied and left.

The Church was silent, beautifully peaceful, with only one other person who lit some tea candles, blessed themselves and left shortly allowing Dympna the luxury of having the Church to herself. She took some Holy Water hesitantly, and crossed herself. 'Father, Son and The Holy Spirit.' She whispered. Dympna walked slowly trying not to let her heels make too much noise. She knelt on a pew at the back row, clasped her hands and bowed her head. Silently D prayed, and spoke to an entity she couldn't understand, had lost faith in and yet still wanted and needed to believe in all at the same time.

'I couldn't understand why you took her, why you took my family, why you allowed all of those things into my life. I miss her, I miss Orghlaith so so much – every day of me life.' Dympna said aloud, pausing to wipe her face. She opened her eyes and looked around the Church taking a breath comforted in the notion that there was something bigger than us at work, beyond our knowledge and comprehension and something she could no longer turn her back on, and at that solitary moment Dympna resumed her Faith. After concluding a prayer for her family D left the Church and returned home to Seamus, Erin and the mountain of boxes.

***

There were a few hundred of them in their cap and gowns that day, they shook the hand of the Dean and accepted the scroll paper that suddenly made three years of study worth its while. Proud parents hugged and congratulated sons and daughters and found comfort in the thought that the tuition fees, textbook fees and all other money needed by their kids throughout University had been worth it. Dympna and Seamus looked proudly on with the rest of the family clapping as Erin walked across the stage and accepted her 1st degree in International Politics from Trinity College, Dublin, 2005.